Fans are talking, texting, and blogging about Emma Chase and her sexy *New York Times* bestseller

"Emma Chase will keep you enthralled and captivated. A brilliant 5-star read!!!!" (Neda, *The Subclub Books*) • **"*Tangled* more than earns a brilliant, out-of-this-world hysterical, swoon-worthy five stars. Emma Chase's unforgettable characters are absolutely beyond compare. One of the best reads of 2013."** (Tessa, *Books Wine Food*) • **"It was absolutely amazing! Drew Evans is hands down my favorite leading man."** (Liz, *Romance Addiction*) • **"A 5-heart read. It's perfection in a book. RAWR hot, hilariously funny, and a romance so good you won't want it to end."** (Tamie & Elena, *Bookish Temptations*) • **"*Tangled* is panty-dropping, outrageously funny, and overwhelmingly lovely. I finished it in nearly one sitting because I had to know more of Drew and Kate."** (Angie, *Smut Book Club*) • **"Witty and hilarious insight into a man's head. I fell in love with Drew Evans's playful and cocky attitude and I will never forget him. . . . A sexy hero."** (Lucia, *Reading Is My Breathing*) • **"The characters are insanely hilarious! Drew had my sides splitting and in stitches with his witty and undeniably competitive personality! The funniest and most creative book told by the male point-of-view. You will not be able to put this book down!"** (Stephanie, *Romance Addict Book Blog*)

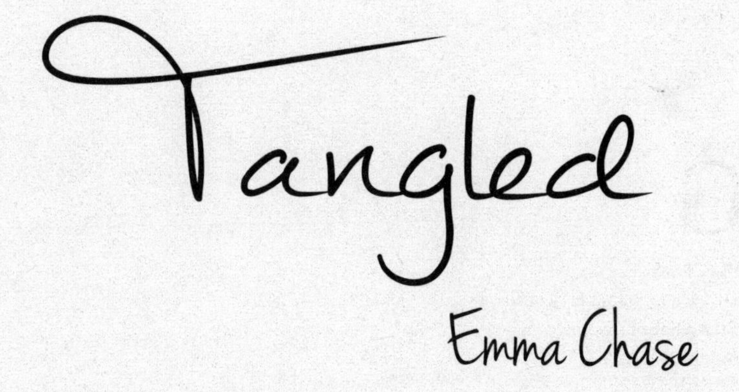

GALLERY BOOKS

New York London Toronto Sydney New Delhi

Gallery Books
A Division of Simon & Schuster, Inc.
1230 Avenue of the Americas
New York, NY 10020

First Gallery Books trade paperback edition January 2014

GALLERY BOOKS and colophon are registered trademarks of Simon & Schuster, Inc.

For information about special discounts for bulk purchases, please contact Simon & Schuster Special Sales at 1-866-506-1949 or business@simonandschuster.com.

The Simon & Schuster Speakers Bureau can bring authors to your live event. For more information or to book an event contact the Simon & Schuster Speakers Bureau at 1-866-248-3049 or visit our website at www.simonspeakers.com.

Manufactured in the United States of America

10 9 8 7 6 5 4 3

Library of Congress Cataloging-in-Publication Data is available.

ISBN 978-1-4767-6177-0
ISBN 978-1-4767-6147-3 (ebook)

To Joe,

for showing me what real love is

and for giving me glimpses every day

into the complicated workings of the male thought process

Acknowledgments

Many thanks to Micki Nuding and everyone at Gallery for believing in me and my work. Sincere gratitude to Omnific Publishing for giving me the opportunity to turn a lifelong dream into a reality. Thanks to my agent, Amy Tannenbaum, and the Jane Rotrosen Agency, for your unending support and guidance. Appreciation and affection to my many online friends whose encouragement helped make this all happen. I am indebted to my family, who taught me through example that humor can be found anywhere, in even the most unexpected situations—especially those. And last but not least, I am grateful to my children—you will always be my proudest accomplishment. Thank you for making me laugh and making me crazy and for inspiring me to never stop trying new things.

Tangled

Chapter 1

Do you see that unshowered, unshaven heap on the couch? The guy in the dirty gray T-shirt and ripped sweatpants?

That's me, Drew Evans.

I'm not usually like this. I mean, that really isn't me.

In real life, I'm well-groomed, my chin is clean-shaven, and my black hair is slicked back at the sides in a way I've been told makes me look dangerous but professional. My suits are handmade. I wear shoes that cost more than your rent.

My apartment? Yeah, the one I'm in right now. The shades are drawn, and the furniture glows with a bluish hue from the television. The tables and floor are littered with beer bottles, pizza boxes, and empty ice cream tubs.

That's not my real apartment. The one I usually live in is spotless; I have a girl come by twice a week. And it has every modern convenience, every big-boy toy you can think of: surround sound, satellite speakers, and a big-screen plasma that would make any man fall on his knees and beg for more. The decor is modern—lots of black and stainless steel—and anyone who enters knows a man lives there.

So, like I said—what you're seeing right now isn't the real me. I have the flu.

Influenza.

Have you ever noticed some of the worst sicknesses in history have a lyrical sound to them? Words like *malaria, diarrhea, cholera*. Do you think they do that on purpose? To make it a nice way to say you feel like something that dropped out of your dog's ass?

Influenza. Has a nice ring to it, if you say it enough.

At least I'm pretty sure that's what I have. That's why I've been holed up in my apartment the last seven days. That's why I turned my phone off, why I've gotten off the couch only to use the bathroom or to bring in the food I order from the delivery guy.

How long does the flu last anyway? Ten days? A month? Mine started a week ago. My alarm went off at five a.m., like always. But instead of rising from the bed to go to the office where I'm a star, I threw the clock across the room, smashing it to kingdom come.

It was annoying anyway. Stupid clock. Stupid beep-beep-beeping.

I rolled over and went back to sleep. When I did eventually drag my ass out of bed, I felt weak and nauseous. My chest ached; my head hurt. See—the flu, right? I couldn't sleep anymore, so I planted myself here, on my trusty couch. It was so comfortable I decided to stay right here. All week. Watching Will Ferrell's greatest hits on the plasma.

Anchorman: The Legend of Ron Burgundy's on right now. I've watched it three times today, but I haven't laughed yet. Not once. Maybe the fourth time's the charm, huh?

Now there's a pounding at my door.

Frigging doorman. What the hell is he here for? He's going to be sorry when he gets my Christmas tip this year, you can bet your ass.

I ignore the pounding, though it comes again.

And again.

"Drew! Drew, I know you're in there! Open the goddamn door!"

Oh no.

It's The Bitch. Otherwise known as my sister, Alexandra.

When I say the word *bitch* I mean it in the most affectionate way possible, I swear. But it's what she is. Demanding, opinionated, relentless. I'm going to kill my doorman.

"If you don't open this door, Drew, I'm calling the police to break it down, I swear to God!"

See what I mean?

I grasp the pillow that's been resting on my lap since the flu started. I push my face into it and inhale deeply. It smells like vanilla and lavender. Crisp and clean and addictive.

"Drew! Do you hear me?"

I pull the pillow over my head. Not because it smells like . . . her . . . but to block out the pounding that continues at my door.

"I'm taking out my phone! I'm dialing!" Alexandra's voice is whiny with warning, and I know she's not screwing around.

I sigh deeply and force myself to get up from the couch. The walk to the door takes time; each step of my stiff, aching legs is an effort.

Frigging flu.

I open the door and brace myself for the wrath of The Bitch. She's holding the latest iPhone up to her ear with one perfectly manicured hand. Her blond hair is pulled back in a simple but elegant knot, and a dark green purse the same shade as her skirt hangs from her shoulder—Lexi's all about the matching.

Behind her, looking appropriately contrite in a wrinkled navy suit, is my best friend and coworker, Matthew Fisher.

I forgive you, Doorman. It's Matthew who must die.

"Jesus Christ!" Alexandra yells in horror. "What the hell happened to you?"

I told you this isn't the real me.

I don't answer her. I don't have the energy. I just leave the door open and fall face-first onto my couch. It's soft and warm, but firm.

I love you, couch—have I ever told you that? Well, I'm telling you now.

Though my eyes are buried in the pillow, I sense Alexandra and Matthew walking slowly into the apartment. I imagine the shock on their faces at its condition. I peek out from my cocoon and see that my mind's eye was spot-on.

"Drew?" I hear her ask, but this time there's concern woven throughout the one short syllable.

Then she's pissed again. "For God's sake, Matthew, why didn't you call me sooner? How could you let this happen?"

"I haven't seen him, Lex!" Matthew says quickly. See—he's afraid of The Bitch too. "I came every day. He wouldn't open the door for me."

I sense the couch dip as she sits beside me. "Drew?" she says softly. I feel her hand run gently through the back of my hair. "Honey?"

Her voice is so achingly worried, she reminds me of my mother. When I was a boy and sick at home, Mom would come into my room with hot chocolate and soup on a tray. She would kiss my forehead to see if it still burned with fever. She always made me feel better. The memory and Alexandra's similar actions bring moisture to my closed eyes.

Am I a mess or what?

"I'm fine, Alexandra," I tell her, though I'm not sure if she hears me. My voice is lost in the sweet-scented pillow. "I have the flu."

I hear the opening of a pizza box and a groan as the stench of rotting cheese and sausage drifts from the container. "Not exactly the diet of someone with the flu, Little Brother."

I hear further shuffling of beer bottles and garbage, and I know she's starting to straighten the mess up. I'm not the only neat freak in my family.

"Oh, that's just wrong!" She inhales sharply, and, judging by the stink that joins the putrid pizza aroma, I'm thinking she just opened a three-day-old ice cream container that wasn't as empty as I'd thought.

"Drew." She shakes my shoulders gently. I give in and sit up, rubbing the exhaustion from my eyes as I do. "Talk to me," she begs. "What's going on? What happened?"

As I look at the troubled expression of my big bitch of a sister, I'm thrown twenty-two years back in time. I'm six years old and my hamster, Mr. Wuzzles, has just died. And just like on that day, the painful truth is ripped from my lungs.

"It finally happened."

"What happened?"

"What you've been wishing on me all these years," I whisper. "I fell in love."

I look up to see the smile form. It's what she's always wanted for me. She's been married to Steven forever, has been in love with him for even longer. So she's never agreed with the way I live my life and can't wait for me to settle down. To find someone to take care of me, the way she takes care of Steven. The way our mother still takes care of our dad.

But I told her it would never happen—it wasn't what I wanted. Why bring a book to the library? Why bring sand to the beach? Why buy the cow when you get the milk for free?

Are you starting to see the picture here?

So I see her beginning to smile, when, in a small voice that I don't even recognize, I say, "She's marrying someone else. She didn't . . . she didn't want me, Lex."

Sympathy spreads across my sister's face like jam on bread. And then determination. Because Alexandra is a fixer. She can unclog drains, patch dented walls, and remove stains from any rug. I already know what's going through her head at this moment: If her baby brother is busted, she'll just put him right back together again.

I wish it were that easy. But I don't think all the Krazy Glue in the world is going to piece my heart back together again.

Did I mention I'm a bit of a poet too?

"Okay. We can fix this, Drew."

Do I know my sister or what?

"You go take a long, hot shower. I'll clean up this disaster. Then, we're going out. The three of us."

"I can't go out." *Hasn't she been listening?* "I have the flu."

She smiles compassionately. "You need a good, hot meal. You need a shower. You'll feel better then."

Maybe she's right. God knows what I've been doing for the last seven days hasn't made me feel any better. I shrug and get up to do as she says. Like a four-year-old with his wooby, I bring my prized pillow with me.

On my way to the bathroom, I can't help but think of how it all happened. I had a good life once. A perfect life. And then it all got shot to shit.

Oh—you want to know how? You want to hear my sob story? Okay, then. It all started a few months ago, on a normal Saturday night.

Well, normal for *me* anyway.

Four months earlier

"Fuck, yeah. That's good. Yeah, like that."

See that guy—black suit, devilishly handsome? Yeah, the guy getting the blow job from the luscious redhead in the bathroom stall? That's me. The *real* me. MBF: Me Before Flu.

"Jesus, baby, I'm gonna come."

Let's freeze-frame here for a second.

For those ladies out there who are listening, let me give you some free advice: If a guy who you just met at a club calls you *baby, sweetheart, angel,* or any other generic endearment? Don't make the mistake of thinking he's so into you, he's already thinking up pet names.

It's because he can't or doesn't care to remember your actual name.

And no girl wants to be called by the wrong name when she's on her knees giving you head in the men's room. So, just to be safe, I went with *baby*.

Her real name? Does it matter?

"Fuck, baby, I'm coming."

She removes her mouth with a pop and catches like a major leaguer as I jizz in her hand. Afterward, I move to the sink to clean up and zip up. Redhead looks at me with a smile as she rinses with a travel-size bottle of mouthwash from her bag.

Charming.

"How about a drink?" she asks, in what I'm sure she thinks is a sultry voice.

But here's a fact for you—once I'm done, I'm *done*. I'm not the kind of guy who rides the same roller coaster twice. Once is enough, and then the thrill is gone and so is the interest.

But my mother did raise me to be a gentleman. "Sure, sweetheart. You go find a table, I'll get us something from the bar." Redhead put in quite an effort sucking me off, after all. She's earned herself a drink.

After leaving the bathroom, she heads for a table, and I go toward the oh-so-crowded bar. I did mention it was Saturday night, right? And this is REM. No, not R.E.M.—*rem*, like REM sleep, as in when you dream. Get it?

It's the hottest club in New York City. Well, at least tonight it is. By next week it will be some other club. But the location doesn't matter. The script is always the same. Every weekend my friends and I come here together but leave separately—and never alone.

Don't look at me like that. I'm not a bad guy. I don't lie; I don't sandbag women with flowery words about a future together and love at first sight. I'm a straight shooter. I'm looking for a good time—for one night—and I tell them so. That's better than ninety percent of the other guys in here, believe me. And most of the girls in here are looking for the same thing I am.

Okay, maybe that's not exactly true. But I can't help it if they see me, fuck me, and suddenly want to bear my children. That's not my problem. Like I said, I tell them how it is, give them a good time and then the cab fare home. Thank you, good night. Don't call me, 'cause I sure as shit won't be calling you.

Finally getting through the crowd to the bar, I order two drinks. I take a moment to watch the writhing, twisting bodies melt into each other on the dance floor as the music vibrates all around.

And then I see her, fifteen feet from where I'm standing, waiting patiently but looking a bit uneasy amongst the arm-raising, money-waving, alcohol-craving herd trying to get the bartender's attention.

I told you I'm poetic, right? The truth is, I wasn't always. Not until this moment. She's magnificent—angelic—gorgeous. Pick a word, any fucking word. The bottom line is, for a moment, I forget how to breathe.

Her hair is long and dark and shines even in the dim light of the club. She's wearing a red backless dress—sexy but classy—that accentuates every perfectly toned curve. Her mouth is full and lush, with lips begging to be ravished.

And her eyes. *Sweet fucking Christ.* Her eyes are large and round and endlessly dark. I imagine those eyes looking up at me as she takes my cock into her hot little mouth. The appendage in question immediately stirs to life at the thought. I have to have her.

I quickly make my way over, deciding then and there that she is the lucky woman who'll have the pleasure of my company for the remainder of the night. And what a pleasure I intend to make it.

Arriving just as she's opening her mouth to order a drink, I intervene with, "The lady will have . . ." I look her over to surmise what she would be drinking. This is a talent of mine. Some people are beer drinkers, some scotch and soda, some an aged wine, others are brandy or sweet champagne. And I can always tell who's what—always. ". . . a Veramonte Merlot, 2003."

She turns to me with a raised brow, and her eyes appraise me from head to toe. Deciding I'm not a loser, she says, "You're good."

I smile. "I see my reputation precedes me. Yes, I am. And you're beautiful."

She blushes. Actually turns frigging pink in the cheeks and looks away. Who blushes anymore? It's goddamn adorable.

"So, what do you say we find someplace more comfortable . . . and private? So we can get to know each other better?"

Without missing a beat, she says, "I'm here with friends. We're celebrating. I don't usually come to places like this."

"What are we celebrating?"

"I just got my MBA and start a new job on Monday."

"Really? What a coincidence. I'm a finance guy myself. Maybe you've heard of my firm? Evans, Reinhart and Fisher?" We're the hottest boutique investment bank in the city, so I'm sure she's duly impressed.

Let's just pause here again, shall we?

Did you see the rounding of this gorgeous woman's mouth when I told her where I am employed? Did you see the widening of her eyes? That should have told me something.

But I didn't notice at the time—I was too busy checking out her tits. They're perfect, by the way. Smaller than what I usually go for, no more than a handful. But as far as I'm concerned, a handful's all you need.

My point is, remember that look of surprise—that will make sense later on. Now, back to the conversation.

"We have so much in common," I say. "We're both in business, we both like a good red. . . . I think we owe it to ourselves to see where this could go tonight."

She laughs. It's a magical sound.

Now I should explain one thing here. With any other woman,

on any other night, I'd be in a cab by now, with my hand up her dress and my mouth making her moan. No question. For me, this *is* working for it. And strangely enough, it's kind of a turn-on.

"I'm Drew, by the way." I hold out my hand. "And you are?"

She holds up her hand. "Engaged."

Undeterred, I take her hand and kiss her knuckle, grazing it ever so slightly with my tongue. I see my reluctant beauty try to suppress a shiver, and I know, despite her words, I'm getting to her.

See, I'm not the type who really listens to what people say. I look at how they say it. You can learn a lot about someone if you just take the time to watch the way they move, the shift of their eyes, the rise and fall of their voice.

Doe Eyes may be telling me no . . . but her body? Her body's screaming, *Yes, yes, fuck me on the bar*. In the span of three minutes, she's told me why she's here, what she does for a living, and allowed me to fondle her hand. Those are not the actions of a woman who is not interested—those are the actions of a woman who does not *want* to be interested.

And I can definitely work with that.

I'm about to comment on her engagement ring; the diamond is so small that even on close inspection, it can't be located. But I don't want to offend her. She said she's just graduated. I have friends who had to put themselves through business school, and the loans can be crushing.

So I go for a different tactic—honesty. "Even better. You don't do places like this? I don't do relationships. We're a perfect fit. We should explore this connection further, don't you think?"

She laughs again, and our drinks arrive. She picks hers up. "Thank you for the drink. I should get back to my friends now. It's been a pleasure."

I give her a wicked smile. "Baby, if you let me take you out of here, I'll give the word *pleasure* a whole new meaning."

She shakes her head with a smile, as if she's indulging a petulant child. Then she calls over her shoulder as she walks away, "Have a good night, Mr. Evans."

Like I said, I am typically an observant man. Sherlock Holmes and I, we could hang out. But I'm so enraptured by the view of that sweet ass, I miss it at first.

Did you notice? Did you catch the little detail that passed me by?

That's right. She called me "Mr. Evans"—but I never told her my last name. Remember that too.

For the moment, I let the dark-haired mystery woman retreat. I intend to give her some slack, then reel her in—hook, line, and sinker. I plan to pursue her the rest of the night if I have to.

She's just that frigging hot.

But then Redhead—yep, the one from the men's room—finds me. "There you are! I thought I lost you." She pushes her body up against my side and rubs my arm intimately. "How about we go to my place? It's just around the corner."

Ah, thanks—but no thanks. Redhead has quickly become a fading memory. My sights are set on better, more intriguing prospects. I'm about to tell her so when another redhead appears beside her.

"This is my sister, Mandy. I told her all about you. She thought the three of us could . . . you know . . . have a good time."

I turn my gaze on Redhead's sister—her twin, actually. And just like that, my plans change. I know, I know . . . I said I don't ride the same coaster twice. But twin coasters?

Let me tell you, no man would pass up a ride like that.

Chapter 2

Have I mentioned that I love my job?

If my firm were Major League Baseball, I'd be MVP. I'm a partner at one of the top investment banks in New York City, specializing in media and technology. Yes, yes, my father and his two closest friends started the firm. But that doesn't mean I didn't bust my ass to get where I am—because I did. It also doesn't mean I don't eat, breathe, and sleep work to earn the reputation I have, because I do.

What does an I-banker do, you ask? Well, you know in *Pretty Woman,* when Richard Gere tells Julia Roberts that his company buys up other ones and sells them off piece by piece? I'm the guy who helps him do that. I negotiate the deals, draw up the contracts, manage due diligence, draft credit agreements, and do many other things I'm sure you have no interest in hearing about.

Now you're probably asking yourself why a guy like me is quoting a chick flick like *Pretty Woman*?

The answer is simple: Growing up, my mother forced "family movie night" on her young children every single week. The Bitch got to choose the featured presentation every other week. She went through this whole Julia Roberts obsession and shoved it down my throat for, like, a year. I could recite the goddamn thing verbatim. Though I have to admit—Richard Gere. He's fucking cool.

Now, back to my job.

The best part about it is the high I feel when I close a deal, a really good deal. It's like winning at blackjack in a Vegas casino. It's like being picked by Jenna Jameson to be in her next porno. There is nothing—and I mean *nothing*—better.

I do the prospecting for my clients, recommend what moves they should make. I know which companies are dying to be bought and which ones need a hostile takeover. I'm the one with the inside information about which media mogul is ready to jump off the Brooklyn Bridge because he spent too much of the company's profits on high-priced hookers.

Competition for clients is fierce. You have to entice them, make them want you, make them believe no one else can do for them what you can. It's kind of like getting laid. But instead of getting a piece of ass at the end of the day, I get a big, fat check. I make money for myself and my clients—lots of it.

The sons of my father's partners also work here, Matthew Fisher and Steven Reinhart. Yes, *that* Steven—The Bitch's husband. Like our fathers, the three of us grew up together, went to school together, and now work at the firm together. The old men leave the real work to us. They check in from time to time, to feel like they're still running things, and then head on out to the country club to get in an afternoon game of golf.

Matthew and Steven are good at the job too—don't get me wrong. But I'm the star. I'm the shark. I'm the one clients ask for and drowning companies fear. They know it and so do I.

Monday morning I'm in my office at nine a.m., same as always. My secretary—the smoking little blonde with the nice rack—is already here, ready with my schedule for the day, my messages from the weekend, and the best damn cup of coffee in the tristate area.

No, I haven't fucked her.

Not that I wouldn't love to. Trust me, if she didn't work for me, I'd hit that harder than Muhammad Ali.

But I have rules—standards, you might say. One of them is no screwing around at the office. I don't shit where I eat, I don't fuck where I work. Never mind the sexual harassment issues it would bring up; it's just not good business. It's unprofessional.

So, because Erin is the only woman besides my blood relatives who I have platonic interactions with, she is also the only member of the opposite sex I've ever considered a friend. We have a great working relationship. Erin is simply . . . awesome.

That's another reason I wouldn't screw her even if she were spread-eagle on the desk begging for it. Believe it or not, a good secretary—a really good one—is hard to find. I've had girls work for me who were dumber than a whole bucket of dirt. I've had others who thought they could make it by just working on their backs, if you know what I mean. Those are the girls I want to meet in a bar on a Saturday night—not the kind I want answering my phones Monday morning.

So now that you have a little insight? Let's go back to my descent into hell.

"I moved your one o'clock lunch with Mecha back to a four o'clock meeting," Erin tells me as she hands me a stack of messages.

Shit.

Mecha Communications is a multibillion-dollar media conglomerate. I've been working on their acquisition of a Spanish-speaking cable network for months, and the CEO, Radolpho Scucini, is always more receptive on a full stomach.

"Why?"

She hands me a folder. "Today—lunch in the conference room. Your father's introducing the new associate. You know how he is about these things."

You ever see *A Christmas Carol*? Of course you have—some version of it's on some channel, somewhere, every day before Christmas. Well, you know when the Ghost of Christmas Past takes Scrooge back in time to when he was young and happy? And he had that boss, Fezziwig, the fat guy who threw the big parties? Yeah, that guy. That's my father.

My dad loves this company and sees all his employees as extended family. He looks for any excuse to throw an office party. Birthday parties, baby showers, Thanksgiving luncheons, President's Day buffets, Columbus Day dinners . . . need I go on?

It's a miracle any actual work gets accomplished.

And Christmas? Forget about it. My father's Christmas parties are legendary. Everybody goes home shitfaced. Some people don't go home at all. Last year we caught ten employees from a rival bank trying to sneak in, just because the soirée is that frigging fantastic. And it's all done to achieve the atmosphere—the vibe—my father wants in this firm.

He loves his employees, and they love him right back. Devotion, loyalty—we've got it in spades. That's part of what makes us the best. Because the people who work here would pretty much sell their first-born for my old man.

Still, there are days—days like today, when I need time to romance a client—that his celebrations can be a royal pain in the ass. But it is what it is.

My Monday morning is packed, so I get to my desk and start working. Then, before I can blink, it's one o'clock and I'm heading to the conference room. I spot a familiar head of bright orange hair attached to a short, stocky-framed body. That would be Jack O'Shay. Jack started at the firm about six years ago, the same year I did. He's a good guy and frequent weekend comrade. Next to him is Matthew, talking animatedly as he pushes a large hand through his sandy-colored hair.

I grab my food from the buffet and join them at their table just as Matthew is recounting his Saturday night. "So then she breaks out handcuffs and a whip. A fucking whip! I thought I was going to lose it right there, I swear to Christ. I mean . . . she went to a convent . . . actually studied to be a goddamn nun, man!"

"I told you, the quiet ones are always into the kinky shit," Jack adds with a laugh.

Matthew turns his hazel eyes to Steven and tells him, "Seriously, dude. You gotta come out with us. Just once, I'm begging you."

I smirk at that because I know exactly what's coming.

"I'm sorry, have you met my wife?" Steven asks, his brow wrinkled in confusion.

"Don't be such a bitch," Jack ribs him. "Tell her you're going to play cards or something. Live a little."

Steven takes off his glasses and wipes the lenses with a napkin as he appears to consider the idea.

"Riiiight. And when she finds out—and Alexandra will definitely find out, I assure you—she'll serve me my balls on a silver platter. With a nice garlic butter dipping sauce on the side and a good Chianti."

He makes a slurping sound à la Hannibal Lecter that has me laughing my ass off.

"Besides," he gloats, replacing his spectacles and stretching his hands over his head, "I got filet mignon at home, boys. I'm not interested in sloppy joes."

"Pussy," Matthew coughs out, while Jack shakes his head at my brother-in-law and says, "Even a nice filet gets old if you eat it every day."

"Not," Steven defends suggestively, "if you cook it a different way every time. My baby knows how to keep my meals spicy."

I put my hand up and plead, "Please. Please just stop there." There are some visuals I don't want in my head. Ever.

"What about you, Drew? I saw you leave with those twins. Were they real redheads?" Jack asks me.

I feel the satisfied smile stretch over my lips. "Oh yeah. They were real." And then I go on to describe my wild Saturday night in vivid, delicious detail.

Okay, let's just stop right now because I can see that judgmental look on your face. And I can hear your high-pitched disapproval too: *What a jerk. He had sex with a girl*—well, in this case, two girls—*and now he's telling his friends all about it. That's sooo disrespectful.*

First of all, if a chick wants me to respect her, she needs to act like someone worth respecting. Second, I'm not trying to be a dick; I'm just being a guy. And all guys talk to their friends about sex.

Let me repeat that in case you missed it:

ALL GUYS TALK TO THEIR FRIENDS ABOUT SEX.

If a guy tells you he doesn't? Dump him, because he's lying to you.

And another thing—I've heard my sister and her little friends have their chats too. Some of the things that came out of their mouths could've made Larry fucking Flynt blush. So don't act like women don't talk just as much as we guys do . . . because I know for a fact they do.

After expounding on the finer points of my weekend, the talk at the table turns to football and the effectiveness of Manning's offense. In the background, I hear my father's voice as he stands at the front of the room, detailing the grand accomplishments of the newest associate, whose file I didn't bother opening this morning. Wharton

School of the University of Pennsylvania, first in her class, interned with Credit Suisse, blah . . . blah . . . blah.

The chatter fades away as my thoughts turn to the part of my Saturday night that I didn't bother telling my friends about: the interaction with one brunette goddess, to be exact. I can still see those dark, round eyes so clearly in my head. That luscious mouth, the luminous hair that could not have possibly been as soft as it looked.

It isn't the first time her image has popped into my head, unbidden, in the last day and a half. In fact, it seems like every hour a picture of some part of her comes to me, and I find myself imagining what happened to her. Or, more to the point, what could have happened if I had stuck around and gone after her.

It's strange. I'm not one to reminisce about the randoms I meet during my weekend adventures. Usually, they fade from my thoughts the moment I escape their beds. But there was just something about her. Maybe it's because she turned me down. Maybe it's because I didn't get her name. Or maybe it was that sweetly toned ass that made me want to grab on and never let go.

As the images in my mind turn to focus on that particular feature, a familiar stirring begins in the southern region, if you catch my drift. I mentally shake myself. I haven't gotten a spontaneous hard-on since I was twelve. What's up with that?

Looks like I'm going to have to call that hottie who slipped me her number in the coffeehouse this morning. Normally I reserve those kinds of activities for weekends, but apparently my dick would like to make an exception.

By this time, I've made it toward the front of the room, in line for the customary handshake of welcome given to all new employees. As I near the head of the line, my father spots me and comes over to greet me with an affectionate slap on the back.

"Glad you made it, Drew. This new girl has some real potential. I want you to personally take her under your wing, help her get her feet wet. You do that, Son, and I guarantee you she'll take off and do us all proud."

"Sure, Dad. No problem."

Great. Like I don't have my own work to take care of. Now I have to hold a newbie's hand as she navigates the dark, scary world of Corporate America. That's just perfect.

Thanks, Dad.

Finally, my turn has come. Her back is to me as I step up. I take in her sleek dark hair that's pulled into a low bun, her tiny, petite frame. My eyes drift down her back as she speaks to someone in front of her. On instinct they fall to her ass and . . . *wait.*

Wait one goddamn minute.

I've seen that ass before.

No fucking way.

She turns around.

Way.

The smile on her face broadens as her eyes connect with mine. Endless, shining eyes that I didn't remember dreaming about till just now. She raises a brow in recognition and holds out her hand. "Mr. Evans."

I feel my mouth open and close, but no words come out. The shock of seeing her again—here of all places—must have momentarily frozen the part of my brain that controls speech. As the synapses start to function once more, I hear my father saying, ". . . Brooks. Katherine Brooks. She's going places, Son, and with your help, she'll be taking us with her."

Katherine Brooks.

The girl from the bar. The girl I let get away. The girl whose mouth I'm still desperate to feel around my cock.

And she works here. In my office, where I have sworn to never . . . ever . . . screw around. Her warm, soft hand slides perfectly into mine, and two thoughts enter my head simultaneously.

The first is: God hates me. The second is: I have been a naughty, naughty boy for most of my life, and this is my payback. And you know what they say about payback, right?

Yep. She's one hairy bitch.

Chapter 3

I am all about self-determination. Will. Control. I determine my path in life. I decide my failures and successes. Screw fate. Destiny can kiss my ass. If I want something badly enough, I can have it. If I focus, sacrifice, there is nothing I can't do.

What is the point of my posturing, you ask? Why do I sound like the featured speaker at a self-help convention? What exactly am I trying to say?

In a nutshell: I control my dick. My dick does not control me. At least, that's what I've been telling myself for the last hour and a half.

See me there, at my desk, mumbling like a goddamn schizophrenic off his meds?

That's me reminding myself of the tenets, the sacred beliefs that have gotten me this far in life. The ones that have made me an uncontested success in the bedroom and in the office. The ones that have never failed me before. The ones that I am dying to throw out the fucking window. All because of the woman in the office down the hall.

Katherine Everyone-Calls-Me-Kate Brooks.

Talk about a frigging curveball.

The way I see it, I could still go for the gold. Technically speaking, I didn't meet Kate at work; I met her in a bar. That means she could forgo the label of "coworker" and retain the "random hookup" status she was originally assigned.

What? I'm a businessman; it's my job to find loopholes.

So, in theory at least, I could definitely nail her and not undermine my own personal laws of nature. The problem with that strategy, of course, is what happens after.

The longing glances, the hopeful eyes, the pathetic attempts to make me jealous. The supposedly "accidental" meetings, the questions about my plans, the seemingly casual walks past my office door. All of which would inevitably escalate into disturbing semi-stalkerish behavior.

Some women can handle a one-night stand. Others can't. And I have definitely been on the wrong end of those who can't.

It ain't pretty.

So, you see, no matter how badly I want to, no matter how hard the little head is trying to lead me down that road, it's not the kind of thing I want to bring into my place of business. My sanctuary—my second home.

It's not going to happen. Period.

That's it. End of discussion.

Case closed.

Kate Brooks is officially scratched off my list of potentials. She is forbidden, untouchable, a no-way-never. Right next to my friends' ex-girlfriends, the boss's daughter, and my sister's best friends.

Well, that last category is a bit of a gray area. When I was eighteen, Alexandra's best friend, Cheryl Phillips, spent the summer at our house. God bless her—that girl had a mouth like a Hoover vacuum. Lucky for me, The Bitch never learned of her friend's two a.m. visits to my room. There would have been hell to pay—I'm talking fire-and-brimstone-of-apocalyptic-proportions hell—if she had.

Anyway, where was I?

Oh, right. I was explaining that I have come to the unequivocal decision that Kate Brooks's ass is one that I, sadly, am never going to tap. And I'm okay with that. Really.

And I almost believe myself.

Right up until she shows up at my door.

Christ.

She's wearing glasses. The dark-rimmed kind. The female version of Clark Kent's. They would be geeky-looking and unattractive on most women. But not on her. On the bridge of that tiny nose, framing those long-lashed beauties, with her hair swept up in that slightly loose bun, they are nothing short of full-out sexy.

As she starts to speak, my mind is suddenly filled with every hot-teacher fantasy I've ever had. They're playing out in my mind right next to the ones about the seemingly sexually repressed librarian who's really a leather-wearing, handcuff-bearing nymphomaniac.

While all this is going on in my head, she's still talking.

What the fuck is she saying?

I close my eyes to stop myself from staring at her glistening lips. So I can actually process the words coming out of her mouth:

". . . father said you could help me with it." She stops and looks at me expectantly.

"I'm sorry, I was distracted. You want to sit down and run that by me again?" I ask, my voice never betraying the horniness inside me.

Once again, to the ladies out there—here's a fact for you: Men pretty much have sex on the brain twenty-four-seven. The exact figure is like every 5.2 seconds or some shit like that.

The point is, when you ask, "What do you want for dinner?" we're thinking about screwing you on the kitchen counter. When you're telling us about the sappy film you watched with your girlfriends last week, we're thinking about the porno we saw on cable last night. When you show us the designer shoes you bought on sale, we're thinking how nice they would look on our shoulders.

I just thought you'd want to know. Don't shoot the messenger.

It's a curse, really.

Personally, I blame Adam. Now there was a guy who had the world by the balls. Walking around naked, a hot chick to satisfy his every whim. I sure hope that apple was tasty, 'cause he really fucked it up for the rest of us. Now we have to work for it. Or, in my case, try desperately not to want it.

She sits in the chair across from my desk and crosses her legs.

Don't look at the legs. Don't look at the legs.

Too late.

They're toned, tan, and as smooth-looking as silk. I lick my lips and force my eyes to hers.

"So," she begins again, "I've been working up a portfolio on a programming company, Genesis. Have you heard of them?"

"Vaguely," I answer, looking down at the papers on my desk to stem the flow of indecent images that the sound of her voice calls forth from my deviant mind.

I am a bad, bad boy. Think Kate will punish me if I tell her how bad I am?

I know. I know. I just can't help myself.

"They posted three million EBIT last quarter," she says.

"Really?"

"Yeah. I know it's not earth-shattering, but it shows they have a solid base. They're still small, but that's part of what has made them good. Their programmers are young and hungry. Rumor has it, they've got ideas that will make the Wii look more like an Atari. And they have the brains to make them happen. What they don't have is the capital."

She stands and leans over my desk to pass me a folder. I'm assailed with a sweet but flowery scent. It's delectable, alluring—not like the grandma whose perfume practically chokes you to death when she walks by you at the post office.

I have the urge to press my face against her neck and inhale deeply.

But I resist and open the folder instead.

"I showed what I have to Mr. Evans . . . uh, your father, and he told me to run it by you. He thought one of your clients—"

"Alphacom." I nod.

"Right. He thought Alphacom would be interested."

I look over the work she's done so far. It's good. Detailed and informative but focused. Slowly, my brain—the one above my shoulders, anyway—starts to shift gears. If there's one topic that has any hope of derailing me from thoughts about sex, it's work. A good deal. I can definitely smell potential here.

It doesn't smell as delicious as Kate Brooks, but it's close.

I motion for her to sit back down. She does. "This is good, Kate. Very good. I could definitely sell this to Seanson. He's Alphacom's CEO."

Her eyes narrow just a bit. "But, you'll keep me on board, right?"

I smirk. "Of course. Do I look like the type who needs to steal other people's proposals?"

She rolls her eyes and smiles. This time, I just can't look away.

"No, of course not, Mr. Evans. I didn't mean to imply . . . It's just . . . You know . . . first day."

"Well, I'd say from the looks of this, you're having one hell of a first day. And, please, it's Drew."

She nods. I lean back in my chair, appraising her. My eyes rake over her from head to toe in a completely unprofessional manner. I know it. But I just can't seem to make myself give a damn.

"So . . . celebrating a new job, huh?" I ask, referring to her comment at REM on Saturday.

She bites her lip, and my slacks tighten as I stir and harden—again. If this keeps up, I'm going to have one hell of a case of blue balls when I get home.

"Yes. New job." She shrugs, then says, "I guessed who you were when you told me your name and the name of your firm."

"You've heard of me?" I ask, truly curious.

"Sure. I don't think there are many in this field who haven't read about Evans, Reinhart and Fisher's golden boy in *Business Weekly* . . . or on Page Six, for that matter."

Her last words refer to the gossip columns on whose pages I frequently appear.

"If the only reason you blew me off is because I work here," I say, "I can have my resignation on my father's desk within the hour."

She laughs and then, with a faint blush coloring her cheeks, replies, "No, that wasn't the only reason." She holds up her hand to remind me of the almost-invisible engagement ring. "But aren't you glad now that I turned you down? I mean, it would have been pretty awkward if something had happened between us. Don't you think?"

My face is completely serious as I tell her, "Would've been worth it."

She raises her brows in doubt. "Even though I'm working under you now?"

Now, come on—she walked right into that one, and she knows it. Working *under* me? How in the hell am I supposed to ignore that?

Yet I merely cock an eyebrow, and she shakes her head and chuckles again.

With a feral smile, I ask her, "I'm not making you uncomfortable, am I?"

"No. Not at all. But do you treat all your employees this way? Because I have to tell you, you're leaving yourself wide open for a lawsuit."

I can't help the smile that comes to my lips. She's such a surprise. Sharp. Quick. I have to think before I speak to her. I like it.

I like her.

"No, I don't treat all my employees this way. Ever. Only one, who I haven't stopped thinking about since Saturday night."

Okay, so maybe I wasn't thinking about her when the twins were double-teaming me. But it's at least partly true.

"You're incorrigible," she says in a way that tells me she thinks I'm cute.

I'm a lot of things, baby. Cute isn't one of them.

"I see something I want, and I go after it. I'm used to getting what I want."

You'll never hear a truer statement about me than that. But let's put things on hold for a minute here, okay? So I can give you the full picture.

See, my mother, Anne, always wanted a big family—five, maybe six kids. But Alexandra is five years older than I am. Five years may not seem like a lot to you, but to my mother it was a lifetime. The way the story goes, after Alexandra, my mother couldn't get pregnant again—and it wasn't for lack of trying. "Secondary infertility," they called it. When my sister was five, my mother had pretty much given up hope of ever having any more kids.

And then guess what? I came along.

Surprise.

I was her miracle baby. Her precious angel from God. Her granted wish. Her answered prayer. And she wasn't the only one who thought so. My father was thrilled, just as grateful to have another child—and a son at that. And Alexandra—this was the pre-Bitch years—was ecstatic to finally have a baby brother.

I was what my family had wanted and waited five years for. I was the little prince. I could do no wrong. There was nothing I wanted that I couldn't have. I was the most handsome, the most brilliant. There was no one kinder, no one sweeter than me. I was loved beyond words—doted on and catered to.

So, if you think I'm arrogant? Selfish? Spoiled? You're probably right. But don't hold it against me. It's not my fault. I am a product of how I was raised.

Now that that's out of the way—back to my office. This next part is big.

"And I think you should know, I want you, Kate."

See the flush on her cheeks, the slight surprise on her face? See how her face turns serious, and she meets my eyes and then looks down at the floor?

I'm getting to her. She wants me too. She's fighting it. But it's there. I could have her. I could lead her right where she is dying to go.

The knowledge makes me swallow a groan as the guy downstairs reacts with a vengeance. I want to walk up to her and kiss her until she can't stand. I want to slide my tongue between those ripe lips until her knees give out from under her. I want to pick her up, wrap her legs around my waist, lean her up against the wall and . . .

"Hey, Drew. There's a traffic jam on Fifty-Third. If you want to make your four o'clock, you should get going."

Thank you, Erin. Way to kill the moment. Awesome secretary—horrible timing.

Kate gets up from her chair, her shoulders stiff, her back straight. She inches toward the door and refuses to look me in the eyes. "So, thanks for your time, Mr. Evans. You . . . ah . . . let me know when you want me."

I raise my brows suggestively at her words. I love that she's flustered—and that I'm the one who did it to her.

Still avoiding eye contact, she grimaces slightly. "About Alphacom and Genesis. Let me know what I should do . . . what you want me to do . . . what . . . oh, you know what I mean."

Before she's out the door, my voice stops her. "Kate?"

She turns to me, her eyes questioning.

I point to myself. "It's Drew."

She smiles. Recovers herself. Her natural confidence finds its way back into her eyes.

Then she meets my gaze full-on. "Right. I'll see you later, Drew."

Once she's out the door, I say only to myself, "Oh, yes. Yes, you will."

As I check my briefcase before leaving for my meeting, I realize that this attraction—no, that's not a strong enough word—this *need* that I have for Kate Brooks isn't just going to go away. I can try and fight it, but I'm only a man, for God's sake. Left unresolved, my desire for her could turn my office, the place I love, into a torture chamber of sexual frustration.

I can't let that happen.

So, I have three options: I can quit. I can get Kate to quit. Or I can entice her to share one profoundly pleasurable night with me. Get it out of both of our systems—consequences be damned.

Guess which one I'm going to pick?

Chapter 4

Turns out I didn't get blue balls after all. I met up with the coffeehouse girl that night. She's a yoga instructor.

Nice.

What? Come on, don't be like that. I want Kate, no question. But don't expect me to act like a monk until it happens. The thing women don't understand is that a guy can want one woman and still fuck another one. Hell, a guy could *love* a woman and still fuck *ten* others. It's just the way it is.

Sex is a release. Purely physical. That's all. At least to men it is.

Okay, okay—calm down—don't start throwing shoes at me or something.

At least to *this* man it is. Better?

Maybe you'll understand my point of view if I put it this way. You brush your teeth, right? Well, suppose your favorite toothpaste is Aquafresh. But the store is out. All they have is Colgate. What are you going to do? You're going to use the Colgate, right?

You may want to brush with Aquafresh, but when all is said and done, you use what you have to keep those pearly whites clean. See my way of thinking? Good.

Now, back to my tale of heartache and pain.

I've never seduced a woman before.

Shocking, I know.

Let me clarify. I've never *had* to seduce a woman before, not in the typical sense. Usually, it just takes a look, a wink, a smile. A friendly greeting, maybe a drink or two. After that, the only verbal exchange involves short one-word phrases like *harder, more, lower* . . . you get the point.

So the whole conversing-a-woman-into-bed concept is pretty new to me, I'll admit. But I'm not worried. Why not, you ask?

Because I play chess.

Chess is a game of strategy, planning. Of thinking two steps ahead of your next move. Of guiding your opponent right where you need her to be.

For the two weeks following her first day, dealing with Kate, for me, is exactly like playing chess. A few suggestive words, some innocent but seductive caresses. I won't bore you with details of every conversation. I'll just say that things are progressing nicely; everything is going according to plan.

I figure it'll take another week—two, tops—till I'm able to claim that golden treasure between her creamy thighs. I already know how it will play out. I've spent hours, in fact, imagining it, fantasizing about it.

Want to hear it?

It will happen in my office, one night when we're both working late—the only ones left. She'll be tired, stiff. I'll offer to rub her neck, and she'll let me. Then I'll lean down and kiss her, starting at her shoulder, trailing up her neck, tasting her skin with my tongue. Finally, our lips will meet. And it will be hot—fucking scorching. And she'll forget all about the reasons why we shouldn't: our mutual place of work, her stupid fiancé. The only thing she'll be thinking of is me and the things my expert hands will be doing to her.

I have a couch in my office. It's suede—not leather. Does suede stain? Hope not. Because that's where we'll end up—on that sorrowfully underused couch.

Now let me ask you this: Have you seen those commercials that say how life can change in an instant?

Yes, yes, I'm going somewhere with this—just bear with me.

You know the ones I'm talking about, don't you? Where the happy family is driving down Main Street on a bright sunny day and then . . . BAM. Head-on collision with a semi. And Daddy goes flying out the window because he didn't have his seat belt buckled.

They're designed to scare the shit out of us. And they do. But the fact remains they are also chock-full of truth. Our goals, our priorities, can change instantaneously—usually when we least expect it.

So, after two weeks of strategizing and fantasizing, I'm sure that Kate Brooks will be my next one-nighter. I can't remember wanting someone as much as I want her. I've definitely never waited for a woman as long as I've waited for her. But the point is, for me, it's a done deal—a foregone conclusion—not an *if*, but simply a *when*.

And then, on Monday afternoon, my father calls me into his office.

"Sit down, Son. There's some business I'd like to discuss."

My father often calls me in here to talk about things he's not yet ready to share with the rest of the staff. "I just got off the phone with Saul Anderson. He's looking to diversify. He's coming to the city next month to shop around for ideas."

Saul Anderson is a media tycoon. Big money—the kind of guy who makes Rupert Murdoch look like a peon. Got a napkin? 'Cause I think I'm drooling.

"Next month? Okay, I can work with that. No problem." I feel the excitement pumping in my veins. This is how a shark must feel after somebody dumps a great big bucket of bloody chum in the water. It's a rush.

"Drew . . ." my father interrupts, but my mind's too busy whirling with ideas to hear him.

"Any clue what he's looking to get into? I mean, the possibilities are pretty endless."

"Son . . ." my father tries again.

You can see it coming, can't you?

Yet I ramble on. "Cable stations are cash cows. Social media's in the toilet right now, so we could pick up some real bargains. Film production is always a safe bet, and that would cut down on the overhead when they replay on his own network."

"Drew, I'm going to give the account to Kate Brooks."

Hold the fucking phone. *Care to repeat that for me?*

"What?"

"She's good, Drew. I'm telling you, she's damn good."

"She's been here for two weeks!"

Dogs are territorial. You know that, right? That's why at the park they seem to have a never-ending supply of piss, which they insist on stopping every four seconds to spread around. It's because they believe it's their park. And they want the other dogs to know it, to know that they were there first. It's the nonverbal way of pretty much saying, "Fuck off—find your own park."

Men are the same way.

Not that I'm going to piss a circle around my desk or anything, but this firm is *mine.* I've nurtured these clients since they were tiny corporations. I've watched, like a proud papa, as they grew to sturdy conglomerates. I've wined them, I've dined them. I've put in hour after hour, years of sleepless nights. My job isn't just what I do—it's who I am. And I will be damned if Kate Brooks is going to walk her ass in here and take that away from me.

No matter how fine an ass it might be.

"Yes," my father says, "and have you seen some of the stuff she's come up with in these two weeks? She's the first one in and the last one to leave—every day. She's fresh and thinks outside the box. She's come up with some of the most innovative investments I've ever seen. My instincts are telling me to give her the ball and see what she'll do with it."

What are the early warning signs of dementia, exactly?

"She'll frigging fumble—that's what she'll do!" I yell. But I know from experience dramatics will get me nowhere with my father, so I pinch the bridge of my nose to try and calm down. "Okay, Dad, I hear what you're saying. But Saul Anderson is not a client you pass off to someone just to see if they can cut it. He's someone you give to your best and brightest. Someone you know can take him all the way to the end zone. And that's me."

Isn't it? I wonder as uncertainty clouds his features.

As my father's silence stretches on, my stomach twists in my gut. It's not that I have a daddy complex or anything, but I'd be lying if I said I didn't enjoy the pride my father takes in my performance at the office. I'm his right-hand man. His go-to guy. When we're down by two with five left on the clock, you can bet your ass I'm the only one John Evans will pass the ball to.

Or at least I used to be.

I'm accustomed to having his undivided confidence. The fact that confidence seems to be wavering is . . . well . . . it fucking hurts.

"Tell you what." He sighs. "We've got a month. Come up with a presentation. Have Kate do the same. Whoever can knock my socks off gets a crack at Anderson."

I should be insulted, really. What he's asking is the equivalent of telling an Oscar winner he's got to audition to play a frigging extra. But I don't argue. I'm too busy planning my next move.

So, you see what I was saying about life?

Just like that, Kate Brooks has changed from a woman I couldn't wait to do the nasty dance with to someone I can't wait to crush under my boot. My adversary. My competition. My enemy.

It's not her fault. I know. Now ask me if I care.

Nope—not even a little.

In full-out combat mode, I return to headquarters—otherwise known as my office. I give Erin a few orders and work the rest of the afternoon. Around six o'clock, I have Erin call Kate into my office.

Always keep the home-field advantage. Play on your own turf. Remember that.

She comes in and sits down, her expression unreadable.

"What's up, Drew?"

Her hair is down, framing her face in a long, glossy curtain. For a second, I imagine what it would feel like tickling my chest, draping across my thighs.

I shake my head. *Focus, Evans, focus.*

She's wearing a dark burgundy suit with matching heels. Kate is into the high heels. I think because she's naturally petite, the height advantage they give makes her feel more confident at the office.

Guys love heels. We associate them with all kinds of fantastic sexual positions. If you want a man to notice you, you cannot go wrong with a pair of shiny four-inch stilettos, I swear.

As my eyes continue to roam over her from head to toe, a problem, shall we say, arises. Although my mind recognizes that Kate Brooks is now my rival, apparently my cock hasn't gotten the memo.

And he, judging from his reaction, still wants to make friends.

So I picture Miss Gurgle, my fifth-grade science teacher, in my mind. She was a beast of a woman. A retired female wrestler—not the bikini kind. She had a mole on her right cheek that was so big, we were sure it was the head of a twin that hadn't separated in the womb. It was disgusting but strangely hypnotic at the same time—you couldn't help but stare at it. It jiggled when she spoke, like a bowl full of Jell-O.

I shudder slightly, but it does the trick. All's clear down below.

"Saul Anderson is coming to the city next month," I say at last.

Her brows rise. "Saul Anderson? Really?"

"Really," I tell her, all business. No more pleasure for her. "My father would like you to put together a mock presentation. A run-through, as if you were really going to pitch a client. He thinks it would be good practice for you."

I know, I know . . . you think I'm a scumbag. I'm not even giving her a fair chance. Well, get over it. This is business. And in business—like war—all is fair.

I expect her to be excited. I expect her to be grateful. She isn't either of these.

Her lips press together in a tight line, and her expression turns serious. "Practice, huh?"

"That's right. It's not a big deal; don't put yourself out. Just throw something together for him. A hypothetical."

She folds her arms in front of her chest and tilts her head to the side. "That's interesting, Drew. Considering your father just told me he hasn't decided who's getting Anderson yet. That it would come down to you or me, whoever put together the more impressive strategy. The way he explained it, it sounded like a very big deal."

Uh-oh.

When I was twelve, Matthew and I snagged a *Hustler* magazine from a convenience store. My father caught me with it in my room before I'd had the chance to hide it under my mattress. The look on my face at this moment is very similar to the one I wore then.

Busted.

"Playing a little dirty, are we?" she asks as her eyes narrow with suspicion.

I shrug. "Don't get ahead of yourself, sweetheart. Anderson's coming to me. My father's just throwing you a bone."

"A bone?"

"Yeah. You've had your lips attached to his ass since you started. I'm surprised he can still stand up straight. He figures this will get you off his back for a little while."

Always strike first—remember that too. The team who scores first? They're almost always the team who wins. Look it up if you don't believe me.

Yes, I'm trying to shake her confidence. Yes, I'm trying to throw her off her game.

Sue me.

I told you my history. I told you how I grew up. I never had to share my toys; I don't plan on sharing my clients.

Ask any four-year-old—sharing sucks.

When she speaks, her tone is lethal, sharp as a fucking machete. "If we're going to work together, Drew, I think we should get a few things straight. I'm not your sweetheart. My name is Kate—Katherine. Use it. And I'm not a kiss-ass. I don't have to be. My work speaks for itself. My intelligence, my determination—that's what got your father to notice me. And obviously he thinks you're a bit lacking in those departments since he's considering me for Anderson."

Ouch. Certainly goes right for the jugular, doesn't she?

"And I know women probably fall all over themselves to get your attention and one of your charming smiles," she continues, "but that's not going to happen with me. I don't plan on being one of your groupies or a notch on your bedpost, so you can save your lines, your smile, and your bullshit for someone else."

She rises to her feet and rests her hands on the edge of my desk, leaning over.

Hey, you know if I just sit up a little bit more, I could see right down her blouse. I love that spot on a woman. That valley just between her—

Stop it!

Mentally, I slap myself. And she goes on.

"You're used to being number one around here. You're used to being Daddy's *special little man*. Well, there's a new player in town. Deal with it. I've worked damn hard to get this job, and I plan on making a name for myself. You don't like sharing the spotlight? Too bad. You can either make room for me at the table, or I'll step on you when you get in my way. Either way, you can bet your ass I'll get there."

She turns to go but then looks back at me, her lips curved into a saccharine smile. "Oh, and I would say good luck with Anderson, but I won't bother. All the luck in Ireland isn't going to help you. Saul Anderson is mine . . . *sweetheart*."

And with that, she turns and stalks out of my office, right past Matthew and Jack, who stand in my doorway openmouthed.

"Well . . . damn," Matthew says.

"Okay, is anyone else turned on right now?" Jack asks. "Seriously, I got wood here 'cause that"—he points in the direction Kate just went—"that was fucking hot."

It *was* hot. Kate Brooks is a beautiful woman. But when she's pissed off, she's spectacular.

Steven walks in with a cup of coffee in his hand. Seeing the looks on our faces, he asks, "What? What'd I miss?"

Matthew all too happily tells him, "Drew is losing his touch. He just got verbally bitch-slapped. By a girl."

Steven nods grimly and says, "Welcome to my world, man."

I ignore the Three Stooges. My attention is still focused on the challenge Kate just threw down. The testosterone pumping through my body screams for victory. Not just a win, but a shutout—nothing short of a full, uncontested knockout will do.

Chapter 5

And so it began—the Olympic Games of investment banking. I'd like to say it was a mature contest between two professional and highly intelligent colleagues. I'd like to say it was friendly.

I'd like to . . . but I won't. 'Cause I'd be lying.

Remember my father's comment? The one about Kate being the first one in the office and the last to leave? It stuck in my mind that whole night.

See, getting Anderson wasn't just about putting on the best presentation, coming up with the best ideas. That's what Kate thought—but I knew better. The man is my father, after all; we share the same DNA. It was also about reward. Who was more dedicated. Who had earned it. And I was determined to show my father that I was that "who."

So, the next day I come in an hour early. Later that morning when Kate arrives, I don't look up from my desk, but I feel it when she walks past my door.

See the look on her face? The slight pause in her step as she sees me? The scowl that comes when she realizes she's the second to come in? See the steel in her eyes?

Obviously, I'm not the only one playing for keeps.

On Wednesday, then, I arrive at the same time to find Kate

typing away at her desk. She looks up when she sees me. She smiles cheerily. And waves.

I. Don't. Think. So.

The day after that, I come in another half-hour earlier . . . and so on. Are you seeing the pattern here? By the time the next Friday rolls around, I find myself walking up to the front of the building at four thirty.

Four fucking thirty!

It's still dark. And as I get to the door of the building, guess who I see across from me, arriving at the exact same time?

Kate.

Can you hear the hiss in my voice? I hope you can. We stand there looking each other in the eyes, clutching our extra-large caffeine-filled double-mocha cappuccinos in our hands.

Kind of reminds you of one of those old westerns, doesn't it? You know the ones I'm talking about—where the two guys walk down the empty street at high noon for a shootout. If you listen hard, you can probably hear the lonely call of a vulture in the background.

At the same moment, Kate and I drop our beverages and make a mad dash for the door. In the lobby, she pushes the elevator button furiously while I head for the stairs. Genius that I am, I figure I can take them three at a time. I'm almost six feet—long legs. The only problem with this, of course, is that my office is on the fortieth floor.

Idiot.

As I finally reach our floor, panting and sweating, I see Kate leisurely leaning against her office door, coat off, a glass of water in hand. She offers it to me, along with that breathtaking smile of hers.

It makes me want to kiss her and strangle her at the same time. I've never been into S&M. But I'm beginning to see its benefits.

"Here you go. You look like you could use this, Drew." She hands me the glass and flounces away. "Have a nice day."

Right.

Sure, I'll do that.

'Cause it's just starting out *great* so far.

I'm sure I've mentioned this before, but I'll go over it again just so we're clear. For me, work trumps sex. Every time. Always.

Except for Saturday nights. Saturday is club night. Guy night. Hook-up-with-gorgeous-girls-and-screw-their-brains-out night. Despite my renewed diligence at work as I vie against Kate for Anderson, my Saturday night does not change. It is sacred.

What? Do you want me to go frigging insane? All work and no play makes Drew a cranky boy.

So, that Saturday night I meet a brunette divorcée at a bar called Rendezvous. I've found myself gravitating toward brunettes for the last couple weeks.

You don't need to be Sigmund Freud to figure that one out.

Anyway, it's a great night. Divorced women have a lot of pent-up anger—a lot of buried frustration—which never fails to translate into a good, long, hard fuck. It's exactly what I'm looking for and just what I need.

But, for some reason, the next day I'm still tense. Edgy.

It's like I'd asked the waitress for a beer, and she brought me a soda. Like I ate a sandwich when what I really wanted was a nice juicy steak. I'm full. But far from satisfied.

At the time, I don't know why I feel like that. But I bet you do, don't you?

To do my job properly, I need books—lots of them. The laws, codes, and regulations involved in what I do are detailed and change frequently.

Luckily for me, my firm has the most extensive collection of pertinent reference materials in the city. Well, except for maybe the city library. But have you seen that place? It's like a frigging castle. It takes forever to find out where something should be, and when you do, it's most likely checked out already. My firm's private library is much more convenient.

So, Tuesday afternoon, I'm at my desk working with one of the aforementioned references when who should grace me with her presence?

Yep—the lovely Kate Brooks. She is looking particularly delicious today.

Her voice is hesitant. "Hey, Drew? I was looking for this year's *Technical Analysis of the Financial Markets,* and it's not in the library. Do you have it by any chance?" She bites her lip in the adorable way she does whenever she's nervous.

The book in question is actually sitting right on my desk. And I'm just about done with it. I could be the better man—the bigger person—and give it to her.

But you don't really think I'm going to do that, do you? Have you learned nothing from our past conversations?

"Yeah, I do have it, actually," I tell her.

She smiles. "Oh, great. When do you think you'll be finished with it?"

I look to the ceiling, seemingly deep in thought. "Not sure. Four . . . maybe five . . . weeks."

"Weeks?" she asks, gazing down at me.

Can you tell she's annoyed?

I know what you're thinking. If I want to eventually—after the whole Anderson thing is over—do the horizontal tango with Kate, why don't I try being just a little bit nicer to her? And you're right. That does make sense.

But the Anderson thing isn't over yet. And as I've said before—this, my friends, is war. I'm talking DEFCON-1, gloves-off, I'll-knock-you-down-even-if-you-are-a-girl war.

You wouldn't give a bullet to a sniper who's got his gun aimed at your forehead, would you?

Plus, Kate is too damn hot when she's angry for me to pass up a chance to see her fired up again, just for my own twisted pleasure. I look her up and down appreciatively as I speak before giving her my patented boyish smile that almost all women are helpless against.

Kate, of course, not being one of those women. *Figures.*

"Well, I suppose if you ask nicely . . . and throw in a shoulder rub while you're at it . . . I might be persuaded to give it to you now."

The truth is, I would never demand anything that resembled a sexual favor in exchange for something work related. I'm a lot of things. A bottom-feeding scumbag like that isn't one of them.

But that last comment could definitely be construed as flat-out, old-school sexual harassment. And if Kate ever told my father I'd said that to her? *Jesus H. Christ,* he would fire me faster than you could say, "Up shit creek without a paddle." Then he'd most likely knock me on my ass for good measure.

I'm walking one high fucking tightrope here. Yet, though the possibility exists, I'm 99.9 percent sure that Kate won't rat me out. She's too much like me. She wants to win. She wants to beat me. And she wants to do it all on her own.

She puts her hands on her hips and opens her mouth to rip into me—most likely to describe just where I can shove my book, I'd guess. I lean back with an amused smile, eagerly anticipating the explosion . . . that never comes.

She tilts her head to the side, closes her mouth, and says, "You know what? Never mind."

And with that, she walks out the door.

Huh.

Kind of anticlimactic, don't you think? I thought so too.

Wait for it.

A few hours later, I'm down in the library looking for an enormous reference titled *Commercial and Investment Banking and the International Credit and Capital Markets.* All of *Harry Potter* would fit into one chapter of this sucker. I scan the stacks for where it should be—but it's not there.

Somebody else must have it.

I turn my attention to a much smaller, but just as important, volume called *Investment Management Regulation, Fourth Edition.* Only to find that it too is missing.

What the hell?

I don't believe in coincidences. I take the elevator back to the fortieth floor and march purposefully through Kate's open door.

I don't see her right away.

That's because stacked on and around her desk, in neat skyscraper-high columns, are books. About three dozen of them.

For a moment, I freeze, my mouth open and my eyes wide with shock. Then, inanely, I wonder how the hell she got them all up here. Kate weighs a buck-ten at best. There've got to be several hundred pounds of pages in this room.

It's then that her shiny dark head emerges over the horizon. And, once again, she smiles. Like a cat with a mouthful of bird.

I hate cats. They're kind of evil looking, don't you think? Like they're just waiting for you to fall asleep so they can smother you with their fur or piss in your ear.

"Hi, Drew. Did you need something?" she asks me with phony benevolence.

Her fingers tap rhythmically on two gigantic hardcovers. "You know . . . help? Advice? Directions to the public library?"

I swallow my response. And frown at her. "No. I'm good."

"Oh. Okay, great. Bye-bye, now." And with that, she disappears back down behind the literary mountain.

Brooks—two.

Evans—zip.

After that, things get nasty.

I'm ashamed to say that both Kate and I sink to new lows in professional sabotage. It never actually wanders over to the realm of the illegal. But it's definitely close.

One day I come in to find all the cables missing from my computer. It doesn't do any lasting damage, but I have to wait an hour and a half for the IT guy to show up and reconnect it.

The next day, Kate comes in to discover that "someone" has switched all the labels on her disks and files. Nothing was erased, mind you. But she pretty much has to look through every single one if she wants to find the documents she needs.

A few days after that, at a staff meeting, I "accidentally" spill a glass of water on some information Kate has compiled for my father. Something that probably took her five or so hours to put together.

"Oops. Sorry," I say, letting the smirk on my face tell her how very unsorry I am.

"It's fine, Mr. Evans," she assures my father as she wipes up the mess. "I have another copy in my office."

How very Boy Scoutish of her, don't you think?

Later—about halfway through the same meeting—do you know what she does?

She fucking kicks me! In the shin, under the table.

"Hmph," I groan, and my hands fist reflexively.

"You all right, Drew?" my father asks.

I can only nod and squeak, "Something in my throat." I cough dramatically.

See, I'm not about to go crying to Daddy either. But *sweet Christ* it hurt. You ever been kicked in the shin by a four-inch pointy shoe? For a man, there is only one area that's more painful to be kicked.

And that is a place that dare not speak its name.

After the throbbing in my leg dies down a bit, I hide my hand behind some upturned papers while my father's speaking. Then I flip Kate the finger. Immature, I know, but apparently we're now both functioning at the preschool level, so I'm guessing it's okay.

Kate sneers at me. Then she mouths, *You wish.*

Well—she's got me there, now, doesn't she?

We're in the homestretch. A month of mortal combat has passed, and tomorrow is my father's deadline. It's around eleven o'clock and, besides the cleaning service working the night shift, Kate and I are the only ones left in the building.

I've had this fantasy a hundred times. Though, I have to say, it's never included us in our respective offices, glaring at each other across the hallway, each making the occasional obscene hand gesture.

I glance over and see her reviewing her charts. What is she thinking? Is this the Stone Age? Who the hell uses poster board anymore? Anderson is definitely mine.

I'm just putting the finishing touches on my own impressive PowerPoint presentation when Matthew walks into my office. He's heading to the bars. Never mind that it's a Wednesday night; that's just Matthew. A few short weeks ago, that was me too.

He looks at me for the longest time, saying nothing. Then he sits on the edge of my desk and says, "Dude, just fucking do it already."

"What are you talking about?" I ask, my fingers never pausing over the keyboard.

"Have you looked at yourself lately? You need to just walk over there and get it done."

And now he's annoying me. "Matthew, what the hell are you trying to say?"

But all he comes back with is, "You ever see *War of the Roses*? Is that how you want to end up?"

"I have work to do. I don't have time for this right now."

He throws his hands up. "Fine. I tried. When we find you two in the lobby under the fallen chandelier, I'll tell your mother I frigging tried."

I stop typing. "What the fuck do you mean?"

"I mean you and Kate. It's obvious you have a thing for her."

I glance over at her office when he says her name. She doesn't look up. "Yeah, I do have *a thing* for her. An extreme dislike of her. We can't stand each other. She's a pill. I wouldn't fuck her with a ten-foot dildo."

Okay, that's not true. I'd *so* fuck her. But I wouldn't like it.

Yeah—you're right. That's not true either.

Matthew sits in the chair across from my desk. I can feel him staring at me again. Then he sighs. And says, like it's supposed to be some awe-inspiring revelation, "Sally Jansen."

I look at him blankly.

Who?

"Sally Jansen," he says again, then clarifies, "third grade."

The picture of a small girl with light brown pigtails and thick glasses comes to mind.

I nod. "What about her?"

"She was the first girl I ever loved."

Wait. What?

"Didn't you used to call her Smelly Sally?"

"Yes." He nods solemnly. "Yes, I did. And I loved her."

Still confused.

"Didn't you get, like, the entire third grade to call her Smelly Sally?"

He nods again and, trying to sound sage, says, "Love makes you do some stupid shit."

I guess so, because . . .

"Didn't she have to leave early twice a week to go to a therapist because you ragged on her so much?"

He ponders this a moment. "Yes, that's true. You know, there's a fine line between love and hate, Drew."

"And didn't Sally Jansen switch schools later that year because—"

"Look, the point here, man, is that I liked the girl. Loved her. I thought she was awesome. But I couldn't deal with those feelings. I didn't know how to express them the right way."

Matthew's not usually this in touch with his feminine side.

"So you picked on her instead?" I ask.

"Sadly, yes."

"And this has to do with Kate and me because . . . ?"

He pauses a beat and then gives me . . . the look. The slight shake of his head, the grimace of sad disappointment. That look right there is worse than a mother's guilt, I swear.

He stands, slaps me on the arms, and says, "You're a smart guy, Andrew. You'll figure it out." And with that, he leaves.

Yeah, yeah, I know what Matthew was trying to say. I get it, all right. And I'm telling you—straight up—he's crazy.

I don't spar with Kate because I like her. I do it because her existence is screwing with the trajectory of my career. She's a nuisance. A fly in my soup. A pain in my ass. As aching as that mother of a beesting I got on my left cheek at summer camp when I was eleven.

Sure, she'd be a great lay. I'd ride the Kate Brooks Express any time. But it would never be anything more than a good screw. That's all, folks.

What? Why are you looking at me like that? You don't believe me?

Then you're as crazy as Matthew.

Chapter 6

Pressure's a funny thing. It makes some people snap. Like the MIT student who decided to take out half the student body with a long-range rifle because he got a B-plus on a final. It makes some people choke. Two words: *Jorge Posada*. Enough said. Pressure makes some people fall. Crumble. Freeze.

I am not one of those people. I thrive on pressure. It propels me, drives me to succeed. It is my element. Like water to a fish.

I get to work the next day bright and early. Dressed to kill, with my game face on.

It's go time.

Kate and I arrive at my father's office door at nine a.m. on the dot. I can't help but check her out. She looks good. Confident. Excited. Apparently she reacts to stress the same way I do.

My father explains that Saul Anderson called to say he would be coming to town ahead of schedule. As in tomorrow night.

Lots of businessmen do this. Push meetings up at the last minute. It's a test. To see if you're prepared. To see if you can handle the unexpected. Lucky for me—I am and I can.

And then we begin. I insist on ladies first.

I watch Kate's presentation like a kid watches a gift under the tree on Christmas Eve. She doesn't know that, of course. My face is the very definition of bored indifference. On the inside, though, I can't wait to see what she's got.

And I'm not disappointed. Don't tell anyone I said this—I'll deny it until death—but Kate Brooks is pretty fucking incredible. Almost as good as I am.

Almost.

She's direct, clear, and persuasive as hell. The investment plans she lays out are unique and imaginative. And destined to make a shitload of money. Her only weakness is that she's new. She doesn't have the connections to necessarily make what she's proposing happen. Like I've said before, part of this business—a big part—is having the inside track. The hidden info and dirty secrets that outsiders can't get to. So although Kate's ideas are strong, they're not altogether viable. Not a slam dunk.

Then it's my turn.

My proposals, on the other hand, are rock fucking solid. The companies and investments I outline are well known and secure. Granted, my projected profits aren't as high as Kate's, but they're certain. Dependable. Safe.

Once I'm done, I sit beside Kate on the couch. See us there? Kate's hands are folded neatly in her lap, her back straight, a sure, satisfied smile on her lips. I lean back on the couch, my stance relaxed, my own confident smile a mirror image of hers.

For those of you out there who think I'm a shit heel? Watch carefully. You're going to love this part.

My father clears his throat, and I can read the excited gleam in his eyes. He rubs his hands together and smiles. "I knew my instincts were right on this one. I can't tell you how impressed I am with what you've come up with. And I think it's obvious who should move forward with Anderson."

Simultaneously, Kate and I smirk at each other, gloating triumph written all over our faces.

Wait for it. . . .

"Both of you."

Irony's really a bite in the ass, isn't it?

Our eyes turn to my father, and the grins drop from our faces faster than an Acme safe in a Road Runner cartoon. Our shocked voices speak at the same time.

"What?"

"Excuse me?"

"With your artistic flair for investing, Kate, and your concrete know-how, Drew, you two will be perfect together. An unbeatable team. You can both work on the account. When he signs with us, you can share him—the workload and the bonuses—fifty-fifty."

Share him?

Share him?

Has the old man lost his freaking mind? Would I ask him to share something he's worked his ass off for? Would he let someone else drive his 1965 cherry Mustang convertible? Would he open his bedroom door and let some other guy screw his wife?

Okay, that was too far. I take it back—considering his wife is my mother. Forget I ever referred to my mother and screwing in the same sentence. That's just . . . wrong. On so many levels.

But for the love of God, tell me you see my point.

My father must have finally looked at our faces, because he asks, "That's not a problem, is it?"

I open my mouth to tell him what a major goddamn problem it is. But Kate beats me to the punch.

"No, Mr. Evans, of course not. No problem at all."

"Wonderful!" He claps his hands together and stands. "I've got tee-off in an hour, so I'll leave you two to it. You've got until tomorrow night to coordinate your proposals. Anderson will be at Le Bernardin at seven."

And then he looks me dead in the face. "I know you won't let me down, Andrew."

Shit.

I don't care if you're sixty, when a parent uses your full name, it pretty much sucks all the argument right out of you.

"No, sir, I won't."

And with that, he's out the door. Leaving Kate and me sitting on the couch, our expressions dazed, like survivors of a nuclear blast.

"'No, Mr. Evans, of course not,'" I whine. "Could you be any more of a kiss-ass?"

She hisses, "Shut up, *Andrew*." Then she sighs. "What the hell are we supposed to do now?"

"Well, you could do the noble thing and bow out." Yeah—like that'll happen.

"In your dreams."

I smirk. "Actually, my dreams involve you bending over something . . . not bowing."

She makes a disgusted sound. "Could you be any more of a pig?"

"I was kidding. Why do you have to be so fucking serious all the time? You should learn how to take a joke."

"I can take a joke," she tells me, sounding insulted.

"Yeah? When?"

"When it's not being delivered by a childish jackass who thinks he's God's gift to women."

"I am not childish."

God's gift on the other hand? My record speaks for itself.

"Oh, bite me."

I wish.

"Nice comeback, Kate. *Very* mature."

"You're a jerk."

"You're a . . . an Alexandra."

She pauses a second and looks at me blankly. "What the hell does that even mean?"

Think about it. It will come to you.

I rub my hand down my face. "Okay, look, this is getting us nowhere fast. We're screwed. We both still want Anderson, and the only way we're going to get him is if we somehow get our shit together. We've got . . . thirty hours to do that. Are you in or not?"

Her lips come together in flat-out determination.

"You're right. I'm in."

"Meet me in my office in twenty minutes, and we'll get to work."

I expect her to argue with me. I expect her to ask why we have to meet in *my* office—why we can't work in *her* office—like a nagging housewife. But she doesn't.

She just says, "Okay." And leaves the room to get the rest of her things.

I'm surprised.

Maybe this won't be as bad as I thought.

"That is the stupidest fucking idea I have ever heard!"

Nope, it's much worse.

"I've researched Anderson. He's the old-fashioned type. He's not going to want to go blind staring at your laptop all night. He's going to want something concrete, tangible. Something he can take home. That's what I'll give him!"

"This is a multibillion-dollar business meeting—not a fifth-grade science fair. I'm not walking in there with frigging poster board!"

It's after midnight. We've been in my office for a little over twelve hours. Except for these few minute details, every aspect of our presentation has been banged out, negotiated, compromised.

I feel like I just bartered a goddamn peace treaty.

By now, Kate has released her hair and lost her shoes. My tie is off, the top two buttons of my shirt open. Our appearance could make things feel friendly—intimate—like an all-night study session in college.

If we weren't trying to rip each other's throats open, of course.

"I don't give a shit if you agree or not. I'm right about this. I'm bringing the poster board."

I give in. I'm too tired to fight about paper. "Fine. Just—shrink it down."

We ordered food a few hours ago and worked through dinner. I had pasta with chicken, while Kate preferred a turkey club with fries on the side. Much as I hate to admit it, I'm impressed. Obviously, she doesn't subscribe to the "I can only eat salads in front of the opposite sex" rule of thumb a lot of chicks swear by. Who gave women that idea? Like a guy's going to say to his friend, "Dude, she was one fugly chick, but once I saw her chomping that romaine, I just had to nail her."

No man wants to fuck a skeleton—and nibbling crackers and water like a prisoner of war at dinner isn't attractive. It just makes us think about what a cranky bitch you're going to be later on because you're starving. If a guy's into you? A cheeseburger deluxe is not going to scare him away. And if he's not? Ingesting all the greens on Peter Cottontail's farm isn't going to change that, trust me.

Now back to the battle royal.

"I'm doing the talking," I tell her firmly.

"No, no way!"

"Kate—"

"These are my ideas, and I'm presenting them!"

She's purposely trying to make me nuts. She's deliberately trying to drive me off the deep end. She's probably hoping I'll throw myself out the window, just to get away from the annoyance that is her. Then she'll have Anderson all to herself.

Well, her evil little scheme isn't going to work. I'm going to stay calm. I'm going to count to ten. I won't let Kate get to me.

"Saul Anderson," I say, "is an old-fashioned businessman—you just said it yourself. He's going to want to talk to another business-*man,* not someone he sees as a glorified secretary."

"That is the most sexist comment I've ever heard. You're disgusting!"

Calm goes straight out the window and down about forty stories.

"I didn't say *I* thought that way—I said *he* thinks that way! Fucking Christ Almighty!"

And it's true. I don't care what you're packing in your pants or which way you roll. A pecker, a cooch, or both—it's all the same to me. As long as you get the job done right, that's all that matters. But Kate seems determined to think the worst of me.

I push my hands through my hair in an effort to vent some of the frustration that makes me want to shake the shit out of her.

"Look, this is the way it is. Trying to pretend certain biases don't exist won't make them go away. We have a better shot at signing Anderson if I do the talking."

"I said no! I don't care what you think. Absolutely not."

"God, you're so fucking stubborn. You're like a menopausal pissed-off mule!"

"I'm stubborn! *I'm* stubborn? Well, maybe I wouldn't have to be if you weren't King of the Control Freaks!"

She's right about the control thing. But what can I say? I like things done the right way—my way. I won't apologize for that. Especially not to Ms. Stick Up Her Ass.

"At least I know when to back off—unlike you. You walk around like an uptight overachiever on crystal meth!"

By this time, we're both on our feet, less than a foot apart facing each other. Without her heels, I have a major height advantage, but Kate doesn't seem intimidated.

She pokes me in the chest as she argues. "You don't even know me. I am not uptight."

"Oh, please. I've never seen someone who needs to get laid as badly as you do. I don't know what the hell your fiancé is doing with you. But whatever it is? He's not doing it right."

Her mouth opens, forming a big ole O at my little dig against her betrothed. Out of the corner of my eye, I see her hand come up, ready to slap me across the face.

This is not the first time a woman has tried to slap me. You're not surprised, are you?

Like a pro, I catch her wrist before she makes contact with my cheek and hold her arm down at her side. "Gee, Kate, for a woman who claims she doesn't want to screw me, you're certainly eager to make this physical."

Her other hand comes up to try and slap me from the other side, but I block her again and am now securely holding both her hands at her hips. I smirk. "Gotta do better than that, baby, if you want a piece of me."

"I hate you!" she yells in my face.

"I hate you more!" I shout.

Admittedly, not my wittiest comeback—but it was the best I could manage under the circumstances.

"Good!"

It's the last word she gets out.

Before my mouth descends on hers.

And our lips crash together.

Chapter 7

I've kissed hundreds of girls. No—make that thousands. I only really remember a handful of them. But this kiss? This is one I won't forget any time soon.

She tastes . . . *Jesus,* I've never done drugs, but I imagine this is what that first snort of cocaine feels like, that first shot of heroin. Goddamn addictive.

Our lips clash and move over each other, angry and wet.

I can't stop touching her. My hands are everywhere: her face, her hair, down her back, grasping at her hips. Pulling her closer, desperate to feel more of her—wanting her to feel exactly what she's doing to me.

Needing air, I rip my mouth from hers and attack her neck. I feast on her, like a starving man. And that's exactly what I am—ravenous for her. I inhale as I lick, suck, and nibble my way from her jaw to her ear.

She's whimpering incoherently, but I get the idea. The sound of her voice, wild and sexy, makes me groan. And her scent. *Sweet Christ,* she smells like . . . flowers and sugar. Like one of those decorative confectionary roses on the top of a cake.

Fucking delicious.

And her hands aren't idle either. She grasps my biceps, and the heat of her hands seeps through my dress shirt. She scrapes her nails down my back and dips her fingers below the waist of my slacks, first grazing then cupping my ass.

I'm dying. I'm burning. My blood is liquid fucking fire, and I feel like we're going to go up in smoke before we ever make it to the couch. Kate gasps as I draw her earlobe into my mouth and dance across the flesh below it with my tongue.

"Drew? Drew, what are we doing?"

"I don't know," I moan in a rough voice. "Just . . . don't stop touching me."

She doesn't.

And I'm back at her mouth. Plunging my tongue into her, sliding it against hers in the same way I'm dying to slide my cock into her wet, welcoming body. I feel her hips push forward against mine. And any blood left in my body descends, making me harder than I've ever been in my life.

Weeks of want and frustration are coursing through me. I've brushed with Colgate for far too long—and it's tasted like shit.

"Do you know how much I want this? Want you? God, Kate . . . I've fucking dreamed about this . . . begged for it. You make me . . . ah, I can't get . . . enough of you."

Her hands are on my chest now, rubbing, scratching, moving down my abs, until one hand brushes against the front of my pants, and I hiss in pure agonizing pleasure. Before I can inhale, she's stroking my dick through my pants, and I thrust forward. Any semblance of control or finesse is gone.

My hands come up to her breasts, and she arches her back to bring them closer. I squeeze, and she moans again. I skim across where I know her nipples are, frustrated by her blouse and bra. I want to tug and pinch those beauties until they're two sharp peaks. Her mouth is on my neck, kissing, and I raise my chin.

It's never been like this. I've never been like this. I've never felt so much for any woman, no matter that it's a mixture of anger and lust.

"Drew . . . Drew, I can't do this. I love Billy," she pants.

Her confession doesn't affect me like you'd think it would. Mostly because she still has one hand on my cock when she says it. Her actions speak the complete opposite of her voice. Hands and hips that are pulling me closer, stroking me, pleading for more.

"That's good, Kate. Fine. Love Billy. Marry Billy. Just please . . . God . . . please just fuck me."

I don't even know what I'm saying. Don't even know if I'm making sense. One thought and one only drums in my head like a primal melody:

More.

I bring my chin down, wanting to taste her mouth again. But instead of her lips . . . I make contact with her palm. I open my eyes to find her hand covering my mouth, blocking me. Her chest is heaving, rising and falling in brisk, rapid pants.

And then I see her eyes. And I feel like I just took a wrecking ball to the chest. Because her eyes are wide with panic . . . and confusion. I try to say her name, but it's muffled by her hand.

I hear a sob in her voice as she says, "I can't do this, Drew. I'm sorry. Billy . . . this job . . . this is my life. My whole life. I . . . I can't."

She's trembling. And suddenly, my need, my lust, and my still-raging hard-on are all pushed to the back burner, behind the overwhelming desire to comfort her. To tell her it's okay. Everything will be all right.

Anything. I'll say anything to take that look off her face.

But she doesn't give me the chance. The moment she takes her hand off my mouth, she runs out the door. And she's gone before I can draw a breath. I should go after her. I should tell her it's okay that she put the brakes on. That this hasn't—and won't—change anything. Though that's one big fat lie, and we both know it, don't we?

But I don't follow Kate. And the reason is simple: Have you ever tried to run with a boner staring up at you?

No?

Well, it's damn near impossible.

I collapse onto the couch and rest my head back. Looking up at the ceiling, I pinch the bridge of my nose with my fingers. How is it that something as simple as sex just became so frigging complicated? I don't know either.

Christ, I'm so hard. I want to cry—I'll admit it. I'm not ashamed. I want to weep from the throbbing ache in my groin that will have no relief. The idea of going out and finding a substitute for Kate never even enters my head. Because my dick knows what my brain is just starting to admit.

There is no substitute for Kate Brooks. Not for me. Not now.

I look down at the tent in my lap. The one that shows no indication of going down anytime soon.

It's going to be a long, long night.

Chapter 8

The next day, Kate doesn't come into the office until eleven o'clock. I don't need to tell you that this is unusual for her.

She's avoiding me. I know this because I've done it myself on more than one occasion. Discreetly sneaking over to the other side of the club when I happen to vaguely recognize one of my previous hookups. But to actually be on the receiving end of this? It sucks.

I don't get the privilege of speaking with her until two, when she comes striding into my office—looking drop-dead gorgeous. Her hair is pinned up in what Alexandra would call a French twist. She's wearing a black dress that flows out slightly at the knee, with matching high heels and a black blazer.

She puts a small stack of poster board on my desk, her charts and graphs shrunk down to notebook-size like we agreed. "Okay. You're right. You should lead with Anderson. I'll be second chair."

She talks like nothing ever happened. Like she wasn't quivering in my arms and setting me on fire with her hands in this very office just a few short hours ago. She's all business. Completely unaffected. And it pisses me off.

Badly.

Indifference is not exactly a reaction I'm used to from women. Frankly, it's a little hard to take.

I feel my jaw clench as I tell her, "Good. That's the best way to go."

Now, if you haven't guessed, I'm not the touchy-feely type. I'm not one to talk my feelings to death like some New Age, meditating freak of nature. But I expected something from her. Some acknowledgment of what happened last night—of the attraction that's still pulling at both of us. I thought she would be the one to bring it up.

She's a woman, after all.

When all I get is silence, I can't help but push. "Kate, about last night—"

She cuts me off. "Last night was a mistake. It will not happen again."

Do you know anything about child psychology? No? Well here's a lesson for you. If you tell a kid they can't do something, guess what's the first thing they're going to try and do the minute you're not looking? Exactly.

Men are the same way. It's *so* going to happen again. But she doesn't need to know that at the moment.

"Okay."

"Good."

"Great."

She whispers, "Fine."

Fine's a funny word, don't you think? I don't think there's another like it in the English language that says so much while actually saying so little. How many wives have told their husbands, "I'm fine," when they really mean, "I want to cut your balls off with a butcher knife"? How many men have told their girlfriends, "You look fine," when they really mean, "You need to go back to the gym and work out—a lot." It's the universal way of saying we're just peachy—when we're really anything but.

"Fine," I repeat, looking down at the papers on my desk.

And then she's out the door, and I spend the next ten minutes staring after her, replaying last night over and over in my mind.

Hey, you know another word that can mean the opposite of what it's supposed to?

Fucked.

Which is exactly what I'm going to be if I don't get my head out of my ass and back in the game by seven o'clock tonight.

Our dinner meeting is well under way. Although I've done a lot of the talking, it's Kate who has Saul Anderson completely charmed. If I wasn't in such a pissy mood, I'd admit that she's working this meeting like a pro. But I am, so I'm not telling anyone but you.

She laughs at some story Anderson just finished telling before he excuses himself to go to the john. I take a drink of my wine, wishing it was whiskey.

Kate turns to me, freshman excitement dancing in her eyes. "So this is going really well, isn't it? I mean, I definitely think he's interested, don't you?"

I shrug. "Depends on what you're trying to sell him."

"What are you talking about? I'm selling us—our proposal, our investment firm."

I'm being a prick—yes, I know.

"Really? 'Cause it seems like you're offering him something else entirely."

"What are you trying to say?"

"Come on, Kate. You went to Wharton. I think you can figure out exactly what I'm saying."

"I have been completely professional . . ."

"You'd be more subtle if you ripped open your blouse and shoved your tits in his face."

Okay, that was uncalled for. And I actually consider apologizing.

But before I can form the words, ice-cold liquid seeps through my pants and into my crotch. From the glass of water Kate just poured into my lap.

"Are you fucking crazy?" I whisper harshly, trying not to make a scene as I jump up and wipe at the stain with a napkin.

"Everything all right here?"

It's Anderson. He's back and looking from me to Kate. I shrug awkwardly as Kate smiles and tells him, "Everything's fine."

There's that word again. See what I mean?

"Drew just had a little mishap with his water glass. You know boys—can't take them anywhere."

Anderson laughs and sits back down while I weigh my chances for an acquittal. The one I'll need after I strangle Kate Brooks.

An hour later, we're waiting for coffee and dessert. Kate has left the table. I'm thinking her bladder must have been seconds from rupturing for her to actually leave me alone with Anderson.

He observes me for a moment and then says, "I like what I've seen here tonight, Drew. Very impressive."

"Thanks, Saul."

In business, always use first names. It's not disrespectful. It shows that you're an equal—in the same league. That's huge.

"And based on what you've shown me, I'm ready to give Evans, Reinhart and Fisher my business."

Yes! Break out the champagne, baby.

"I'm pleased to hear that. I think this deal is going to be very profitable for both—that is, all of us." Can't forget Kate, right? As if she would let me. "You can put your complete confidence in Kate and me. We won't let you down."

He fingers his crystal glass. "Right. About that. Before I sign, I have only one contingency."

This kind of thing happens all the time. Not a big deal.

"Go ahead, Saul. I'm sure we can provide whatever you need."

"I'm happy to hear that. So, why don't you have that darling girl of yours—Kate—bring the contracts by my place tonight, around midnight." He hands me a business card, and I feel like there's a boulder in my stomach.

Can you feel it too?

"Here's where I'm staying. You have her bring the papers . . . alone."

You know on TV when there's one of those awkward, shocking moments, and all you hear are the crickets in the background?

Well chirp fucking chirp. This is one of those moments.

"I'm not sure I—"

"Oh, sure you do, Drew. You know how it is. When a man's working late and needs a little . . . comfort. A distraction."

How about my foot up your ass, Saul? How'd that be for distraction?

"And that girl of yours is one prime piece. My business will bring your firm millions in revenue. And that's not including the additional clients you'll get once word gets around that I'm with you. I'd say a little after-hours servicing is a small price to pay, wouldn't you?"

He makes sense—in a sick, perverted, registered-sex-offender kind of way. But do you think that matters? Hell no. I stand up. I'm afraid of what I'll do if I have to look at his smug, shit-eating grin another minute.

I throw a dozen bills on the table and tell him, "That's not the kind of business we're in. If that's the sort of deal you're looking for, Forty-Second Street is about ten blocks that way. I'm no pimp, and Katherine Brooks is certainly not a whore. This meeting is over."

Aren't you proud of me? I am. Though what I just said was in no way satisfying, it was professional—dignified. I kept it together. I didn't even call him the ass-licking, dick-bag piece of steaming dog shit that I think he is. Go me.

I walk toward the bar area in the next room, and I'm fuming. Can you see the steam coming out of my ears? No? Well, obviously you're not looking hard enough. That guy's got some set of balls. To fucking suggest that Kate . . . Kate is more than just a pretty face. She's brilliant. And funny. And—okay, maybe she's not nice, but I'm sure she could be if she didn't hate my guts. In any case, she deserves better—more respect—than what she just got. So much more.

That's when I see her, walking past the bar on her way back from the restroom. She spots me and walks over, a smile spread across her face.

"So? How'd it go? He's with us, isn't he? I knew it, Drew! I knew the minute we showed him our projections he was done. And I know working together hasn't been the easiest thing, but I think your father was right. We do make a pretty good team, don't we?"

I swallow hard. I look down at her hand on my arm and then back up into those sweet, innocent eyes, and . . . I just can't do it. I can't tell her.

"I blew it, Kate. Anderson's not interested."

"What? What do you mean? What happened?"

I stare at my nine-hundred-dollar shoes. "I screwed up. Can we just get out of here?"

When I look back up, her face is a mask of confused sympathy. Here I just told her that I blew the account—our account—and there's not a trace of anger in her expression. God, I'm such an asshole.

"Well, let me talk to him. Maybe I can fix this."

I shake my head, "No, you can't."

"Let me at least try."

"Kate, wait . . ." But she's already walking away, toward the table where Anderson still sits.

You ever been on the freeway, stuck in bumper-to-bumper traffic? And when you finally get to the head of the line, you realize the backup is because of an accident? Maybe not a bad one—maybe just a fender bender that's already been moved to the side of the road. And all that traffic—all that wasted time—is because every driver who passes the scene has to slow down and take a look.

It's ridiculous, isn't it? And you swear that when you pass by, you're not going to look—just on principle alone. But when you get there, and you're driving past the dented doors and flashing lights and smashed bumpers, what do you do?

You slow down and look. You didn't want to, but you can't help it. It's morbid. Absurd. But that's human nature for you. Watching Kate walk up to Anderson feels just like looking at the aftermath of an accident. And no matter how much I want to—I just can't look away.

She stands next to his chair, a perfect, professional smile on her lips. If you look closely, you'll see the moment when what he's asking for registers in her mind. See how her smile freezes? Her brow wrinkles slightly because she can't actually believe he's suggesting what he is. And then she's stiff and unsure. Should she tell him to go fuck a duck? Should she laugh it off or politely refuse? While the wheels are turning in Kate's head, Anderson takes his finger—can you see the slime dripping off it?—and trails it slowly down her bare arm.

And that's it. I snap out of my stupor. And I see red. Bright, neon, Technicolor red.

You ever see *A Christmas Story*? You know toward the end when Ralphie beats the ever-loving shit out of the bully? I hope to God you've seen it. Because then you'll know exactly what I mean when I say I'm about to go real fucking Ralphie on this son of a bitch.

I walk over and put myself in front of Kate. "Touch her again and I'm going to throw you through that windowpane. They'll be picking pieces of you up off Fifty-First for days."

He chuckles. Sounds like the Crypt Keeper, doesn't he?

"Calm down, Son."

Son? Is this dipshit for real?

"You know something, Drew? I like you."

Now *there* is a concept that scares the piss out of me.

"I need a man like you around," he continues. "Someone who's not afraid to speak his mind. To tell me what he really thinks. It seems as though my . . . *contingency* isn't going to be met. But I'm going to sign with you and your firm anyway. What do you think of that?" He leans back in his chair and takes a sip of his wine. Completely confident in the fact that I will disregard anything he's said or done for the chance to get my hands on his money.

"I'm going to say a great big *no* to that, Saul. See, we have this company policy: We don't deal with limp-dick, Viagra-popping, dirtbag motherfuckers who try to use their position to coerce women—young enough to be their daughters—into bed. Go peddle your shit somewhere else. We aren't buying."

Our stares are locked on each other like two wolves on the Discovery Channel when he says, "Think carefully, Son. You're making a mistake."

"I think the only mistake I've made is wasting our time here with you. That's something I don't plan on doing a second longer. We're done here."

And then I turn to Kate and tell her softly, "We're leaving."

With my hand on her lower back, we walk to the coat-check room. I hold her coat for her and help her into it. With my hands on her shoulders, I ask, "You okay?"

She doesn't look back at me, "I'm fine."

Right. And we all know what that means, don't we?

For many men, their car is equivalent to the perfect woman. We can build her to look exactly how we want, we can ride her hard and she won't complain, and we can easily trade her in when a newer, younger model comes along. It's pretty much the ideal relationship.

I drive an Aston Martin V12. There're not many things in this world that I love, but my car is one of them. I got her after I closed my first deal. She's a beauty. She's my baby. Not that you would know that by the way I'm driving at the moment. It's the typical pissed-off-guy mode of driving. A death grip on the steering wheel, hard turns, fast stops, a smack on the horn at the slightest provocation. I don't think about how my attitude might be interpreted by Kate, until her small voice comes from the passenger seat.

"I'm sorry."

I glance quickly at her. "You're sorry for what?"

"I never meant to send out those kinds of signals, Drew. I would never come on to a client. I didn't realize that . . ."

Christ.

Why do women always do this? Why are they so eager to blame themselves when someone treats them like shit? A guy would take a cheese grater to his tongue before admitting he screwed up.

When we were sixteen, Matthew was dating Melissa Sayber. One day while he was in the shower, Melissa went through his sock drawer and found notes from the two other girls he was banging at the same time. She went apeshit. But you know what? By the time Matthew was done talking to her—after he flushed the evidence—not only did he convince her that she had read the notes wrong, but she was apologizing to him for going through his stuff. Unbelievable, right?

I pull over to the side of the road and turn to face her. "Listen to me, Kate—you didn't do anything wrong."

"But you said, about my blouse . . . and his face . . ."

Great. She thinks she was asking for it because that's what I fucking told her. Perfect.

"No, I was being an asshole. I didn't mean it. I was just trying to get a rise out of you. Look, in this business some guys are just power-high pricks. They're used to getting whatever they ask for, women included."

I don't want to see the similarities between Saul Anderson and myself. But they're kind of hard to miss. Listening to him tonight made me feel . . . shitty . . . about how I've treated Kate the last few weeks. My father wanted me to help her, mentor her. Instead I let my cock and my overactive sense of competition lead the way.

"And you're a gorgeous woman. This won't be the last time something like this happens. You have to have a thick skin. You can't let anyone rattle your confidence. You were perfect at that meeting. Really. Should've been a home run."

She gives me a small smile. "Thank you."

I turn back onto the road, and we drive in silence. Until she says, "God I could use a drink right now."

Her comment throws me. It seems like such an un-Kate thing to say. She's a straight arrow. No nonsense. The kind of girl who hardly drinks, doesn't eat trans fats, and vacuums behind the couch three times a week. It's then that I realize that although the woman next to me occupies a permanent space in my thoughts, I really don't know much about her. Not any more than I did when I first approached her all those weeks ago at REM.

It's an even bigger shock when I admit to myself that I want to.

At this juncture in my life, my idea of getting to know a woman consists of finding out if she likes it slow and sweet or hard and dirty—top, bottom, or from behind. But the interactions I've had with Kate are different from any other woman. *She's* different.

She's like a Rubik's Cube. So frustrating at times that you want to toss it out the goddamn window. But you don't. You can't. You're compelled to keep playing with it until you figure it out.

"Seriously?" I ask.

She shrugs. "Well, yeah. It's been a rough night—a rough few weeks, actually."

I smile and shift my baby into fifth gear. "I know just the place."

Don't worry. I don't plan on plying her with alcohol until she gives up the goodies. But . . . if she happens to get wasted and tries to rip my clothes off in the alley behind the bar, don't expect me to beat her off with a stick either.

All kidding aside, this is a new beginning for Kate and me. A fresh start. I'll be a perfect gentleman. Scout's honor.

Then again, I never was a Boy Scout.

Chapter 9

"First time you got drunk?"

"Thirteen. Just before a school dance. My parents were out of town, and my date, Jennifer Brewster, thought it'd be mature to have a vodka and orange juice. But all I could find was rum. So we had rum and orange juice. We ended up puking our guts out behind the gym. To this day, I can't smell rum without wanting to hurl. First kiss?"

"Tommy Wilkens. Sixth grade, at the movies. He put his arm around me and stuck his tongue down my throat. I had no idea what was happening."

We're playing First and Ten. For those of you who are unfamiliar with this drinking game, I'll explain. One person asks about a first—your first trip to Disneyland, the first time you got laid, doesn't matter. And the other person has to tell about that first. If they haven't done it for the first time yet—or won't answer—they have to drink their shot. Then they have to tell you something they *have* done at least ten times. Which one of us suggested this game? I've already missed five firsts. I have no clue.

"First time you fell in love?"

Make that six. I pick up my vodka and toss it back.

We're in a darkened corner of a small local bar named Howie's. It's a low-key place, kind of like the bar on *Cheers*. The patrons are laid-back, easygoing. Not the slick, couture-wearing Manhattanites with whom I typically spend my weekend nights. I like it here, though. Except for the karaoke. Whoever invented karaoke is evil. He should be shot between the eyes with a dull bullet.

Kate cocks her head to the side, appraising me. "You've never been in love?"

I shake my head. "Love is for suckers, sweetheart."

She smiles. "Cynical much? So you don't believe love is real?"

"Didn't say that. My parents have been happily married for thirty-six years. My sister loves her husband, and he worships her."

"But you've never?"

I shrug. "I just don't see the point. It's a whole lot of work and not much payoff. Your odds of making it for even a few years are only fifty-fifty at best. Too complicated for my tastes."

I prefer simple and straightforward. I work, I fuck, I eat, I sleep; on Sundays I have brunch with my mother and play basketball with the guys. Effortless. Easy.

Kate sits back in her chair. "My grandmother used to say, 'If it's not difficult, it's not worth it.' Besides, don't you get . . . lonely?"

On cue, a busty shot girl comes to our table and leans over with her hand on my shoulder and her cleavage in my face. "You need anything else, cutie?"

That pretty much answers Kate's question, huh?

"Sure, honey. Could you bring us another round?"

As the waitress moves away, Kate's eyes meet mine before rolling to the ceiling. "Anyway. Give me your ten."

"I've had sex with more than ten women in one week."

Cancún. Spring break 2004. Mexico is awesome.

"Uck. Is that supposed to impress me?"

I grin proudly. "It impresses most women." I lean forward and lower my voice as I rub my thumb slowly against hers. "Then again, you're not most women, are you?"

She licks her lips, her eyes on mine. "Are you flirting with me?"

"Definitely."

Shot Girl brings our drinks. I crack my knuckles. I'm up. Time to get . . . intimate.

"First blow job?"

I tried. I held out for as long as I could. I couldn't resist any longer.

The smile drops from Kate's face. "You have serious issues. You know that, right?"

Borrowing some peer pressure from *The Breakfast Club,* I goad, "Come on, Claire—just answer a simple question."

Kate picks up her drink and knocks it back impressively.

I am both shocked and appalled. "You've never given a blow job?"

Please, God, don't let Kate be one of those women. You know the ones I mean—cold, unadventurous, the ones who just don't do *that.* The ones who insist on *making love,* which means fucking in the missionary position only. They're the reason men like Eliot Spitzer and Bill Clinton risk the destruction of their political careers, 'cause they're just that desperate for a happy ending.

She flinches as the vodka burns down her throat. "Billy doesn't like . . . oral sex. He doesn't like to give it, I mean."

She's got to be drunk. There's no way in holy hell that Kate would be telling me this were she not completely and utterly shit-faced. She hides it well, don't you think? But she still hasn't answered my question.

As for her fiancé—he's a pussy. No pun intended. My mother always told me, "Anyone worth doing is worth doing well." Okay, she didn't actually say those exact words, but you get the picture. If I'm not eager to go down on a chick, then I'm not screwing her. Sorry if that's crude, but that's just how it is.

And this is *Kate* we're talking about here. I'd eat her for breakfast every day of the week and twice on Sunday. And I can't think of a single man I know who would disagree with me.

Billy is a total fucking idiot.

"So, since he's never . . . you know. He doesn't think it's fair that I should do it to him. So, no . . . I've never . . ."

She can't even say it. I have to help her out. "Given head? Sucked him off? Been tea-bagged? Blown his balls and his mind?"

She covers her face and giggles. I'm pretty sure it's the most adorable thing I've ever seen. She takes her hands off her face and blows out a breath. "Moving on. My ten. I've been with Billy Warren for over ten years."

I choke on my beer. "Ten years?"

She nods. "Almost eleven."

"So you started dating when you were . . ."

"Fifteen. Yeah."

So, if I'm hearing her correctly, what she's most likely saying is no man has ever gone down on her? Don't mean to beat a dead horse, but I just can't wrap my mind around this. That's what she's saying, right?

I could cry. What a fucking sin. Spare the karaoke guy—save the bullet for Kate's boyfriend.

"How long have you been engaged?"

"About seven years. He asked me the week before I left for college."

Those two sentences tell me exactly what kind of man shithead Billy happens to be. Insecure, jealous, clingy. He knew his girl was out of his league, that she was going places and would most likely leave him in the dust. So what does he do? He asks her to marry him, pretty much trapping her before she knew any better.

"That's why the ring is so . . . you know . . . small. But it doesn't matter to me. Billy worked for six months to get me this ring. Bussing tables, mowing lawns, killing himself. This tiny stone means more to me than the biggest rock at Tiffany's."

And those few sentences tell me exactly what kind of woman Kate Brooks is too. A lot of Manhattan women are all about flash—the brand of the car, the name on the bag, the size of the ring. Superficial. Empty. I should know; I've slept with most of them. But Kate is the real deal. Genuine. She's all about quality, not quantity.

She reminds me of my sister, actually. Even with all the money we grew up with, Alexandra doesn't really give a rat's ass about labels or what other people think. That's how she ended up with a guy like Steven. He and Alexandra started dating in high school, when he was a sophomore and she was a senior. That maneuver made him a legend at St. Mary's Prep. To this day, his name is invoked in her hallowed halls with reverence.

What's that? Yes, I went to Catholic school. You're surprised? You shouldn't be. My profanity has a certain religious flavor that can only be learned through a lifetime of Catholic education. *Jesus H. Christ . . . Goddamn it . . . Jesus, Mary, and Joseph . . . fucking Christ*

Almighty . . . holy fucking shit—and that's just what we heard from the priests. Don't get me started on the nuns.

Anyway—where was I? That's right, Steven and Alexandra.

Steven is not the most handsome guy, nor the most suave. He's not a player; he never was. Then how did he manage to bag a prize like my sister, you ask?

Confidence.

Steven never doubted himself. Never thought for a second that he wasn't good enough for The Bitch. He refused to be intimidated. He always exuded that quiet self-assurance that women are attracted to. Because he knew that no one could ever love my sister the way he did. So when Alexandra left for college years before Steven could join her, did he worry? Hell no. He wasn't afraid to let her go. Because he knew with absolute certainty that one day she would come back. To him.

Obviously Billy No-Blow Warren wasn't so sure.

Two hours later, Kate and I are certifiably drunk. See us there? Staring at the stage, sipping our beers with those glazed looks on our faces. You can learn a lot about a person when they're drunk, and I have learned a boatload about Kate. When she drinks—she's a talker.

Think she's a screamer too? Never mind; that part comes later.

Kate's hometown is Greenville, Ohio. Mom still lives there, running the western-themed diner her family owns. It sounds like a real Middle America type of place. The kind where the locals eat breakfast before work and teenagers congregate after a football game. Kate waitressed there during her high school years. She didn't mention a dad, though, and I didn't ask. And despite being valedictorian, Kate used to be quite the wild child. That explains why she holds her liquor so well. Apparently, she and the shithead spent their youth breaking into roller-skating rinks after hours, shoplifting, and singing in a band together.

Oh yeah, that's what the donkey dick still does for a living. He's a musician. You know what that means, right?

Yep—unemployed.

Why is Kate still with this loser? That's the million-dollar question, kids. I'm not a snob. I don't care if you pump gas or run the register at Mickey fucking D's. If you're a man, you work—you don't leech off your girlfriend.

"Karaoke sucks," I grunt as the blond transvestite at the microphone finishes the song "I Will Survive."

Kate tilts her head to the side. "She's . . . he's . . . not so bad."

"I think my ears are bleeding." I motion to the other comatose faces around the bar. "And they're dying a slow death."

Kate sips her beer. "It's just the wrong song for this kind of place. The right one would wake them up."

"You're nuts."

She slurs just a little. "Betcha I could do it."

"No way. Not unless you plan on doing a singing striptease."

And that, boys and girls, is a show I would give my left nut to see.

She takes my cell phone off the table and wags her finger at me. "No pictures. Can't have any evidence." Then she gets up and walks onstage. Hear the groans of pain from my bar mates as the music begins? It's a preemptive response to what they assume will be more auditory torture from another tanked-up, tone-deaf *American Idol* reject.

But then she starts to sing:

I don't stand a chance
When you look at me that way
I'll do anything you want me to
Anything for you
And I'll shout it for the whole world to know
Oh, honey, that's what you do to me
And I don't mind at all

Good freaking God.

Her voice is deep, and perfect, and arousing. Like a phone-sex worker at one of those nine-hundred numbers. It floats around the room and washes over me like . . . like verbal foreplay. My body reacts instantly to the sound. I'm as hard as a fucking rock.

You know I'm not a girl who cares to see
Or gives a damn what anyone thinks of me
I go down hard, I stand my ground
But whenever you come around
I'm helpless
Baby, I don't stand a chance
Every time you look at me that way
It brings me to my knees

She starts swaying her hips in time to the music, and I imagine how perfect she would look on her knees. I can't take my eyes off of her. She's mesmerizing . . . hypnotic.

And I'm changing, never thought I'd be like this
But you showed me a better way
I'll do anything for your kiss
In all my days I've never seen
A man who means everything to me
I can leave everything else in the dust
But it's you I just can't give up

She has the full attention of every man in the place. But her eyes . . . those stunning onyx eyes . . . are looking right at me.

And it makes me feel like a god.

I've never let anyone get this close to me before
Distance keeps me safe and keeps me sane
But now you've got my heart twisted with yours
Better than it's ever been, there's a lot to lose
But even so much more to win
Oh, baby . . .

She tosses her hair back, and I picture her doing just that as she rides me with long and hard strokes. *Jesus.* I've gotten lap dances from some of the best strippers in the city, and I've never come in my pants—not once. But that's exactly what I'm going to do if this song doesn't end real fucking soon.

I feel so helpless
When you look at me that way
I'll do anything for you
Only for you

The bar erupts into hoots and whistles and clapping hands as Kate walks off the stage. Sounds like a frigging rodeo. She smiles giddily as she walks toward me. I stand up, and she stops just inches away.

She looks up at me and raises one brow. "Told you I could wake them up."

I softly say, "That was . . .You . . . are amazing."

I want to kiss her. More than I want to fucking breathe. Images of last night flash in my mind. Of how goddamn good she felt in my arms. I *need* to kiss her. The smile slowly slides off her face, and I know she needs it too. I push a strand of her hair back behind her ear and lean in. . . .

And the shrill scream of her cell phone comes between us.

Kate blinks like she's waking up from a trance and picks up her phone. "H-Hello?" She flinches and pulls the phone from her ear to gain some distance from the shouting voice on the other end. "No . . . Billy, I didn't forget. I just had a difficult evening. No . . . yes . . . I'm at a bar called Howie's. It's on . . ." She stares at her phone a moment, and I'm guessing the dipshit just hung up on her. Her eyes are completely sober now.

"I have to go outside. Billy's coming to pick me up."

Won't this be a treat? I get to meet a walking, talking asshole. It'll be like Freak Night at the carnival.

While we wait outside on the sidewalk, Kate turns to me. "What are we going to say to your father?"

And there's the question I've avoided asking myself all night. The old man's a stand-up guy—chivalrous. Traditional. I'd like to think he'd be proud of my defending Kate's honor. But he's also a businessman. And the truth is, I could have defended Kate and still signed Anderson. It's what I should have done. It's what I would have done had it been anyone but her on the negotiating table.

"I'll handle my father."

"What? No. No, we're a team, remember? We both lost this client."

"I'm the one who went off on the guy."

"And I'm the one who didn't stop you. Now, I appreciate what you did for me, Drew, really. You were pretty magnificent, actually."

Maybe it's just the vodka, but her words make me feel all warm and fuzzy inside.

"But I don't need a white knight," she goes on. "I'm a big girl, and I can certainly handle whatever your father may dish out. We'll talk to him together on Monday morning. Agreed?"

This clinches it: Kate Brooks is one incredible woman.

"Agreed."

It's then that a black Thunderbird roars down the street and stops in front of us. Yes—I said Thunderbird. Can you say Totally Eighties Weekend? A guy with an average build and light brown hair gets out of it.

Is it just me, or does he look like a douche bag to you too? The old-fashioned kind. Your grandma's vinegar-and-water type of douche.

With a frown, he zeros in on Kate before looking me over. And then he looks even more pissed. Maybe dumbass isn't as stupid as I thought; he recognizes competition when he sees it.

He comes around and opens the passenger door for Kate. She sighs and gives me a tight smile. Then she takes two steps toward the car and trips on a crack in the sidewalk. I move to catch her, but Needle Dick is closer and beats me to it. He holds her at arm's length, the anger on his face turning to disgust.

"Are you fucking wasted?"

I don't really appreciate his tone. Someone needs to teach him some fucking manners.

"Don't start, Billy. I've had a bad night," Kate tells him.

"A bad night? Really? As in having the biggest gig of your life and your girlfriend not showing up? Was it that bad, Kate?"

Gig? Did he really just say gig? She actually sleeps with this moron? You have *got* to be kidding me.

She pulls out of his grasp. "You know what . . ." She starts off strong—and then deflates. "Just . . . let's go home." She gets in the car and Bitch Boy slams it closed behind her. He glares at me as he walks around to the driver's side.

Kate rolls down the window. "Good night, Drew. And thanks . . . for everything."

I give her a smile despite my growing desire to smash her fiancé's face in. "Anytime."

And the Thunderbird roars away. Leaving me, for the second night in a row, aching for Kate Brooks. I rub my hand down my face as a voice comes from behind me.

"Hey, cutie. I just got off. Want to get off with me?"

It's Shot Girl. She's decent looking—nothing to write home about—but she's there. And after seeing Kate take off with the spineless weasel she's marrying, I refuse to spend the rest of the evening alone.

"Sure, baby. I'll get us a cab."

I'll come back for my car later—when I'm actually sober enough to drive without wrapping it around a lamppost.

It's a lousy lay. Some advice: Being as still and silent as a corpse when a guy is fucking you will never be remembered as a stellar sexual experience.

The other reason it sucks is because I can't get Kate out of my head. I keep comparing Shot Girl to her, and the former, of course, comes up disappointingly short.

You think I'm a sleazeball for saying that? Come on—are you going to tell me you never imagined that it was Brad Pitt sticking it to you instead of your beer-bellied husband? That's what I thought.

Still think I'm a scumbag? Then you're in luck. I'll be getting just what you think I deserve very soon.

Chapter 10

My father was not pleased with how I handled the Anderson situation. I'd been rash, unprofessional, blah, blah, blah. And because of my seniority, he held me more accountable for losing the client than Kate.

But the fact that I was on the shit list at the office for a while didn't hit me as hard as you'd think. Mostly because I have no regrets over how I'd reacted. If I had it to do all over again, I wouldn't change a thing. So, maybe my father was disappointed in me, but to tell you the truth, by the time he got done reaming me out, I was pretty fucking disappointed in him too.

Also, in the four weeks following that disastrous meeting, things between Kate and me have continued to evolve. We still trade punches at work, but they're more jabs to the chest, meant to sting, rather than right hooks to the jaw, designed to knock each other on our respective asses. We share ideas, help each other out. My father was right about that, at least. Kate and I complement each other, balance each other's strengths and weaknesses.

Somewhere along the line, she's become more to me than just a set of legs I want to crawl between. More than a pair of pants I desperately want to get down.

Now she's Kate—a friend. A friend who causes my dick to stand at attention every time she walks into the room, but that's my cross to bear, I guess. Because as much as I still want her, and as sure as I am a part of her wants me, Kate is just not the cheating kind.

At least not the kind who could live with herself afterward.

Now, I know what you're thinking: *But what happened?* How did a self-assured, handsome, wickedly charming young man like myself become the flu-infected, sloppy shut-in you first met?

We're getting there—trust me.

To show you the whole picture, there are a few more players you need to meet in the shit-pit soap opera that is now my life. You've seen Dirtbag Warren. He'll be back later, unfortunately.

And now you'll meet Dee-Dee Warren. She's the jackass's cousin. But you shouldn't hold that against her. She's also Kate's best friend. I'll show you.

"I saw you talking to the brunette with the nice rack. You go back to her place?" Matthew asks me. He, Jack, and I are having lunch at a diner a few blocks from the office. We're discussing our most recent Saturday night.

"We didn't make it that far."

"What do you mean?"

I smirk, remembering what an exhibitionist the girl had been. "I mean that cab will never be the same again. And I think we scarred the driver for life."

Jack laughs. "You're such a fucking dog, man."

"Nah, I saved doggie-style for when we were actually inside her apartment."

Don't give me that look again. We've been over this.

Guys. Sex. Talk.

Besides, despite the wild eagerness of Taxi Girl, the sex was subpar. She wasn't even Colgate. She was more like some generic brand of toothpaste they stock in low-grade hotel rooms, whose name you can't even remember after you brush with it.

"Hey, Kate," Matthew says, looking behind me. I didn't see her approach us.

We'll stop here for just a moment. This is important.

See the look on her face? The thin line of her lips? The slight wrinkle of her brow? She heard what I said. And she doesn't look too happy about it, does she? I missed this the first time around, but you should make a note of it. This moment will come back to bite me in the ass later on.

I turn to look at her. Her expression is now blank and passive.

"You want to join us?" I ask.

"No, thanks. I just finished having lunch with a friend, actually."

And up walks her friend. She's wearing ankle-high black boots, black tights that are ripped at strategic places up and down her legs, a minuscule skirt, a strapless hot-pink top, and a short, knitted gray sweater. Her hair is long, strawberry-blond, and wavy, her lips a shiny red, and her quick amber eyes look us over from beneath a curtain of thick dark lashes.

She's . . . interesting. I wouldn't say pretty, but striking in a sexy street-fashion kind of way.

"Matthew Fisher, Jack O'Shay, Drew Evans, this is Dee-Dee Warren."

On hearing my name, Dee-Dee's eyes turn sharply in my direction. It feels like she's analyzing me—sort of how a guy would look at a car engine right before he busts it up.

"So, you're Drew? I've heard about you."

Kate told her friend about me? Interesting.

"Oh yeah? What've you heard?"

She shrugs. "I could tell you, but then I'd have to kill you." She points her finger at me. "You just keep on being nice to my Katie-girl here. You know, if you'd like to keep your balls attached to your pecker, that is."

Although her tone is light, I get the distinct impression Dee-Dee isn't fucking around.

I smile. "I've been trying to show her how nice I can be. She keeps turning me down."

She chuckles. Then Matthew interjects smoothly, "So, Dee-Dee . . . is that short for something? Donna, Deborah?"

Kate grins mischievously. "Delores. It's a family name—her grandmother's. She hates it."

Delores gives Kate the stink eye.

Shifting into pickup mode, Matthew replies, "Delores is a gorgeous name, for a gorgeous girl. Plus, it rhymes with *clitoris* . . . and I really know my way around them. Big fan."

Delores smiles slowly at Matthew and runs one finger across her lower lip. Then she turns to the rest of us and says, "Anyhoo. I have to jet, gotta get to work. Nice meeting you, boys." She hugs Kate and throws Matthew a wink as she walks away.

"She's got to get to work?" I ask. "I thought the strip clubs didn't open until four."

Kate just smiles. "Dee's not a stripper. She just dresses like that to throw people off. So they're shocked when they find out what she really does."

"What does she do?" Matthew asks.

"She's a rocket scientist."

"You're fucking with us." Jack voices what all three of us are thinking.

"Afraid not. Delores is a chemist. One of her clients is NASA. Her lab works on improving the efficiency of the fuel they use in the space shuttles." She shudders. "Dee-Dee Warren with access to highly explosive substances . . . it's something I try to not think about every day."

After a beat, Matthew speaks up. "Brooks, you've got to hook me up. I'm a nice guy. Let me take your friend out. She won't regret it."

Kate thinks a moment. "Okay. Sure. You seem like Dee's type." She hands him a business card. "But I have to warn you. She's the love-'em-and-leave-'em-with-bruises type of girl. If you're looking for a good time for a night or two, then definitely call her. If you're looking for anything deeper than that, I'd stay away."

We're speechless. And then Matthew rises from the table, walks up to Kate, and kisses her on the cheek. I suddenly have the urge to put my hand down his throat and rip his tonsils out.

Is that wrong?

"You . . . are my new best friend," he tells her.

Kate misreads the scowl on my face. "Don't pout, Drew. It's not my fault your friends like me better than you."

She means Steven too. A few days ago, he was frantically trying to find the perfect place to take The Bitch for their wedding anniversary. Apparently, Kate's neighbor is the maître d' at Chez, the most exclusive restaurant in the city. She was able to get him a table for that evening.

Alexandra must have done things to Steven that night that I don't even want to contemplate. Because ever since, Steven Reinhart would happily take a bullet to the chest for Kate Brooks.

"It's the boobs," I tell her. "If I had a set like yours, they'd like me better too."

A few weeks ago, that comment would have pissed her off. Now she just shakes her head and laughs.

The night before Thanksgiving is officially the biggest bar night of the year. Everyone goes out. Everyone is looking for a good time. Usually, Matthew, Jack, and I start the night at my father's day-before-Thanksgiving office party and work our way out to the clubs afterward. It's tradition.

So you can imagine my surprise when I enter the large conference room and see Matthew's arm around the woman who I can only assume is his date for the evening—Delores Warren. Since he met her two and a half weeks ago, Matthew's been MIA on the weekends, and I'm starting to suspect why. I'll have to talk to him tomorrow.

Beside them are my father and Kate.

And for the second time in my life, Kate Brooks leaves me

breathless. She's wearing a deep burgundy dress that hugs her in all the right places and strappy heeled shoes that send my imagination spinning into X-rated territory. Her hair falls around her shoulders in soft shining waves. My hand twitches to touch it as I walk toward her.

Then someone in the middle of the room moves—and I see that she's not alone.

Fuck me.

Everyone brings their significant other to these kinds of things. I shouldn't be surprised that the dickwad is here. He pulls at the tie of his suit like a frigging ten-year-old, obviously uncomfortable in it. *Pussy.*

I button the jacket of my own perfectly tailored Armani and make my way over.

"Drew!" my father greets me. Though things between him and me were tense for a few days, they quickly went back to normal. He never can stay pissed at me for long.

Look at this face. Could you?

"I was just telling Mr. Warren," he says, "about that deal Kate closed last week. How lucky we are to have her."

Have her? The word *lucky* doesn't even come close.

"It's all an act," Delores teases. "Beneath her corporate suit and that good-girl persona beats the heart of a true rebel. I could tell you stories about Katie that would put hair on your eyeballs."

Kate turns stern eyes on her friend. "Thank you, Dee. Please *don't*."

Cum Stain smiles, puts his arm around Kate's waist, and rests his lips on the top of her head.

I need a drink. Or a punching bag. Now.

Words fly out of my mouth like well-aimed bullets: "That's right. You were quite the little delinquent back in the day, weren't you, Kate? Dad, did you know she used to sing in a band? That's how you supported yourself through business school, right? Guess it beats pole dancing."

She chokes on her drink. Gentleman that I am, I hand her a napkin.

"And Billy here, that's what he still does. You're a musician, right?"

He looks at me like I'm a pile of dog crap that he just stepped in. "That's right."

"So, tell us, Billy, are you like a Bret Michaels kind of rocker? Or more of a Vanilla Ice?" See how his jaw clenches? How his eyes narrow? *Bring it, Monkey Boy. Please.*

"Neither."

"Why don't you grab your accordion, or whatever you play, and pop up on stage? There's a lot of money floating around this room. Maybe you could book a wedding. Or a bar mitzvah."

Almost there.

"I don't play those types of venues."

This should do it.

"Wow. In this economy, I didn't think the poor and jobless could be so picky."

"Listen, you piece of—"

"Billy, honey, could you get me another drink from the bar? I'm almost done with this one." Kate pulls on his arm, cutting off what I'm sure would have been a brilliant retort.

Are you feeling the sarcasm?

And then she turns toward me, and she doesn't sound nearly as friendly. "Drew, I just remembered I have some documents to give you about the Genesis account. They're in my office. Let's go."

I don't move. I don't answer her. My eyes are still locked in a staring contest with Shit for Brains.

"It's a party, Kate," my father says, clueless. "You should save the work for Monday."

"It'll just take a minute," she tells him with a smile—before grabbing my arm and dragging me away.

Once we're in her office, Kate slams the door behind us. I straighten my sleeves, then smile benevolently. "If you wanted to be alone with me that badly, all you had to do was ask."

She doesn't appreciate my humor. "What are you doing, Drew?"

"Doing?"

"Why are you insulting Billy? Do you know how hard it was for me to get him to come here tonight?"

Poor Billy. Stuck in a room with the big bad successful bankers.

"Then why did you frigging bring him?"

"He's my fiancé."

"He's an asshole."

She looks up sharply. "Billy and I have been through a lot together. You don't know him."

"I know he's not good enough for you. Not by a long shot."

"Please stop trying to embarrass him."

"I was just pointing out the facts. If the truth embarrasses your boyfriend, then that's his problem, not mine."

"Is this a jealousy thing?"

For the record? I have never been jealous a day in my life. Just because when I see them together I can't decide if I want to puke or punch his fucking lights out—she calls that *jealousy*?

"Don't flatter yourself."

"I know you have this thing for me, but—"

Wait one goddamn minute. Let's back the fuck up, shall we?

"*I* have a thing for *you*? I'm sorry, was it *my* hand grabbing *your* crotch in my office a couple months back? Because I remember it the other way around."

And now she's pissed. "You're such a bastard sometimes."

"Well, then we're a perfect fit, 'cause you're a first-class bitch most of the time."

Fire dances in her eyes as she raises her half-filled glass.

"Don't you fucking dare. You throw that drink at me, I'm not responsible for what I do after."

I'll give you a minute to guess what she does.

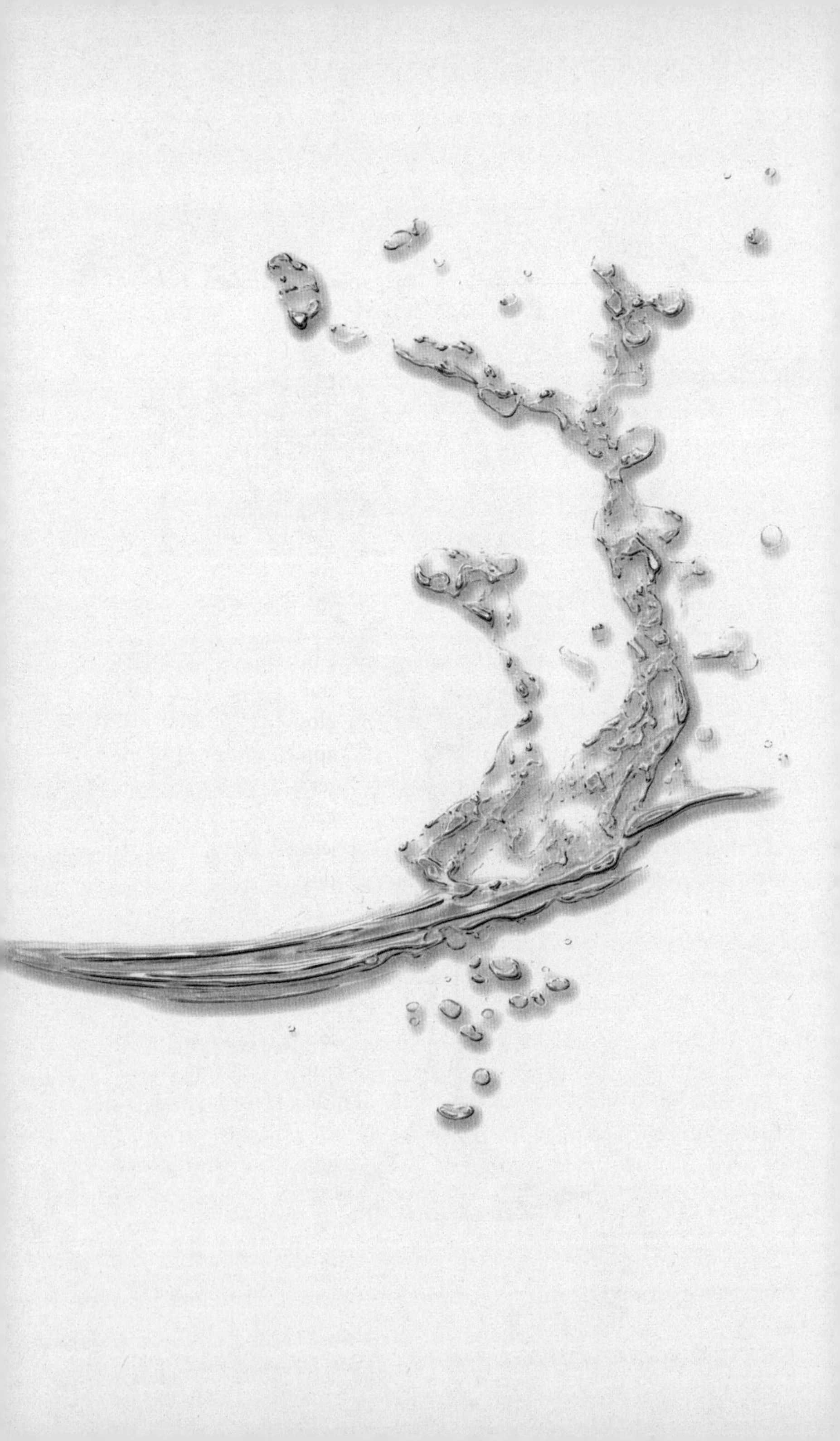

Yep. She threw the drink at me.

"Goddamn it!" I grab the tissues from her desk and wipe my dripping face.

"I'm not one of your random sluts! Don't you ever talk to me like that again."

My face is dry, but my shirt and jacket are still soaked. I throw the tissues down. "Doesn't matter. I'm leaving anyway. I have a date to get to."

She scoffs. "A date? Wouldn't a date involve actual conversation? Don't you mean you have a quick fuck to get to?"

I close my hands around her waist and pull her in. In a low voice I tell her, "My fucks are never quick—they're long and thorough. And you should be careful, Kate. Now you're the one who sounds jealous."

Her palms are flat against my chest, and my face is just inches from hers.

"I can't stand you."

"Feeling's mutual," I tell her quickly.

And then we're at it again—my mouth, her lips—joined hot and heavy. My hands are buried in her hair, cradling her head. Her hands grip the front of my shirt, holding me close.

I know what you're thinking. And, yes, apparently arguing for Kate and me is akin to foreplay. It seems to get us both all charged up. I just hope we get to come before we kill each other.

Just when things are starting to get good, there's a pounding on the door. Kate either doesn't hear it or, like me, she doesn't give a damn.

"Kate? Kate, you in there?"

The cocksucker's voice cuts through the lust that has us stuck together like glue. Kate pulls away. She stares at me a minute, her eyes guilty, her fingers resting on the lips I just tasted.

You know what? *Screw this*. Do I look like a goddamn yo-yo to you? I don't play games with people—I don't appreciate being played with. If Kate can't decide what she wants, I'll decide for her. Stick a fork in me; I'm fucking done.

I step up to the door and open it wide, giving Shithead plenty of room as he walks in.

Then I smile. "You can have her now. I'm finished."

And I don't even think about looking back as I walk out.

Chapter 11

Thanksgiving is held at my parents' country house upstate every year. It's always a small family affair. There are my parents, of course. You've met my father. My mother is an older, shorter version of Alexandra. For all her strong feminist beliefs—she'd been a top-notch attorney before motherhood lured her away—she loves playing the happy homemaker. After she and my father hit the big time financially, she also dedicated herself to various charitable organizations. It's what she still does with most of her time now that Alexandra and I have flown the nest.

Then there's Steven's father, George Reinhart. Picture Steven thirty years from now with thinning hair and a serious case of crow's feet. Mrs. Reinhart passed away when we were teenagers. To my knowledge, George hasn't been out on a single date since. He spends a lot of time at work, quietly crunching numbers in his office. He's a great guy.

And that brings us to the Fishers, Matthew's parents. Can't wait for you to see them. They're a fucking riot. Frank and Estelle Fisher are the most mellow people I've ever met.

They're almost catatonic.

Imagine Ward and June Cleaver after they've smoked a giant bong of marijuana. That's Frank and Estelle. You'd think Matthew's parents would be a little more high-strung, wouldn't you? I have a theory. They had Matthew later in life, and I think he sucked out any energy they had left—like a parasite.

Topping off the mix are Matthew, Steven, Alexandra, and me.

Oh—and of course the other woman in my life. I can't believe I haven't mentioned her before. She is the only female to ever truly hold my heart in her hand. I am her slave. She asks, and I do.

Gladly.

Her name is Mackenzie. She's got long blond hair and the biggest blue eyes you'll ever see. She's almost four. See her there? On the other end of the seesaw I'm currently riding?

"So, Mackenzie, have you decided what you want to be when you grow up?"

"Yep. I wanna be a princess. And I wanna marry a prince and live in a castle."

I need to talk to my sister. Disney is dangerous. Corrosive brainwashing bullshit, if you ask me.

"Or, you could go into real estate. Then you could buy the castle yourself, and you won't need the prince."

She thinks I'm funny. She laughs.

"Uncle Drew. How's I gonna have a baby wit no prince?"

Oh, boy.

"You've got plenty of time for babies. After you get your master's in business, or your medical degree. Oh, or you can be a CEO and start a day care at your office. Then you can bring your babies to work with you every day."

"Momma don't go to a office."

"Momma sold herself short, sweetie."

My sister was a brilliant trial attorney. She could have gone all the way to the Supreme Court. Seriously. She was that good.

Alexandra worked throughout her entire pregnancy and had a nanny all lined up. Then she held Mackenzie in her arms for the first time. She told the nanny the same day her services wouldn't be needed. Not that I blame her. I couldn't imagine a more important job than making sure my perfect niece grows up happy and healthy.

"Uncle Drew?"

"Yes?"

"Is you gonna die alone?"

I smirk. "I don't plan on dying for a long time, honey."

"Momma says you gonna die alone. She tol' Daddy that you gonna die, and it be days till a cleanin' lady find your rottin' corpse."

Lovely. Thank you, Alexandra.

"Wha's a corpse, Uncle Drew?"

Wow.

I'm saved from having to answer when I see Matthew walking down the back steps into the yard.

"Hey, sweetie, look who's here!" She hops off the seesaw and flings herself into Matthew's open arms.

Before you ask, the answer is no—when she is older, my little darling will never hook up with a guy like me. She'll be too smart for that. I'll make sure of it. Guess that makes me a hypocrite, huh? That's okay. I can live with that.

Matthew puts Mackenzie down and walks over. "Hey, man."

"What's up?"

"You go out early last night?" he asks me. "You never came back to the party."

I shrug. "My head wasn't in it. I hit the gym and went to bed."

The truth is I spent three hours pounding the hell out of the punching bag, imagining all the while that it was Billy Warren's face.

"You hung out with that Delores chick?"

He nods. "Her, Kate, and Billy."

I shake my head. "That guy licks ass."

Mackenzie walks over to us and holds up a glass jar half-filled with dollar bills. I slide a dollar into it.

"He's not so bad."

"Idiots annoy me."

Mackenzie holds up the jar again, and in goes another dollar.

The jar?

It was invented by my sister, who apparently thinks my language is too harsh for her offspring. It's the Bad Word Jar. Every time someone—usually me—swears, they have to pay a dollar. At this rate, that thing is going to put Mackenzie through college.

"So what's the deal with you and Delores?"

He smiles. "We're hanging out. She's cool."

Usually Matthew is more forthcoming with the details. It's not like I get off on his stories, but you have to understand, Matthew and I have been friends since birth. That means every kiss, every breast, every hand job, blow job, pearl necklace, and lay has been shared and discussed.

And now he's stonewalling me. What's up with that?

"I'm assuming you've nailed her?"

He frowns. "It's not like that, Drew."

I'm confused. "Then what's it like, Matthew? You haven't hung out in over two weeks. I can understand you being too pussy whipped to come out if you're getting some. But if not, what's the deal?"

He smiles in a nostalgic, remembering-a-happy-moment kind of way. "She's just . . . different. It's hard to explain. We talk, you know? And I'm always kind of thinking about her. It's like the minute I drop her off, I can't wait to see her again. She just . . . amazes me. I wish you knew what I meant."

And the scary thing is—I know *exactly* what he means.

"You're in dangerous territory, man. You see what Steven goes through. This path leads to the Dark Side. We always said we wouldn't go there. You sure about this?"

Matthew smiles, and in his best Darth Vader voice tells me, "You don't know the power of the Dark Side."

It's dinnertime. My mother makes a big show of bringing out the turkey, and everyone *oohs* and *ahhs* before my father carves it up. That's right—Norman fucking Rockwell's got nothing on us.

As bowls are passed and plates are filled, my mom says, "Drew, honey, I'm going to pack you up a big bag of leftovers. I don't even want to think about how you're eating in that apartment with no one to cook a decent meal. And I'll put dates on the containers so you'll know when to throw it out. The last time I looked in your refrigerator, it was like some sort of science experiment was growing in there."

Yes—my mommy loves me. Told you so.

"Thanks, Mom."

Matthew and Steven make loud, wet kissy noises at me. With both hands, I flip each of them the bird. Beside me I see Mackenzie looking at her fingers trying to copy the move. I quickly put my hand over hers and shake my head. I show her Mr. Spock's Vulcan salute instead.

After we say grace, I announce, "I think Mackenzie should come live with me."

No one reacts. No one looks up. No one pauses. I've made this suggestion several times since my niece was born.

Alexandra says, "The turkey's delicious, Mom. Very juicy."

"Thank you, dear."

"Hello? I'm serious here. She needs a positive female role model."

That gets The Bitch's attention. "What the hell am I?"

Mackenzie slides the jar toward her mother, and in goes a dollar. We all bring small bills to the table on holidays now.

"You're a stay-at-home mom. Which is very commendable, don't get me wrong. But she should be exposed to career women too. And for God's sake, don't let her watch *Cinderella*. What kind of example is that? A mindless twit who can't even remember where she left her damn shoe, so she has to wait for some douche bag in tights to bring it to her? Give me a frigging break."

I'm not sure how much I owe after that little speech. I pass Mackenzie a ten. Did I say that jar would put her through college? I meant law school. I'm going to need to hit an ATM soon.

Steven joins in. "I think Alexandra is the perfect role model for our daughter. There's no one better."

Steven is a beaten man. And Matthew wants to join his club.

Unreal.

Alexandra smiles at him. "Thank you, honey."

"You're welcome, dear."

Matthew and I start coughing, "Whipped . . . brown nose."

Mackenzie looks at us suspiciously, unsure if we need to pay up or not.

Alexandra scowls.

I continue. "I should bring her to the office with me. She should meet Kate, don't you think, Dad?"

My mother asks quickly, "Who's Kate?"

My father answers between bites. "Katherine Brooks, new employee. Brilliant girl. And quite the firecracker. She gave Drew a run for his money when she first started."

My mother looks at me with glittering, hopeful eyes. The way Paula Deen looks at a tub of lard, imagining the delicacy just waiting to be made. "Well, this Kate sounds like a lovely young lady, Drew. Maybe you should have her over to the house for dinner."

I roll my eyes. "We work together, Mom. She's engaged. To a jackass, but that's another story."

Another dollar bites the dust.

My sister interjects. "I think Mom's just surprised to actually hear you refer to a woman by name. Usually it's 'the waitress with the nice butt' or 'the blonde with the big boobs.'"

Though her observation is accurate, I ignore it. "The point is, she's a terrific example for Mackenzie of how much a woman can accomplish." Despite her terrible taste in men. "I'd be . . . I think we'd all be really proud if she grew up to be half the professional Kate is."

Alexandra looks surprised by my statement. Then she smiles warmly. "Mackenzie and I can take a trip into the city next week. We'll get together with you for lunch and meet the illustrious Kate Brooks."

We eat in silence for a few minutes, and then Alexandra says, "That reminds me. Matthew, could you escort me to a charity dinner the second Saturday in December? Steven is going to be out of town." She looks toward me. "I would ask my darling brother to do it, but we all know he spends his Saturday nights with the city slu—" She glances at her daughter. "Undesirables."

Before Matthew can answer, Mackenzie puts her two cents in. "I don't think Uncle Matthew can come, Momma. He been too busy bein' pussy whipped. Wha's *pussy whipped,* Daddy?"

As soon as the words leave her angelic little lips, a horrendous chain reaction is set off:

Matthew chokes on the black olive in his mouth, which flies out and nails Steven right in the eye.

Steven doubles over, holding his eye and yelling, "I'm hit! I'm hit!" and then goes on about how the salt from the olive juice is eating away at his cornea.

My father starts coughing. George stands up and begins pounding on his back while asking no one in particular if he should perform the Heimlich.

Estelle knocks over her glass of red wine, which quickly seeps into my mother's lace tablecloth. She makes no move to clean up the mess, but instead chants, "Oh my goodness. Oh my goodness."

My mother runs around the dining room like a chicken with its head cut off, searching for non-cloth napkins to wipe up the stain, all the while assuring Estelle that everything's fine.

And Frank . . . well . . . Frank just keeps eating.

While the chaos continues around us, Alexandra's death-ray glare never wavers from Matthew and me. After squirming under it for about thirty seconds, Matthew caves. "It wasn't me, Alexandra. I swear to Christ it wasn't me."

Chickenshit.

Thanks, Matthew. Way to leave my ass blowing in the wind. Remind me never to go to war with him as my wingman.

But as The Bitch glower is turned full force on me alone, I forgive him. I feel like at any moment I'll be reduced to a smoking pile of Drew ash on the chair. I dig deep and give her the sweetest Baby Brother smile I can manage.

Take a look. Is it working?

I'm so fucking dead.

See, there's one thing about Bitch Justice you should know. It's swift and merciless. You won't know when it's coming; all you can be certain of is that it will come. And when it does, it will be painful. Very, very painful.

Chapter 12

On Monday morning, I'm in the conference room waiting for the staff meeting to start. Everyone's here. Everyone, that is, except Kate. My father glances at his watch. He's got an early tee-off this morning, and I know he's eager to get there. I scratch behind my ear.

Where the hell is she?

Finally, Kate comes barreling in with her coat still on and a bunch of folders falling out of her hands. She looks . . . terrible. I mean, she's beautiful, she's always beautiful. But take it from someone who's watched her closely—Kate is having a bad day. See how pale she is? And when the hell did those dark circles crawl under her eyes? Her hair's thrown up in a messy bun, which would be sexy as hell if she didn't look so . . . ill.

She smiles nervously at my father. "Sorry, Mr. Evans. It's been a morning."

"No problem, Kate. We're just getting started."

As my father rattles off his announcements, I don't take my eyes off her. She doesn't look at me once.

"Kate, do you have those projections for Pharmatab?"

It's the deal my father was talking to the ass-muncher about at the office party. The one Kate closed last week. She looks up, her big brown eyes making her look all the more like a deer caught in headlights.

She doesn't have them.

"Ahh . . . they're . . . um . . ."

I lean forward and announce, "I have them. Kate gave them to me last week to look over. But I left it on my desk at home. I'll get it to you ASAP, Dad." My father nods, and she closes her eyes in relief.

After the meeting is over, everyone slowly files out, and I walk up beside Kate. "Hey."

She looks down at the folders she's carrying and adjusts the coat on her arm. "Thank you for what you did in there, Drew. It was really decent of you."

I know what I said the other day—that I was finished with her. I didn't mean it. I was talking out of my ass, blowing off some sexually frustrated steam. You know that. Think Kate knows? Think she gives a damn?

"I have to do the decent thing once in a while. Just to keep you on your toes." I give her a small smile that she doesn't return.

And she still hasn't fucking looked at me. What's wrong with her? My heart begins to hammer in my chest as I run through all the possibilities. Is she sick? Did something happen to her mother? Was she mugged on the frigging subway?

Jesus.

Kate walks into her office and closes the door, leaving me standing on the outside. This is where men got the shitty end of the stick, people. When God gave Eve that extra rib? He should have given us something extra too. Like mental telepathy.

I once heard my mother tell my father that she shouldn't have to explain why she was pissed. That if he didn't already know what he'd done wrong, then he wasn't really sorry for it. What the fuck does that even mean? News flash, ladies: We can't read your thoughts. And frankly, I'm not entirely sure I'd want to. The female mind is a scary place to be.

Men? We don't leave a lot of room for doubt: *You're a dick. You fucked my girlfriend. You killed my dog. I hate you.* Direct. Clear. Unambiguous. You girls should try it sometime. It would bring us all one step closer to world peace.

I back away from Kate's door. Looks like I won't be finding out what her deal is any time soon.

Later that day, I sit in a café across from Matthew, not eating my sandwich.

"So, Alexandra get to you yet?"

He's referring to the Thanksgiving Day Massacre—in case you've forgotten. I nod. "I got the call yesterday. Apparently I've committed myself to volunteer next month at the Geriatric Society of Manhattan."

"It could've been worse."

"Not really. Remember Steven's aunt Bernadette?"

Old women have a thing for me. And I don't mean a pinch-my-cheek, pat-me-on-the-head kind of thing. I mean a grab-my-ass, rub-my-junk, why-don't-you-push-my-wheelchair-into-the-broom-closet-so-we-can-get-nasty kind of thing.

It's fucking disturbing.

Matthew's now laughing his ass off. Thanks for the sympathy, man.

The bell above the door to the café jingles. I look up and decide that maybe God doesn't hate me after all. Because Billy Dumbass Warren just walked in. His face, at any other time, would definitely put a dent in my good mood. But at this moment? He's just the donkey dick I need to see. I'll be nice.

I approach him. "Hey, man."

He rolls his eyes. "What?"

"Listen, Billy, I was just wondering, is everything okay with Kate?"

He snarls, "Kate isn't any of your fucking business."

Let the record show, I'm trying. And he's being a prick. Why am I not surprised?

"I see what you're saying. But this morning, she really didn't look well. Do you know why?"

"Kate is a big girl. She can take care of herself. She always does."

"What are you talking about?"

And then it hits me. Like a bucket of ice-cold Gatorade after a football game.

"Did you do something to her?"

He doesn't answer. He looks down. That's all the answer I need. I grab him by the front of his shirt and pull him up quick. A second later, Matthew's there telling me to calm down. I shake the jerk off just a little. "I asked you a question, motherfucker. Did you do something to Kate?"

He tells me to get my hands off him, and I shake him harder.

"Answer me!"

"We broke up! We broke the fuck up, all right?"

He means *he* broke up with *her*.

He pushes my hands off and shoves me. I let him. He straightens his shirt, glaring. But I just stand there. Stunned. His finger stabs my chest. "I'm out of here. You ever put your hands on me again, I'm laying you out, dickhead."

And with that, he leaves. Matthew watches him go, then asks, "Drew, what the hell was that about?"

Ten years—almost eleven. She loved him. That's what she said. *Ten frigging years*. And he dumped her.

Fuck.

"I have to go."

"But you didn't finish your sandwich." Food's important to Matthew.

"You have it. I have to get back to the office."

I sprint out the door to . . .

Well, you know where I'm going.

Her office door is still closed. But I don't knock. Quietly, I walk in. She's sitting at her desk.

Crying.

Have you ever been kicked in the stomach by a horse?

Me neither. But now I know what it feels like.

She looks so small behind that desk. Young and vulnerable and . . . lost. My voice is soft and careful. "Hey."

Kate glances at me, surprised, and then she clears her throat and wipes her face, trying to pull it together. "What do you need, Drew?"

I don't want to embarrass her, so I pretend not to notice the wetness that still clings to her cheekbones. "I was looking for that file . . ." Slowly, I step closer. "Do you . . . uh . . . have something in your eye?"

She plays along and wipes at her eyes again. "Yeah, it's an eyelash or something."

"You want me to take a look? Those eyelashes can be dangerous if left untreated."

For the first time today, her eyes meet mine. They're like two dark shining pools. "Okay." Kate stands up, and I guide her toward the window. I put my hands on her cheeks, gently holding her face. Her beautiful, tear-streaked face.

I've never wanted to do physical damage to someone as badly as I do Billy Warren in this moment. And I'm pretty sure I can get Matthew to help me bury whatever's left of him in the backyard.

I wipe her tears away with my thumbs. "Got it."

She smiles, even as more tears spring up. "Thanks."

I'm done pretending now. I pull her in against my chest. She lets me. I put my arms around her and smooth the back of her hair with my hand. "Do you want me to talk to him? Was it . . . was it because of . . . me?"

I can't imagine the scumbag was very happy finding us in Kate's office like he did last week—with her looking freshly fucked and all. And no, I haven't gone insane. The last thing I want to do is help her get back with the asshole. But goddamn it, she's killing me here.

One tear at a time.

She laughs into my chest. It sounds bitter. "It was me." Kate looks up at me and smiles sadly. "I'm not the same girl he fell in love with."

It must have been hard for her to hear those words. It's the oldest guy trick in the book. The blame game: *"It's not me, honey. It's you."*

She shakes her head. "He packed up all of his things and moved out on Saturday. He said a quick, clean break would be better. He's staying with Dee-Dee until he can find his own place."

She looks toward the windows for a moment, then sighs dejectedly. "It's been coming for a while, I think. It really wasn't a shock. For so long, my focus was on school . . . and then work. Everything else came second. I stopped . . . I couldn't . . . give him what he needed.

"It's just . . . Billy held my hand the day we buried my father. He taught me to drive a stick shift and convinced me I was good enough to sing in front of actual people. Billy helped me fill out my college application and opened the acceptance letter for me because I was too nervous to look. When I was in the MBA program, he worked three jobs so I didn't have to work at all. Billy was there the day I graduated, and he came with me when I wanted to move to New York. He's always been such a huge part of my life. I don't know who I'll be without him."

Women. No offense. But she doesn't even realize what she just said. These are *her* accomplishments. Challenges *she's* lived through. Shithead was just along for the ride. In the background. Like wallpaper. You can change the color of the walls anytime, and it might look different, but the room's still the same.

"I know who you'll be: Kate Brooks, Investment Banker Extraordinaire. You're smart and funny, and you're stubborn and gorgeous and . . . perfect. And you'll still be perfect without him."

Our eyes hold for a minute, and then I enfold her in my arms until her tears subside. Her voice is muffled as she whispers, "Thank you, Drew."

"Anytime."

It's not until late that night, as I crawl between the cool sheets of my bed, that the ramifications of today's events really hit me.

I sleep naked, by the way. You should try it. If you haven't slept naked, you haven't lived. But that's beside the point.

The fact that hasn't occurred to me until now is—Kate Brooks is single. Free. Available. The only real obstacle that stood between her and me and my office couch just shot himself in the foot. *Holy shit.* This is what Superman must have felt like when he turned back time and pulled Lois out of that car. It's a do-over. A second shot. Recommencing liftoff.

I fold my hands behind my head and settle back into my pillows with the biggest, brightest can't-wait-for-tomorrow smile you have ever seen.

It's been four days since I found out Dipshit broke up with Kate. That next day, she came into work looking like herself again. For all intents and purposes, she seemed completely over the moron. But Mackenzie caught a cold, so Alexandra had to reschedule our lunch for next week. With the weekend Kate had, it was probably for the best.

Oh yeah. Just one more little detail you should know: I haven't gotten laid in twelve days.

Twelve days.

Two hundred and eighty-eight sex-free hours. I can't calculate the minutes—it's too depressing. Remember all work and no play makes Drew a cranky boy? Well, at this point, Drew is practically a goddamn psychopath, okay?

Twelve days may not seem like a long time for you amateurs out there, but for a guy like me? It's a frigging record. I haven't had a drought like this since the winter of '02. That January, a massive blizzard blanketed the tristate area with twenty-eight inches of snow. Only official vehicles were allowed on the roads, so I was stuck in the penthouse with my parents.

And I was *seventeen.* A year in a guy's life when a light breeze is capable of giving him a boner. I spent so much time in the bathroom, my mother thought I had a virus. Finally, after the seventh day, I couldn't take it anymore. I braved the elements and walked to Rebecca Whitehouse's condo uptown. We humped like bunnies in the janitor's closet of her parents' building.

She was a nice girl.

Anyway, once again, I've been reduced to jerking off in the shower. It's humiliating. I feel so dirty. Not that there's anything wrong with a good rub-and-tug in the morning to start the day off right. Particularly if, like me, you had to bypass last weekend's typical Saturday score night because of family-related holiday obligations. But if that's the only action you're getting? Well, that's just . . . sad.

The reason behind my recent extended sexual famine? I blame Kate. It's all her frigging fault.

Apparently, I've grown a conscience. I don't know when it happened, I don't know how it happened, but I am not happy about it.

If I could, I would squash that Jiminy Cricket fucker like the roach he is.

Because you know how some people have gaydar? Well, I have dump-dar. That means I can pick out a recently dumped female a mile away. They're easy pickings. All you have to tell them is that their ex is an idiot for letting them go, and they'll be begging you to nail them.

Kate now falls into the aforementioned dumped category. Should be a sure thing, right?

Wrong. Here's where Jiminy rears his ugly little bug head.

I can't bring myself to make a move. The idea makes me feel like a goddamn predator. It's hard to tell if she's still raw. She doesn't seem to be, but you never know. She could just be putting up a good front. And if she is—hurt and vulnerable—that's not how I want her. When it happens for Kate and me, I want her ripping at my clothes, and her own for that matter, because she can't wait a second longer to have me pounding into her. I want her moaning my name, scratching my back, and screaming because of the sheer magnificence of it.

Damn it, there I go again. I've got a hard-on just thinking about it.

What a mess. I can't fuck Kate, and I don't want to fuck anyone else. It's my own personal Perfect Storm. Told you I'd get what I deserve. Are you happy now?

I turn off the lights in my office and walk over to Kate's. She doesn't see me right away, so I cross my arms and lean against the doorframe, just watching her. Her hair's down, and she's standing, bent over her desk, looking at her computer. And she's singing:

No more drinks with the guys
No more hitting on girls
I'd give it all up

And it'd be worth it in the end
If you were my lady
I would comprehend
How it feels to have something real
I would want to be a good man . . .

She really does have a great voice. And the way she's bending over her desk like that . . . I just want to walk up behind her and . . . *Christ.* Never mind. I'm just torturing myself.

"Rihanna better watch her back." She looks up at the sound of my voice, and her face breaks into a wide, embarrassed grin. I request, "Don't stop on my account. I was enjoying the show."

"Very funny. Show's over."

I crook my finger at her. "Come on. I'm kicking you out. It's after eleven on a Friday night, and you haven't eaten yet. I know a place. My treat. They make a great turkey club."

Kate turns off her screen and grabs her bag. "Oohh, they're my favorite."

"Yeah, I know."

We grab a table in the bar area and order. The waitress brings our drinks, and Kate takes a sip of the margarita I ordered for her. "Mmm. This is just what I wanted right now."

I told you I was good at the drink thing—remember? We talk comfortably for a few minutes, and then . . . watch this.

Kate's eyes go wide as saucers, and she dives under the table. I look around. *What the hell?* I duck my head and take a peek at her. "What are you doing?"

She looks panicked. "Billy's here. Upstairs, in the loft over the dance floor. And he's not alone." I start to lift my head when she yells, "Don't look!"

Jesus Christ—this is ridiculous. So much for being over the dickwit.

"It's just . . . I can't let him see me like this."

Now I'm confused. "What are you talking about? You look great." She always looks great.

"No, not in these clothes. He said it wasn't attractive that I was so driven. It was one of the reasons he wanted to break up. That I . . . He said I was too . . . masculine."

You have got to be fucking kidding me. I'm masculine. Hillary Clinton is masculine. Kate Brooks doesn't have a goddamn masculine cell in her body. She's all woman, believe me.

But I know what the fucker was going for. Kate is intelligent, outspoken, ambitious. Lots of men—like the shit-eating asshole, for instance—can't handle a woman like that. So they twist it around. Make those qualities seem unappealing. Something to be ashamed of.

Screw this. I grab Kate's hand and drag her out from under the table. She looks around quickly as I lead her to the dance floor.

"What are you doing?"

"Giving you back your dignity."

I bump into several people on the way, making a slight ripple, so I'm sure Douche Bag will notice us. "By the time I'm done, Billy Warren will be kissing your feet, your ass, and any other body part you tell him to, to get you back."

She tries to pull out of my grasp. "No, Drew, that's not really . . ."

I turn to face her and put my arms around her waist. "Trust me, Kate." Her body's close to mine, her face so near I can see the green speckles in her eyes. Why the fuck am I doing this again?

"I'm a guy. I know how we think. No guy wants to see a girl that used to be his with someone else. Just go with me on this."

She doesn't answer. She just raises her arms around my neck, bringing us together—chest to chest, stomach to stomach, thigh to thigh.

It's agony. Exquisite, delicious agony.

With a mind of its own, my thumb draws slow circles on her lower back. The music swirls around us, and I feel buzzed—not from the alcohol, but from the feel of her. I want to ignore the perfect way her body fits against mine. I try to remember my noble intentions. I should glance up to see if Dirtbag is watching us. I should, but I don't. I'm too caught up in the way she's looking at me.

Maybe I'm deluding myself, but I swear it's desire I see swimming in those dark beauties. Naked, uninhibited want. I lean in and brush my nose against hers, testing the waters.

I'm not doing this for me. Really. I'm not doing this because being this near to her is the closest to heaven that I'll ever get.

This is for her. Part of the plan. To win back the scumbag who doesn't deserve her.

I press my lips against hers softly. It's tender at first, and then she melts against me. That's when I start to lose it. She opens her mouth, and I slide my tongue in slowly. Then harder, firmer, more intense, like the downhill swoop of a roller coaster.

I forgot how good she tastes. More decadent than the richest chocolate. Sinful. It's different from the other times we've kissed. Better. There's no anger behind it, no frustration or guilt or a point to prove. It's unhurried, languid, and fucking sublime.

Our lips separate, and I force myself to look up, catching Warren's devastated glare before he disappears into the crowd. I turn back to Kate and touch my forehead to hers. Our breaths mingle—mine panting, hers gasping slightly.

"It worked," I tell her.

"What?"

I feel her fingers playing with the hair at the nape of my neck. And when she speaks, her voice is breathy. Needy. "Drew . . . could you? Drew . . . do you want . . . ?"

"Anything, Kate. Ask me anything and I'll do it."

Her lips part, and she stares at me a moment. "Would you . . . kiss me again?"

Thank. You. God.

And as for you, Jiminy? Piss off.

Chapter 13

The ride to my apartment is an exercise in stunt driving. Trying desperately to keep my mouth on Kate and not get us killed. She sits on my lap straddling my waist, kissing my neck, tonguing my ear—driving me out of my frigging mind. I've got one hand on the steering wheel and the other wedged between us, gliding over her stomach, her neck, and those perfect breasts that tease me through her half-open shirt.

Do not try this at home, kids.

Her skirt bunches high on her thighs as she grinds herself on my straining cock. She's so damn hot against me, I have to use every ounce of will not to let my eyes roll back into my head. I kiss her hard and watch the road over her shoulder. She slides up and down, jerking me off slowly with the pressure. Fucking Christ, dry humping never felt so good.

Control? Restraint? They went bye-bye a long time ago.

Finally, I pull into the parking garage of my building. I grab the first spot I see and drag us out of the car. My hands on her ass, her legs locked around my waist, I carry Kate to the elevator, our lips and tongues dancing furiously.

I didn't lock my car. I don't think I even closed the door.

Fuck it.

They can steal it. I have more important matters at hand.

I stumble into the elevator and push the button for the top floor before slamming Kate back against the wall and thrusting against her like I've been dying to do. She moans long and deep into my mouth. It's like that scene out of *Fatal Attraction,* without the creepiness.

Making it to my door, I grope for the lock with one hand still holding Kate against me. She nibbles on my ear and whispers, "Hurry, Drew."

I would have kicked the fucking thing open at this point if the key wasn't already turning. We fall into my apartment, and I kick the door shut with my foot. I peel her legs off me, and her feet slide to the floor, creating a delicious friction along the way. I need my hands free.

With our mouths still joined, I start unbuttoning the rest of her blouse. Kate is not so skilled—or she's just impatient. She digs her fingers into the front of my shirt and pulls. Buttons scatter on the floor.

She just ripped my shirt open.

How hot is *that*?

I get to the clasp on her bra and pop it open. I'm an expert at those things. Whoever invented the front-clasp bra? God bless you.

Kate pulls her lips away and smooths her palms over my chest and down my abs. Her eyes are filled with wonder as they follow her hands' path. I watch as my own fingers skim across her collarbone, down between flawless breasts, and over that valley I love before coming to rest at her waist.

"God, Drew. You're so . . ."

"Beautiful," I finish for her.

I pull her up against me again, wrapping my arms around her and lifting her feet off the floor as I back up toward the couch. Did I think dancing with her was heaven? No. Her bare chest against mine—that is what heaven feels like. Fucking paradise.

I kiss down her jaw and suck at the tender flesh of her neck. I love Kate's neck—and judging from the sounds vibrating in her throat, she loves what I'm doing. I sit back on the couch, taking her with me with her torso resting against mine, her closed legs between my spread knees. She pulls my lips back to hers for one more kiss before standing up and backing away.

We're both out of breath and staring, practically attacking each other with our eyes. She bites her lip, and her hands disappear behind her back. I hear the hiss of a zipper, and then her skirt is slowly sliding to the floor. It's the sexiest goddamn thing I have ever seen.

Kate stands in front of me in black lace boy-short panties, an open white blouse, and high heels. Her lips are swollen, her cheeks are flushed, and her hair is tousled from my hands. She's a goddess . . . fucking divine. And the way she's looking at me almost has me coming right here and now. I reach for my wallet and pull the condom out, resting it on the cushion next to me.

Kate walks out of her skirt and toward me . . . leaving her high heels on.

Christ Jesus.

She kneels between my legs and unbuttons my pants, keeping her blazing eyes locked on mine. I lift up, and she peels my pants and boxers off. My cock springs up, proud and hard and so fucking ready. Her eyes go down, and she looks me over. I let her get her fill; I'm not really the shy type.

But when a devilish smile comes to her lips and she leans toward my dick, I grab her and pull her back to my mouth. I don't know what she was planning—well, I have an *idea*—but if I don't get inside her soon, I think I'm actually going to die.

I lift her at the waist, and her knees rest on either side of me. I hold her up with one hand while the other pushes the lace between her legs to the side. I dip two fingers inside her. *Jesus.* She's ready too. I slide my fingers all the way in, and we both moan loudly. She's wet . . . and hot. She molds snugly around my fingers, and my eyes close, knowing just how incredible she'll feel around my cock. I pump my fingers in and out, and she starts riding my hand. She's whimpering . . . moaning . . . gasping my name.

Music to my frigging ears.

I can't take it anymore. I grab the condom and rip the packet open with my teeth. Kate rises up as I start to roll it on. Then she pushes my hands away. And she rolls it on for me.

Sweet fucking Christ Almighty.

I pull at her lace panties. I want her bare, nothing in the way.

With a rip and a snap, I tear them off. Her dark curls and shiny lips beckon me, and I swear to God I'll give them all the attention they deserve later. But I can't wait.

My eyes are on hers . . . those dark chocolate eyes that pulled me in the moment I first saw them.

Gorgeous.

Slowly, she sinks down on me. For a moment, neither of us moves. Or breathes. She's tight . . . Fuck . . . even through the rubber, I feel her walls stretching for me.

I whisper her name like a prayer. "Kate."

I take her face in my hands and bring her down to me. I can't not kiss her. She rises up, pulling me almost completely out before smoothly sliding down, taking me back inside.

Holy God.

Nothing has ever felt this good—nothing. My hands grasp her hips, helping her ride my cock with steady strokes. Our mouths are open against each other, kissing and panting.

I pull myself up to sit straighter, knowing the added pressure against her clit will make it better for her. And I'm not wrong. She comes down on me harder, faster, my hands digging into her hips. I kiss her neck and bend my head, licking my way to a hardened nipple. I take it in my mouth, sucking and rolling my tongue around, making her hand fist in my hair as she moans.

I'm not going to last. There's no way. I've waited for this too long, wanted it too much. I brace my feet on the floor and start thrusting up, stabbing into her, pushing her hips down hard as I do. It's bliss. Hard, deep, wet rapture, and I never want it to end.

She throws her head back and moans louder. "Yes . . . yes . . . Drew."

I'm cursing and calling her name, both of us almost mindless. Out of control. Because it feels that fucking good.

She screams my name, and I know she's coming.

God, I love her voice.

And then she's contracting all around me—her pussy around my cock, her legs against my thighs, her hands on my shoulders—all clenching taut and stiff. And I'm right there with her.

"Kate, Kate . . . fuck . . . Kate."

I thrust up again and again. Then I come long and hard. White-hot pleasure shoots through my body unlike anything I have ever felt before. My head falls against the back of the couch.

After the spasms die down, my arms come up around Kate, bringing our chests together and her head against my neck. I feel her heartbeat start to return to normal. And then she's laughing, low and satisfied.

"God . . . that was so . . . so . . ."

Now I'm smiling too. "I know."

Earth-shattering. Off the Richter scale. Powerful enough to take out a small island country.

I stroke my hand through her hair . . . so frigging soft. I lean down and kiss her again. So goddamn perfect.

What a great night. I think this could very well be the best night of my life. And it's only just started.

Kate squeals as I stand up and carry her, wrapped around me, to my bedroom.

I've never brought a woman to my bedroom before. It's a rule. No random hookups in my apartment—never even considered it. If one of those girls actually knew where I lived? Can you say Stalker Psycho, anyone?

But I don't think twice about setting Kate down in the middle of my bed. She watches me, on her knees, as I strip off my buttonless shirt and get rid of the used condom. Biting her lip with a smile, she peels off her own blouse, which was still hanging on her arms. Oh yeah—and she's still got her heels on.

Nice. So very, very nice.

I crawl over to her and rest on my knees in the center of the bed. I cradle her face in my hands as I kiss her long and hot. I'm all set to go again. My dick pokes her in the stomach where it stands firm and ready. But this round, I want to take my time. I've admired her body for months—and now I plan to explore every fucking inch of it, up close and personal.

I lean forward and lay her back. Kate's hair fans out behind her onto my pillows. She looks like some mythical imp, some fabled pagan sex deity from a Roman legend.

Or a well-acted porno.

Her knees fall open naturally, and I settle between them. Christ . . . she's already damp. I can feel how wet she is against my stomach when she pushes up and rubs against me. Silently begging for it—again.

I kiss my way down her neck and collarbone, coming face-to-face with her pebbled nipples. Kate's hands knead my shoulder blades as I lick a circle around one dusky pink center. Her breathing's fast and urgent. I flick my tongue over her nipple quickly until she groans my name.

The minute the word leaves her lips, I close my mouth over her and suckle hard. For a few minutes, I alternate licking, sucking, and scraping her pointy little peak. Her reaction is so frigging primal, I can't help but switch to the other tit and give that beauty the same attention.

By the time I work my way lower, Kate is writhing under me, bucking and rubbing herself on any part of my body she can reach.

It's shameless.

Beautiful.

And as badly as I want her right now, as goddamn good as it feels to have her grinding against me—I'm in complete control of what I'm doing. I'm in charge. And there's one thing I can't wait to do. Something I've fucking dreamed of doing ever since that night at Howie's. I lick a trail down the center of her stomach, then crawl lower. I slip her shoes off and lick another path up her inner thigh till I'm eye level with my target: her neat patch of dark curls.

Kate is shaved short, trim, and the skin surrounding her snatch is as smooth as silk. I know because I'm nibbling my way around that manicured little triangle right now. Guys love a pussy that's almost completely bare. And no, it has nothing to do with perverted prepubescent fantasies. The idea that a woman is nearly bald there is just . . . naughty. *Such* a turn-on.

I rub my nose into her tiny, coarse patch and inhale. Kate gasps and moans above me—eyes closed, mouth open.

Just so you know, men don't expect a woman to smell like

Winter Pine or Niagara Falls or whatever the fuck those feminine products say. It's a pussy—it's supposed to smell like one. *That's* the fucking turn-on.

Kate's scent in particular has me salivating like a famished frigging animal. I rub again, kissing her plump outer lips. *Mother of God.*

Her hands clench the blanket.

"God, you smell so good, I want to eat you all night."

And I just actually might.

I lick up her wet slit, and she arches off the bed with a moan. I push her hips down with my hands, holding her immobile as I do it again, and she cries out louder.

"That's it, Kate—let me hear you."

I'm well aware that this—that I—am the first man to ever do this to her. And yes, as a guy, that fact makes it even better.

You know who Neil Armstrong is, don't you?

Now tell me who the second guy was. Hell, tell me any other guy you know who made it to the moon after him. You can't, can you? That's why this is such a rush.

She'll never forget this.

She'll always remember . . . me.

Maybe that's chauvinistic and egotistical, but it's the truth.

Up and down, over and over, I lick her from end to end. Her cream is sweet and thick. Goddamn delicious. I push her thighs apart, spreading her wider, and push in and out of her—fucking her with my tongue. Her head rolls side to side as high-pitched moans echo from her throat. She's incoherent, and her toes dig into my shoulders, but I don't let up. No freaking way. In one motion, I suck Kate's firm little clit into my mouth and slip two fingers inside her.

Then I'm the one moaning. Her hot juice coats my fingers, almost burning. I can't stop my hips from rotating and rubbing against the bed. *Fuck.* Still pumping in and out with my hand, I flatten my tongue and rub steady, hard circles on her clit.

"Drew! Drew!"

Hearing Kate scream charges me up even more. I move my fingers faster, in time with my tongue, and look up . . . needing to see her lose it. I'm going to come just watching her. The look on her face is of full-blown ecstasy, and I don't know which one of us is getting off more.

"Oh God, oh God, oh God . . . God!"

Then she's rigid—stiff as a fucking board. Her hands pull my hair, her thighs tighten around my head, and I know she's there.

After several moments she loosens her hold, and I slow my tongue to leisurely paced licks. When Kate relaxes her limbs even more, I sit up, wipe my face with my hand, and slide on a fresh condom.

Oh yeah—I'm just getting started.

I lean over her, and she pulls me down and kisses me hard. She pants against my lips, "So . . . incredible."

Smug, conceited satisfaction pumps through my veins, but I can't even smile. I need to fuck her too goddamn much. I slide in easily. She's slick but tight—like a wet fist. I feel her clench around me as I pull out slow and glide back in.

I start to thrust faster. Harsher. My arms are straight on either side of her head so I can watch the pleasure that flickers across her face. Her tits bounce every time I surge forward, and I almost lower down to suck on one.

But then she opens her eyes and looks up at me. And I can't look away. I feel like a king—like a fucking immortal. And any self-control I had just vanished. I push into her, fast and merciless. Pure heated pleasure swells in my stomach and down my thighs.

Sweet Jesus.

Our bodies slap together over and over, hard and quick. I hook one arm under her knee and raise her leg up over my shoulder. She feels even tighter, and I can't help but moan, "Kate . . ."

"Yes, like that. God, yes! Drew . . ." And then she goes stiff under me again, her eyes closing as a strangled moan leaks from her lips.

That's when I let go. I ram into her one last time before the most intense orgasm of my life rushes through me. I groan loud, flooding the condom inside her to the frigging brim. My arms collapse, and my full weight falls on her. She doesn't seem to mind. The moment I'm down, she's kissing me—my eyes, my cheeks, my mouth. I struggle to catch my breath, and then I'm kissing her back.

Un-fucking-believable.

Chapter 14

I read an article once that said having sex extends the human life span. At this rate, Kate and I are going to live forever. I've lost count of the number of times we've done it. It's like a mosquito bite—the more you scratch, the more it itches.

I'm just glad I bought the extra-large box of condoms at Costco.

And in case you couldn't tell from my reactions, I'll just come out and say it: Kate Brooks is a fantastic lay. A spectacular piece of ass. If I wasn't sure that Billy Warren was a complete dumbass fuckwit before, now—since I've sampled what he threw away—I'm completely certain of it.

She's adventurous, unapologetically demanding, spontaneous, and confident. A lot like me. We're a perfect fit, in more ways than one.

When we finally come up for air, the night sky outside my window is just turning gray. Kate is lying quietly, her head on my chest, her fingers tracing its contours and occasionally stroking the dusting of hair there.

I hope after everything I've told you that this doesn't come as a shock, but I don't "cuddle." Typically, after a woman and I are done, there is no spooning, no snuggling, no frigging pillow talk. I might, on occasion, have a nap before I head out the door. But I can't stand it when a girl braids herself around me like some mutant octopus. It's annoying and uncomfortable.

With Kate, however, the old rules just don't seem to apply. Our warm skin is meshed together, our bodies aligned, her ankle over my calf, my thigh under her bent knee. It feels . . . peaceful. Soothing in a way I can't fully describe. I have absolutely no desire to move from this spot.

Unless it's to roll over and nail her again.

She breaks the silence first. "When did you lose your virginity?"

I laugh. "Are we playing First and Ten again? Or are you wondering about my sexual history? Because if that's it, I think you're a little too late, Kate."

She smiles. "No. It's not like that. I just want to know you . . . more."

I sigh as I think back. "Okay. My first time was . . . Janice Lewis. My fifteenth birthday. She invited me to her house to give me my present. It was her."

I feel her smile against my chest. "Was she a virgin too?"

"No. She was just shy of eighteen—a senior."

"Ah. The older woman. So she taught you everything you know?"

I smile and shrug. "I picked up a few tricks over the years."

We fall quiet again for a few minutes, and then she asks, "Don't you want to know about mine?"

Don't even have to think about that one.

"Nope."

Don't want to spoil the mood, but we'll pause here a second.

When it comes to a woman's past, no guy wants to hear about it. I don't care if you've fucked one guy or a hundred—keep it to yourself.

Let me put it this way: When you're out at a restaurant and the waiter brings your meal, do you want him to tell you about every single person who touched that food before you put it in your mouth?

Exactly.

I also think it's pretty safe to assume that her first time was with Warren—that he was her one and only. And he is the last fucking person I want to be discussing at this particular place and time.

Now, back to my bedroom.

I turn on my side so I'm facing Kate. Our faces are close, our heads sharing one pillow. Her hand's tucked under her cheek in an innocent kind of way.

"There *is* something I want to know, though," I say.

"Ask away."

"Why'd you go into I-banking?"

I come from a long line of white-collar professionals. Alexandra and I weren't expected to follow in our parents' footsteps—it just sort of happened that way. People always gravitate toward what they know, what's familiar.

Like professional athletes. Have you ever noticed how many Juniors there are in major-league baseball? It's to distinguish them from their Hall of Fame fathers. The Manning quarterbacks—same deal. But I wonder what attracted Kate to investment banking considering her adolescent years of petty crime.

"The money. I wanted a career where I knew I'd make a lot of money."

I raise my eyebrows. "Really?"

She looks at me knowingly. "You were expecting something more noble?"

"Yeah, I guess I was."

Her smile dims. "The truth is, my parents got married young—had me young. They bought the diner in Greenville. Mortgaged it to the gills. We lived above it. It was . . . small . . . but nice."

Her smile fades a little more. "My father was killed when I was thirteen. Car accident—drunk driver. After that, my mom was always busy. Trying to keep the diner going, trying to keep herself from falling apart."

When she pauses again, I put my arm across her and pull her in until her forehead rests against my chest. And then she goes on:

"She barely kept us above water. I wasn't deprived or anything, but . . . it wasn't easy. Everything was a struggle. So, when they told me I was going to be valedictorian, and I received a full scholarship to Wharton, I figured—okay—investing it is. I never wanted to be helpless or dependent. Even though I had Billy, it was important to me to know I'd be able to support myself, by myself. Now that I can, all I really want to do is take care of my mom. I've been asking her to move to New York, but so far she's said no. She's worked her entire life. . . . I just want her to rest."

I don't know what to say. For all my snide comments about my family, I'm pretty sure I'd lose my frigging mind if something happened to any one of them.

I raise her chin so I can look into her eyes. Then I kiss her. After a few minutes, Kate turns around. I wrap my arms around her waist and pull her right up against me. I press my lips to her shoulder and settle my face in her hair. And even though it's technically morning, that's just how we stay until we both fall asleep.

Every healthy man in the world wakes up with a stiffy. A fatty. Morning wood. I'm sure there's some medical explanation for the phenomenon, but I just like to think of it as a little present from God.

A chance to begin the day with your best dick forward.

I can't remember the last time I slept next to a woman. Waking up beside one, however, definitely has its benefits. And I'm prepared to take full advantage of them.

With my eyes still closed, I roll over and search for Kate. I plan on teasing her awake before giving her a "good morning" from behind. It's the only acceptable wake-up call, in my book. But as my hand slides over the sheets, it finds only empty space where she's supposed to be. I open my eyes, sit up, and look around. There's no sign of her.

Huh.

I listen for movement in the bathroom or the sound of running water from the shower. But there's only silence. Deafening, isn't it?

Where'd she go?

My heart rate kicks up a notch at the thought that she snuck out while I was asleep. It's a move I've performed myself—on several occasions—but one I'd never expect from Kate.

I'm just about to get out of bed when she appears in the doorway. Her hair's pulled up in one of those elastic bands that women always seem to pull out of thin air. She's wearing a gray Columbia

T-shirt—*my* gray Columbia T-shirt—and I'm momentarily fascinated by the way her tits jiggle beneath the lettering as she walks.

Kate sets the tray she's carrying on the bedside table. "Good morning."

I pout. "It could've been. Why'd you get up?"

She laughs. "I'm starving. My stomach was growling like a caged troll. I was going to cook breakfast for us, but the only thing I could find in your kitchen was cereal."

Cereal is the perfect food. I could eat it at every meal. And not the healthy bran-and-oats shit your parents shoved down your throat. I only go for the good stuff: Lucky Charms, Fruity Pebbles, Cookie Crisp. My cabinet is a veritable smorgasbord of highly sugared puffed wheat.

I shrug. "I order out a lot."

She hands me a bowl. Apple Jacks—good choice. Between bites, Kate says, "I borrowed a T-shirt. Hope you don't mind."

I crunch my breakfast of champions and shake my head. "Not at all. But I really like you better out of it."

See how she looks down? How her lips curve into a soft smile? See the color that rises in her cheeks? Good God—she's blushing again. After last night? After the cursing, the screaming, the scratching? *Now* she blushes?

Adorable, right? I think so too.

"I didn't think cooking in the nude was very sanitary."

I put my now-empty bowl back on the tray. "Do you like to cook?" In the months we've worked together, I've learned a lot about Kate, but there's still more I want to know.

She nods and finishes her cereal. "You grow up over a diner, it kind of rubs off on you. Baking is sort of my thing. I make great cookies. If we can get the ingredients later, I'll make them."

I smile devilishly. "I'd love to eat your cookie, Kate."

She shakes her head at me. "Why do I have the feeling you're not talking about the chocolate chip variety?"

Remember that gift from God? I can't let it go to waste. That would be a sin—and I really can't afford any more of those. I drag her onto the bed and pull the T-shirt over her head.

"'Cause I'm not. Now, about that cookie . . ."

"Queen to B-seven."

"Bishop to G-five."

Games are fun.

"Knight to C-six."

"Check."

Games without clothes? They're more fun.

Kate's brow furrows as she stares at the chessboard. This is our third match. Who won the other two? Please, like you even need to ask.

We've been trading stories while we play. I told her about the time I broke my arm skateboarding when I was twelve. She told me about the day she and Delores dyed her hamster's fur pink. I told her about the nickname Matthew and I have for Alexandra. (Kate pinched my nipple after that one. Hard. She remembered the day I called her "an Alexandra" in my office.)

It's comfortable, easy, enjoyable. Not as enjoyable as screwing—but a close second. We're lying on the bed on our sides, our heads resting on our hands, the board in the middle.

Oh—and in case you forgot, we're naked.

Now, I know some women have issues with their bodies. Maybe you've got a little extra junk in the trunk? Get over it. Doesn't matter. Naked kicks Modest's ass every single time. Men are visual. We wouldn't be fucking you if we didn't want to look at you.

You can write that down if you like.

Kate has no problem being naked. She's definitely comfortable in her own skin. And it's sexy—damn sexy.

"Are you going to move or just burn a hole in the board looking at it?"

"Don't rush me."

I sigh. "Fine. Take all the time you need. There's nowhere for you to go anyway. I've got you cornered."

"I think you're cheating."

My eyes open wide. "That hurts, Kate. I'm wounded. I don't cheat. I don't need to."

She raises a brow at me. "Do you have to be so cocky?"

"I certainly hope so. And talking dirty will get you nowhere. Stop stalling."

She sighs and accepts defeat. I make my final move. "Checkmate. Want to play again?"

She rolls onto her stomach and bends her knees, so her feet almost touch her head. My cock twitches at the sight.

"Let's play something else."

Twister? Hide the Salami? Kama Sutra charades?

"Do you have Guitar Hero?"

Do I have Guitar Hero? The jousting of our millennia? The coolest video game of all time? Of course I do.

"Maybe you should pick something else," I say. "If I keep beating you like this, it could damage your fragile female ego."

Kate glares at me. "Set it up."

Her eagerness should have been a red flag. It was a slaughter. Absolutely brutal. She kicked my ass—from one end of the apartment to the other.

In my defense, Kate knows how to play a real guitar. That and . . . she made us put clothes on. How frigging mean is that? I kept trying to catch a glimpse of that succulent little ass peeking out from under my T-shirt. It distracted me.

I never had a chance.

So, by now you're probably wondering what the hell I'm doing, right? I mean, this is me. One ride per customer—no rewinds, no repeats. So why am I wasting away my Saturday afternoon playing Adam and Eve with Kate?

Here's the deal: I've worked for months to get her where she is right now. I've spent night after endless night wanting, dreaming, fantasizing about it.

Let's say you get stranded on a desert island and can't eat for a week. And then the rescue ship finally shows up with a big plate of food. Would you take one taste and throw the rest away?

Of course not. You'd scarf down every bite. Devour every crumb. Lick the plate clean.

That's what I'm doing. Hanging out with Kate until I'm . . . full. Don't read any more into it than that.

Did I mention Kate has a tattoo? Oh yeah. A slut tag. A tramp stamp. Call it whatever you like. It's inked just above the swell of her ass, on her lower back. It's a small turquoise butterfly.

It's tasty. I'm tracing it with my tongue right now.

"God, Drew . . ."

After the Guitar Hero disgrace, Kate decided she wanted a shower. And get this—she asked if I wanted to go first.

Silly, silly girl. Like showering single file was even a consideration.

I stand up and tease her from behind. She's hotter than the fucking water that hits us on all sides. I move her hair to the side as I feast on that scrumptious neck. My voice is husky as I tell her, "Open your legs for me, Kate."

She does.

"More."

She does again.

I bend my knees and slide my cock home. *Jesus.* It's been two hours since I was deep inside her like this. Too fucking long—a lifetime.

We moan together. Her breasts are slick from the soap as I slide my fingers to her nipples and play with them in the way I know makes her purr. She drops her head back against my shoulder and scratches her nails up my thighs. I hiss at the sensation and pick up the pace just a little.

Then she leans forward, bending at her waist and bracing her hands against the tiles. I cover them with my own, threading our fingers together. I pump in and out unhurriedly. I kiss her back, her shoulder, her ear. "You feel so fucking good, Kate."

Her head rolls on her neck, and she moans, "God, you feel so . . . hard . . . so big."

That phrase? Hearing that phrase is the dream of every man who has ever lived. I don't care if you're a freaking monk; you want to hear it.

Yeah, I've heard it before. But coming from Kate—in that sweet voice—it's like I'm hearing it for the first and only time.

And then she's begging. "Harder, Drew . . . please."

I do as she asks with a groan. I leave one hand on the wall and bring the other to her clit, so each time I push forward, she bucks up against my fingers. She moans at the contact.

Then she's demanding, "Harder, Drew. Fuck me harder."

When her command reaches my ears, I snap, like the roof caving in on a raging house fire. I push into her until she's pinned against the wall, her cheek resting on the cold tile. I thrust rough and fast. Kate's gratified screams echo off the walls, and we come in perfect sync.

It's long and intense and fucking glorious.

As the pleasure wanes, she turns, wraps her arms around my neck and kisses me slowly. Then her head is on my chest, and we stand together under the spray. I can't keep the awe out of my voice as I say, "God, it gets better every time."

She laughs. "You too? I thought I was the only one who felt it." She looks up at me, bites her lip, and pushes my wet hair back from my eyes. It's a simple gesture. But there's so much emotion behind it. Her touch is gentle, the look in her eyes so cherishing, like I'm the most wonderful thing she's ever seen. Like I'm some kind of . . . treasure.

Normally, a look like that would have me ducking for cover—heading for the nearest exit.

But as I stare at Kate's face, one hand holding her waist, the other moving through her hair, I don't want to run. I don't even want to look away. And I don't ever want to let go.

"No . . . I feel it too."

Chapter 15

I'm not boring you with these sordid details, am I? I could shorten this whole thing by simply saying: Kate and I fucked each other's brains out all weekend.

But that's not really much fun.

And it wouldn't give you the full picture. By taking the long way around, you get all the facts. And a bird's-eye view of all our little moments. Moments that seemed silly and insignificant at the time. But now that I have the flu, they're the only things I can think about.

Every minute of every day.

Have you ever gotten a song stuck in your head? Sure you have; everybody does. And maybe it's a beautiful song, maybe it's even your favorite. But it's still annoying, isn't it? It's second-rate. Because you don't want to just hear it in your brain—you want it on the radio or live in concert. Replaying it in your mind is just a cheap imitation. A mocking, frigging reminder that you're not able to hear the real thing.

Do you see where I'm going with this?

Don't worry, you will.

Now, where was I? That's right—Saturday night.

"This is the perfect pillow."

We just ordered food—Italian—and we're waiting for it to arrive. Kate is sitting on my couch amid an oasis of pillows and blankets. And she's holding one bedroom pillow in her lap.

"The perfect pillow?"

"Yes," she says. "I'm very high maintenance when it comes to pillows. And this one is perfect. Not too flat, not too puffy. Not too hard, not too soft."

I smile. "Good to know, Goldilocks."

We've decided to watch a movie. On-demand cable is the second-greatest invention of our time. The first, of course, being the big-screen plasma TV. I get up to fetch the remote while Kate fishes something out of her bag on the floor.

Have I mentioned we're still naked? We are. *Very.* It's liberating. Fun.

All the good parts are easy to reach. And the view is fantastic.

As I turn to make my way back to the couch, a now-familiar scent assails my nostrils. Sweet and flowery. Sugar and springtime. I look at Kate and find her rubbing lotion on her arms. I grab the bottle from her, like a dog snapping at a bone. "What is this?"

I bring the bottle to my nose and inhale deeply, then fall back against the pillows with a satisfied moan.

Kate laughs. "Don't snort it. It's moisturizer. I didn't realize fighting dry skin got you so revved up."

I look at the bottle. Vanilla and lavender. I take another deep sniff. "It smells like you. Every time you're near me, you smell like . . . like a bouquet of fucking sunshine with brown sugar on top."

She laughs again. "Aw, Drew, I didn't know you were a poet. William Shakespeare would be so jealous."

"Is it edible?"

She makes a face. "No."

Too bad. I'd have poured it on my food like a rich hollandaise. Guess I'll just have to settle for tasting it on Kate.

Now that I think about it—that is the preferable option.

"They make a bubble bath too. Since you like it so much, I'll get some."

It's the first reference she's made about a next time. A hookup at some later date. A future. Unlike my past bump-and-grinds, the suggestion of a second go-round with Kate doesn't fill me with indifference or irritation. Instead, I'm eager—excited—about the prospect.

I stare at her for a moment, soaking in the strange enjoyment that comes from just looking at her. I could make a full-time profession out of watching Kate Brooks.

"So," she asks, "did we decide on a movie?"

She settles up against me, and my arm goes naturally around her. "I was thinking *Braveheart*."

"Ugh. What is it with that movie? Why are all men addicted to it?"

"Ah, the same reason women are obsessed with the freaking *Notebook*. That is what you were going to suggest, right?"

She smiles slyly, and I know I guessed right.

"*The Notebook* is romantic."

"It's fucking gay."

She hits me in the face with the "perfect" pillow.

"It's sweet."

"It's nauseating. I have friends who are flaming homosexuals—and that movie is too gay for them."

She sighs dreamily. "It's a love story, a beautiful love story. The way everyone tried to keep them apart. But then, years later, they found each other again. It was fate."

I roll my eyes. "Fate? Please. Fate's a frigging fairy tale, sweetheart. And the rest of the story is a bonfire of bullshit too. Real life doesn't work like that."

"But that's—"

"*That's* why the divorce rate is so high. Because movies like that give women unreasonable expectations."

And the same goes for romance novels. Alexandra practically took Steven's head off once because he borrowed one of my *Playboys*. Yet every summer, there's The Bitch lying out on the beach with her Fabio-covered soft porn.

Yeah, I said porn. That's what it is.

And it's not even *good* porn: "He moved his trunk-like manhood toward the weeping petals of her womanly center."

Who the fuck talks like that?

"Real guys don't think like Nolan or Niles or whatever the hell that douche bag's name was."

"Noah."

"And any man who would build a room in his house for some chick who blew him off? Any man who would wait years for that same girl to show up at his door, knowing she was with someone else? He's not a man at all."

"What is he?"

"A big, hairy, unwaxed vagina."

Was that too crude?

I'm afraid that it was.

Until Kate covers her mouth with her hands and falls over on the couch, convulsing in a fit of deep, snorting laughter. "Oh . . . my . . . God. You're such . . . a . . . pig. How . . . how do you even come up with these things?"

I shrug. "I call them like I see them. I won't apologize for it."

Her laughter dies down, but the smile's still there. "Okay, no *Notebook*."

"Thank you."

Then her whole face lights up. "Oohh, how about *Anchorman: The Legend of Ron Burgundy*?"

"You like Will Ferrell?"

"Are you kidding? Have you seen *Blades of Glory*?"

It's one of my favorites. "The Iron Lotus? Classic."

She wiggles her eyebrows at me and quotes expertly, "You got some sweet cream to soothe that nasty burn?"

I laugh. "God, I love y—"

And then I choke.

And cough.

And clear my throat.

"I love . . . that movie." I fiddle with the remote, and we lie down on the couch as *Anchorman* starts.

Okay—don't get crazy on me now. Let's just all calm down for a second, shall we? It was a simple mistake. A slip of the tongue. Nothing more.

My tongue's been getting quite the workout lately, so I think it's allowed.

After eating, we continue watching *Ron Burgundy* lying against each other on the couch, her back to my front. My face is in her hair again, inhaling the scent that I've become addicted to. I drift in and out of sleep. Kate's laughter vibrates against my chest as she asks softly, "Is that what you thought of me?"

"Mmmm?"

"When I first started at the firm. Did you think I was a 'scorpion woman'?"

She's referring to a line Will Ferrell just delivered in the movie. I smile drowsily. "I . . . When I first saw you that day in the conference room, it knocked me right on my ass. After that, I just knew nothing would ever be the same."

She must have liked my answer. Because a minute later, she rubs her hips back against me. And my half-erect cock slides between the cheeks of her ass.

I don't care how exhausted a guy is—he could've just worked a thirty-five-hour shift hauling sandbags across state lines—that move will always, always wake him up.

My lips find their way to her neck as my hand skims across her stomach. "God, Kate. I can't stop . . . wanting you."

It's getting kind of ridiculous, isn't it?

I feel her breathing pick up. She turns to face me, and our lips meet. But before we go further, my curiosity gets the better of me, and I pull back. "What did you think of me when we first met?"

Her eyes roll to the ceiling as she contemplates her answer. Then she smiles. "Well . . . that first night at REM, I thought you were . . . lethal. You just radiated sex and charm." Her fingers trace my lips and brows. "That smile, your eyes, they really should be illegal. It was the only time in all my years with Billy that I wished I was single."

Wow.

"And then at the office I'd hear the secretaries talking about you. How you had a different girl every weekend. But after a while . . . I saw that there was so much more to you. You're brilliant and funny. You're protective and caring. You shine so bright, Drew. Everything you do—how you think, the things you say, the way you move—it's . . . blinding. I feel . . . lucky, just being close to you."

I'm speechless.

If any other woman said that to me, I'd agree with her. I'd tell her she *was* lucky to be with me—'cause I'm the best of the best. There's no one better. But coming from Kate? From someone whose mind I envy, whose opinion I actually admire? I just . . . don't have any words. So, once again, I let my actions do the talking.

My mouth presses against hers, and my tongue begs for entrance. But when I try to roll us over so I'm on top, Kate has other ideas. She pushes me on the shoulders until I'm on my back. Then she moves her mouth over my jaw and down my neck, burning a trail down my chest and stomach. I swallow hard.

She takes my cock in her hand and pumps slowly, and I'm already stiff as steel. I was hard the minute she started talking. "Jesus, Kate . . ." I keep my eyes open and watch from above as she wets her lips, opens her mouth, and slides me in. "Fuck . . ." She takes my entire length in deep and sucks hard as she pulls back slowly. Then she does it again.

I'm sort of a connoisseur of blow jobs. For a guy, they're the most convenient kind of sex. No fuss, little mess. If any of you out there have never given one, I'll let you in on a little secret. Once a guy's dick is actually in your mouth, he'll be so happy, it doesn't really matter what you do with it afterward. That being said, there are certain moves that make it better.

Kate pumps me with her hand while increasing the suction at the tip with her hot little mouth.

Like that, for instance.

She swirls her tongue around the head like she's licking a lollipop. Where the fuck did she learn that? I moan helplessly and grip the cushions on the couch. She takes me all the way down her throat once, then twice. Then she switches to fast, short pumps with her mouth and hand.

It's magnificent. I've been blown by the best of them. And I swear to God, Kate Brooks has the technique of a freaking porn star.

I try to hold still, conscious that this really is her first time, but it's difficult. And then her hands are under me—on my ass—urging me upward. She guides my hips back and forth, pushing me in and out of her mouth. *Holy God.* She removes her hands, but my hips continue to move in short, shallow jabs.

I'm close to losing it—but I always give a warning first. If a guy doesn't warn you? Dump him fast. He's a fucking prick.

"Kate . . . baby, I'm . . . If you don't move now . . . God, I'm gonna . . ." Coherent words are apparently beyond my ability at the moment. Still, I think she gets the idea.

But she doesn't move away. She doesn't stop. I look down at the very moment Kate opens her eyes and looks up. And that's all it takes. It's the moment I've fantasized about since I first saw her. Those big brown doe eyes staring up at me as my cock slides between her perfect lips. With a whimper of her name, I fill her mouth with a pulsing stream. Kate moans and takes it all in, swallowing greedily.

After what seems like an eternity, I start to come down. You know when you first step out of a Jacuzzi? How your limbs feel like Jell-O? Yeah—that's me. Right now.

I'm breathing hard and grinning like the village idiot as I pull her up by the shoulders and kiss her deep. Some men are grossed out about kissing a woman whose mouth they just came in. I'm not one of them. "How in holy hell did you learn to give head like that?"

Kate laughs at the wonder in my voice as she spreads out on top of me. "Delores dated this guy in college. He was really into porn. He used to leave movies at our dorm all the time. And, once in a while . . . I'd watch them."

The next time I see Delores Warren? Remind me to drop to my knees and kiss her ass.

Once the movie ended, Kate and I decided to have a full-out Will Ferrell marathon. We're halfway through *Blades of Glory* when my phone rings. We're still on the couch, lying comfortably side by side, and I don't really feel like getting up. Or talking to anyone not currently in the room, for that matter.

I let the answering machine pick up. Jack's voice fills the room, yelling over the sound of pounding music in the background: "Drew! Dude, pick up! Where the fuck are you?" He pauses a moment, and I'm guessing he realizes I'm not going to pick up. "You have *got* to come out tonight, man! I'm at Club Sixty-Nine, and there's someone here who wants to see you."

This doesn't sound promising. I start to sit up, my Y-chromosomal instincts telling me to turn the machine off. *Now.* But I'm not fast enough. And a sultry female voice comes out of Pandora's box. "Dreeewwww . . . it's Staaaacey. I've missed you, baby. I want to take another taxi ride. Remember that night when I sucked your dick so g—"

My hand slaps down on the *off* button.

Then I glance sideways at Kate. Her face is frozen on the TV, her expression indecipherable. I should probably say something. What the fuck should I say? "Sorry, one of my other cum-dumps called?" Nah, for some reason, I don't think that one would go over very well.

She sits up stiffly. "I should probably get going."

Shit. Frigging Jack.

Kate gets up, holding my pillow close against her, covering herself.

Well, that's not a good sign. An hour ago she was pushing her snatch against my face. Now she doesn't even want me looking at it.

Goddamn it.

She walks past me toward the bedroom. Even with my stomach churning, I can't help but admire the sway of her tight ass as she goes by. Predictably, my cock springs up like Dracula rising from his coffin.

When I was ten, we had a dog. He humped everything and anything—from the maid's leg to my parents' four-poster bed. He was insatiable. My parents were mortified whenever company stopped by. But now I realize he really wasn't a bad dog. It wasn't his fault.

I feel your pain, Fido.

I sigh. And get up to follow Kate. By the time I make it to the bedroom, her skirt's on and her blouse is buttoned. She doesn't look at me when I walk in.

"Kate—"

"Do you know where my other shoe is?" Her eyes gaze at the floor, the bed—anywhere but at me.

"Kate—"

"Maybe it's under the bed." She kneels down.

"You don't have to go."

She doesn't look up. "I don't want to get in the way of your plans."

Who has plans? The only plan I had was to gorge myself on the juicy buffet between her thighs. Again.

"I don't—"

"It's okay, Drew. You know, this has been nice . . ."

Nice? She calls what we did last night and all day—in the bedroom, the kitchen, the shower, up against the hallway wall—"nice"? Is she fucking joking?

She must see the look on my face, because she stops midsentence and raises an eyebrow. "I'm sorry, was that the wrong adjective? Did I insult your fragile male ego?"

I stutter indignantly, "Well . . . yeah."

"What word would you prefer?"

FYI—I'm still naked, and if my dick's posture is any indication, it doesn't take Einstein to figure out what I'd really prefer at the moment.

"Stupendous? Transcendent? Unparalleled?" I punctuate each word with a predatory step in her direction.

She matches my forward momentum with nervous steps backward, until her ass bumps up against my dresser. I smirk down at her. "You're a graduate of the most prestigious business program in the country. My honor demands that you come up with something, *anything,* better than 'nice.'"

She stares at my chest a minute. Then she looks up into my eyes. She looks serious. "I should go."

She tries to walk past me, but I grab her arm and pull her back. "I don't want you to go."

No—don't ask me why. I won't answer. Not now. I'm only focused on here—and her. The rest doesn't matter. She looks at my hand on her arm and then at me. "Drew . . ."

"Don't leave, Kate." I pick her up, sit her on the dresser, and step between her legs. "Stay." I kiss her neck and nibble her ear. She shivers. I whisper, "Stay with me, Kate." I look into her eyes. "Please."

She bites her lip. Then smiles slowly. "Okay."

I smile in return. And then my mouth is on hers. The kiss is long and slow and deep. I push her skirt up, skimming the skin of her thighs with my fingertips. She's still not wearing any underwear.

You've got to love the easy access.

I kneel down in front of her. "Drew . . . ?" It's a half question, half moan.

"Shhh. If I'm going to top 'nice,' I need to concentrate."

And there's not a single coherent word between us for the rest of the night.

Chapter 16

Every superhero has a hideout—a sanctuary. At least all the good ones do. I have one too. My own personal Bat Cave. It's where the magic happens. Where I've built the legend that is my career.

My home office.

It's a male haven. A pussy-free zone—in the good kind of way. Every guy should have one. I decorated it myself—each piece, every detail. If my car is my baby, this room is my firstborn. My pride and joy.

Mahogany floors, handwoven Oriental rugs, English leather couches. A stone fireplace and built-in bookshelves line one wall. Behind my desk is a full picture window that offers a priceless view of the city. And in the corner is a card table where the guys and I drink aged Scotch, smoke Cuban cigars, and play poker once a month.

It's the only time Steven is allowed to come out and play.

I'm at my desk, in boxers, working on my laptop. It's what I do every Sunday afternoon.

Kate? No—she's still here. But after our fuck-a-thon last night, I figured I should let her sleep in. Recharge the batteries. I canceled brunch with my mother and blew off the basketball game with the boys. And now I'm staring at the final draft of a contract when a sleepy voice calls me from the doorway.

"Hey."

I look up and smile. "Hi."

She's wearing another one of my T-shirts—the black Metallica one. It goes past her knees. That and the sleep-mussed hair make her look sweet but sexy. Alluring. Compared to Kate, work's not looking so appetizing anymore.

She runs a hand through her hair as her eyes sweep over the room. "This is a beautiful office, Drew. Breathtaking."

Kate is the type of woman who appreciates the importance of an awe-inspiring work space. If you want to be a winner, you need an office that says you already are one. "Thanks. It's my favorite room in the apartment."

"I can see why."

She picks up a frame from one of the shelves and shows it to me. "Who's this?"

It's a picture of Mackenzie and me at the beach last summer. She buried me up to my neck in the sand. "My niece, Mackenzie."

She looks at the photo and smiles. "She's adorable. I bet she worships you."

"Yeah, she does. And I'd pretty much cut my hand off for her if she asked me to, so it's equitable. I'd love for you to meet her one day."

Kate doesn't hesitate. "I'd really like that."

She makes her way over to my chair and perches herself on my knee. I lean forward till my lips find hers—my tongue driving deep into the mouth I now know so well.

She snuggles back against my bare chest. "You're so warm." She rests her head on my shoulder and looks toward my computer. "What are you working on?"

I sigh. "This deal with Jarvis Technologies."

Jarvis is a communications company. They're looking to acquire a broadband satellite subsidiary.

I rub my eyes.

"Problems?"

I'm usually a lone wolf when it comes to business. I don't confide—I don't share. My opinion is the only one that counts. But talking to Kate about business is kind of like talking to myself. I'm actually interested in hearing what she has to say. “Yeah. The CEO is all brains and no balls. I’ve got the perfect deal lined up, but he won’t pull the trigger. He’s nervous about the risk.”

Her finger traces my jaw. “Every acquisition has risks. You have to show him the payoff is worth it.”

“That’s what I’m trying to do.”

She perks up then. “You know, I have something that could help you out. One of my old study partners from Wharton designed a template for a new valuation model. If you run it and the numbers are solid, it might just be enough to persuade Jarvis to take the plunge.”

I’m starting to think Kate’s brain turns me on almost as much as her ass.

Almost.

“It’s on a disk in my bag. I’ll get it for you.”

As she stands to go, I grab the bottom of her shirt and pull her back down on my lap—so there’s no way she can miss the perpetual hard-on I’m sporting. My arms wrap around her waist, trapping her. My mouth’s against her ear.

“Before we get into that, there’s something I want to do first.”

There’s amusement in her voice as she asks, “What do you want to do, Drew?”

I pick her up, sweep everything off my desk, and lay her down.

“You.”

We spend the rest of the day working. And talking. And laughing. I tell Kate about Mackenzie and the Bad Word Jar that’s sucking me dry. She tells me more about growing up in Greenville and her parents’ diner. We eat lunch on the balcony. It’s cold, so Kate sits on my lap to keep warm and feeds me with her fingers.

I can’t remember ever having such a good time. And we aren’t even screwing.

Go figure.

It's after ten. We're getting ready for bed. Kate is in the shower.

Alone.

She took my razor and kicked me out. Unlike women, guys don't need privacy. There is no bodily function a man won't perform in front of an audience.

We have no shame.

But whatever; if Kate needs her space, she can have it. I keep myself busy while I wait for her. I change the sheets. I take the box of condoms out of my drawer—to have a few within easy reach.

Then my heart sinks. And if he could, my dick would cry.

The box is empty. "Fuck."

"My thoughts exactly. Great minds think alike."

I turn at Kate's voice. She stands in the doorway, one hand on her hip, the other braced against the doorframe. She's beautifully, wonderfully naked. Her snatch is shaven even closer than before—just a whisper of dark curls. *Sweet Christ.*

I keep waiting for the time when Kate's body doesn't get to me. When I feel been-there-done-that. So far, it's just the opposite.

It's like . . . eating lobster. If you've never eaten it, you think, "Eh, maybe." But once you've tasted it? The chance to eat it again gets your mouth watering like the goddamn Mississippi River. Because now you know how fucking delicious it really is. Even just the thought of her . . . God. I may end up being the first man in history capable of masturbating without touching himself.

Look, Mom—no hands.

She walks toward me, wraps her arms around my neck, and kisses me slowly, her tongue coming out to trace my lower lip in the sexiest frigging way. I force myself to pull back. "Kate, wait . . . we can't."

Her hand slides into my boxers, around my already hard cock. She gives it a few pumps. "I think someone disagrees with you."

I press my forehead to hers. My voice sounds strangled. "No . . . I mean, we're out. Condoms. I . . . um . . ." I put my hand over hers, stopping her strokes so I'll be able to string a few words together that actually make sense. "I have to go to the store on the corner and get more . . . and then . . . God, then I'll fuck you all night."

Kate looks down and swallows. Her voice is hushed. "Or, we could . . . not . . . use them."

"What?"

I've never gone bareback. Ever. Not even during my younger years. I've always loved my dick much too much to have it shrivel up and fall off.

"I'm on the pill, Drew. And Billy . . . he's a lot of things, but he'd never cheat on me. Have you been . . . tested?"

Sure I have. Once a month, for as long as I can remember. It's a must with my lifestyle. An occupational hazard, you could say. My voice practically squeaks. "Yeah. I . . . I have. I'm good. But . . . are you sure?"

I've been offered a lot of things in bed. Every kind of kinky contraption and role-play you can imagine. Some you probably can't. Fucking without protection has never been one of them. It's not smart or safe. A woman can say she's on the pill, but how do you really know? People can tell you they're clean, but I wouldn't believe them. That would require trust.

And trust has never been a factor in my sex life.

It's not about sharing—getting to know someone and letting them know me. It's about getting off and getting the girl off in the process. Period.

"I want to feel you, Drew. I want you to feel me. I don't want . . . anything between us."

I gaze at her eyes. The way she's looking at me . . . it's just like she did after our shower yesterday. Like she's giving me something—a gift. That's just for me. Only for me. And it's her. Because she trusts me, has faith in me, believes in me. And you know what?

I don't want Kate to ever look at me any other way.

"Kate, these last couple days with you have been amazing. I've never . . . I've just never . . ." I don't even know how to describe what I'm feeling. I have no idea how to tell her. I make my living off the ability to communicate. By being able to verbalize an idea. Describe a plan.

But at this moment words are pitifully inadequate.

So I grab her by the upper arms and drag her against me. She moans in surprise or excitement—I'm not sure which. Her tongue slides against mine, and her hands pull at my hair. Somehow we end up on the bed, side by side, mouths fused together, my boxers on the floor. My hand slides over her tits, down her stomach, and between her legs.

I groan, "Fuck, Kate, you're already wet."

And she is. I've barely touched her and she's dripping for me. *Jesus.* I've never wanted anyone or anything as much as I want her at this moment. She nips at my neck as I slide my fingers inside. Her pussy closes around them like a goddamn glove, and we both moan loudly.

Then Kate's hands are on me, all over me. Cupping my balls, stroking my cock, scratching my chest and back.

I roll her under me. I need her—now. I tease her open with my dick, coating the tip with her sweet cream. Heat rolls off her, from her. She's like a fire—calling to me, drawing me in. I push inside slowly but to the hilt, and my eyes fall closed in perfect fucking ecstasy.

She's bare, unguarded, all around me. She feels . . . more. Wetter, hotter, tighter. More in every way. It's unbelievable.

Kate grips my ass, kneading and massaging and urging me in deeper. But I pull all the way out, just so I can slide back in again.

Christ Almighty.

I set the rhythm. It's not slow or sweet or tender. It's brutal and hot, and fucking amazing.

High-pitched whimpers escape through her parted lips. Then my mouth is on hers again, cutting them off. And we're grasping at each other, desperate and raw.

Like it's the first time. Like it's the last time.

She's curled around me in every way. Her cunt envelops my cock, her legs surround my waist, her arms encircle my neck—all wrapped tight like some exquisite vise. And I'm burrowing into her, wanting to be closer, needing to be deeper. God, I'd fucking crawl inside her if I could and never want out.

Kate's hands find mine. Our fingers fold together, and I bring them, joined, up over her head. Our foreheads touch—every pant, every breath mixing and mingling. Her hips move with mine, like the flow of the ocean. Back and forth. In frenzied unison. Together.

Our eyes lock. "God, Drew . . . don't stop . . . Please, don't ever stop."

I'm drowning in her. I can barely draw a breath. But somehow I grind out, "I won't. I'll never stop."

I feel it when she comes. Every scorching wet inch of her tightens blissfully around me. And it's so good . . . so savagely intense I want to fucking weep from the pleasure. I bury my face in her neck, inhaling her, devouring her. And then I'm coming with her—within her. Bathing her insides with each carnal thrust. Sweet electricity races through me as one word falls from my lips over and over again:

"Kate . . . Kate . . . Kate . . . Kate."

It's miraculous.

After several moments, our bodies still. The only sounds in the room are our rapid breaths and pounding heartbeats.

Then Kate whispers, "Drew? Are you all right?" I lift my head and find her beautiful eyes looking at me with concern. Her hand cups my cheek gently. "You're shaking."

Have you ever tried to take a picture of something really far away? And you look through the lens and the whole scene is a blurry blob? So you mess with the focus; you zoom in and out. And then the camera whirls and seconds later—boom—instant clarity.

Everything snaps into place.

The picture is as clear as crystal.

That's what it's like for me—right now—looking at Kate. Suddenly, it's all so obvious. So frigging clear.

I'm in love with her. Totally. Helplessly. Pathetically.

In love.

Kate owns me. Body and soul.

She's all I think about. She's everything I never thought I wanted. She's not just perfect—she's perfect for me.

I'd do anything for her.

Anything.

I want her near me, with me. All the time.

Forever.

It's not just the sex. It's not just her gorgeous body or her brilliant mind. It's not just that she makes me think or how eager she is to challenge me. It's more than any of that.

It's all of it.

It's her.

I've broken every goddamn rule I've ever set for myself to be with her. And it wasn't just to fuck her.

It was to have her. To keep her.

How did I not see it before? How come I didn't know?

"Hey?" She kisses me softly on the lips. "Where'd you go? I lost you for a minute. Are you okay?"

"I . . ." I swallow harshly. "Kate, I . . ." I take a deep breath. "I . . . I'm fine." I smile and kiss her back. "I think you just wore me out."

She laughs. "Wow. Never thought that would happen."

Yeah—tell me about it.

Chapter 17

I know what you're thinking: *What the fuck?*

If I realized that I'm in love with Kate, and she's obviously infatuated with me—how does she end up back with Billy Why-Don't-You-Just-Die-Already Warren?

Excellent question. We're almost there. But first: a science lesson. What do you know about frogs?

Yes. I said frogs.

Did you know that if you put a frog in boiling water, he'll jump out? But, if you put one in cold water and heat it slowly, he'll stay in. And boil to death. He won't even try to get out. He won't even know he's dying. Until it's too late.

Men are a lot like frogs.

Was I freaked out by my little epiphany? Of course I was. It was huge. Life-changing. No more strange pussy. No more stories for the guys. No more Saturday nights. But none of that mattered anymore. Honestly.

Because it was too late. I was already boiling—for Kate.

That whole night I watched her sleep. And made plans . . . for us. The things we'd do together, the places we'd go—tomorrow and next weekend and next year. I practiced what I would say, how I would tell her about my feelings. I imagined her reaction and how she would confess she felt the same way. It was like a movie, some horrible chick flick that I would never go see. The dashing playboy meets the take-no-prisoners girl of his dreams, and she snags his heart forever.

I should have known then that it was too good to be true. The best things usually are: Santa Claus, the male G-spot, heaven—the list is endless.

You'll see.

We're walking down Fifth Avenue. Instead of wasting precious time driving across town to Kate's apartment, we stopped at Saks on the way to work, where I bought Kate a new navy Chanel suit. Can't have her doing the Walk of Shame into the office, now, can I? When she was trying on clothes for me, I swear, I felt just like Richard fucking Gere in *Pretty Woman*. Kate even bought me a tie.

See?

Then she insisted on stopping by the lingerie department to replace the panties I'd so erotically destroyed. I put up a good fight over that one, but I lost. You ladies ought to know—going commando? That's sexier than leather and lace and whips and chains all put together.

We stop by Starbucks and grab some much needed caffeine. As we walk back outside, I pull Kate close. I cup her cheek and kiss her. She tastes like coffee—light and sweet. She pushes my hair back out of my eyes and smiles.

I'll never get tired of looking at her. Or kissing her. Pussy whipped, thy name is Drew. Yeah I know. It's okay. I don't mind. 'Cause if this is the Dark Side? Sign me up. Seriously. Don't be surprised if I start skipping down the street singing, "Zip-a-dee-fucking-doo-dah." I'm that happy.

Kate and I turn the corner. Holding hands and smiling at each other like two idiots who popped one too many antidepressants. Nauseating, isn't it?

We need to stop here for just a minute. You should look at us. How we are right here, right now—hand in hand. You should remember this moment. I do.

We were . . . perfect.

Then we get to our building. I open the door for Kate and walk in behind her.

And the first thing I see are daisies. Large white daisies with cheerful yellow centers. Some in vases on the security desk, others in bunches tied with ribbon. Some are scattered singly all over the floor, random petals here and there. In the middle of the lobby is a circle of even more daisies. In the center of that circle is Billy Warren. And he's got his guitar.

Fuck. Me.

No, that doesn't quite cover it.

Fuck me with a chain saw.

Yeah—that's about right.

You ever see a singing asshole? Here's your chance:

I was so blind I didn't know
How much it would hurt to let you go
I want to heal us, want to mend
Come back, come back to me again

If I didn't hate him so much—and the jackal who spawned him—I'd have to admit he's not half bad. I watch Kate closely. Every emotion that crosses her face, each feeling that dances in her eyes.

You know when you have a stomach virus? And you lie around all day with a bucket at your side because you feel like you're going to puke at any second? But then there's that moment—when you know it's coming. You break out in that cold, full-body sweat. Your head pounds, and you feel your throat expand to make room for the bile that's charging up from your stomach.

That's me. Right now.

I actually put my coffee down and look around for the nearest garbage can just to be sure I'll make it there in time.

And I need to say I'm sorry
For all the pain I caused
Please give your heart back to me
I'll keep it safe for eternity
We belong together
We've always known it's true
There will never be another
My soul cries out for you.

Any other time, any other girl, I would bury Warren. Without even trying. He can't hold a candle to me. I'm a goddamn Porsche; he's a frigging pickup truck that can't pass inspection.

But this is Kate. They have a history, a decade's worth. And that, kiddies, makes him some major-league competition.

In the dark of night, it's your name I call
I can't believe I almost lost it all
One more chance, one breath, one try
No more reasons to say good-bye

I want to pick Kate up, caveman style, and carry her out of here. I want to lock her in my apartment where he can't see her. Can't touch her. Can't touch us. The whole time I stare at her, but she doesn't turn to look at me.

Not one fucking time.

And I need to say I'm sorry
For all the pain I caused
Please give your heart back to me
I'll keep it safe for eternity
We belong together
We've always known it's true
There will never be another
My soul cries out for you

Why didn't I learn to play an instrument? When I was nine, my mother wanted me to play the trumpet. After two lessons, the tutor quit 'cause I let the dog piss on his mouthpiece.

Why the hell didn't I listen to my mother?

You are my beginning; you'll be my end
More than lovers, more than friends
I want you, I want you

He can't have her. *Go ahead and want all day long, douche bag. Sing from the motherfucking rooftops. Play until your fingers fall off.* It's too little, too late. She's already mine. Kate isn't the type to have sex with just anyone. And she fucked me all weekend like the world was ending. That has to count for something.

Doesn't it?

And I need to say I'm sorry
For all the pain I caused
Please give your heart back to me
I'll keep it safe for eternity
For eternity
You and me

The small crowd that's gathered in the lobby applauds. Dickhead puts his guitar down and walks up to Kate.

If he touches her, I will break his fucking hand. I swear to God.

He doesn't acknowledge me at all. He's focused only on Kate. "I've been calling you since Friday night . . . and I stopped by the apartment a few times this weekend, but you were out."

That's right. She wasn't home. She was busy. Now ask her what she was doing.

Who she was doing.

"I know this is work . . . but do you think we could go somewhere? To talk? Maybe your office?"

Say no.

Say no.

Say no, say no, say no, say no, say no, say no, say no, say no. . . .

"Okay."

Shit.

As she starts to walk away, I grab Kate's arm. "I need to talk to you."

Her eyes question me. "I'll just be a—"

"There's something I have to tell you. Now. It's important." I know I sound desperate, but I really don't give a damn.

She puts her hand over mine, the one still clasping her arm. She's calm—condescending, like she's talking to a child. "All right, Drew. Let me talk to Billy first, and I'll meet you in your office, okay?"

I want to stomp my foot like a two-year-old. No. It's so *not* fucking okay. She needs to know where I stand. I have to stake my claim. Throw my hat in the ring. Get my car in the goddamn race.

But I drop my hand anyway. "Fine. You two have a nice chat."

And I make sure I walk away first.

I stride toward my office. But I can't help but stop at Erin's desk when they walk by. As Kate turns to close her office door, our eyes meet. And she smiles at me.

And for the first time in my life, I don't know what it means.

Is she reassuring me that nothing's changed? That nothing will? Is she saying thank you for bringing that fuck nut crawling back to her? I just don't know.

And it's driving me crazy.

I clench my jaw and stalk toward my own office, slamming the door behind me. And then I pace. Like a soon-to-be father outside the delivery room, waiting to see if everything that means anything to him will come out unscathed.

I should have told her. Last night. When I had the chance. I should have explained how much she means to me. What I feel for her. I thought I had time. I figured I'd ease into it, slowly work up to it.

Stupid.

Why didn't I just fucking tell her?

Goddamn it.

Maybe she already knows. I mean, I brought her to my apartment, I *cuddled* with her. I worshiped her. I fucked her without a rubber—three times. She's got to know.

Erin quietly enters the room. I must look like a disaster, because her face is soft with sympathy. "So, Kate and Billy are talking, huh?"

I snort. "Am I that obvious?"

She opens her mouth, probably to tell me yes, but closes it and starts again. "No. I just know you, Drew."

I nod.

"You want me to take a walk? See what I can see . . . or hear?"

"You think that'll work?"

She smiles. "The CIA would be lucky to have me."

I nod again. "Okay. Yeah. Go do that, Erin. See what's going on."

She walks out. And I go back to wearing a hole in the rug. And pushing my hand through my hair until it sticks up like I've been struck by lightning.

A few minutes later, Erin comes back. "The door's closed, so I couldn't hear anything, but I peeked through the glass. They're sitting in front of her desk, facing each other. He's got his head in his hands, and she's listening to him talk. Her hand is on his knee."

Okay. He's pouring his heart out. And she's being sympathetic. I can live with that. Because then she's going to crush him, isn't she? She's going to tell him to screw off. That she's moved on—found someone better. Right?

Right?

Christ, just fucking agree with me.

"So . . . what should I do?"

Erin shrugs. "All you can do is wait. And see what she says when they're done."

I've never been good at waiting. No matter how hard my parents tried, I could never wait until Christmas morning to find out what I got. I was like a mini Indiana Jones—searching and digging until I found every single gift.

Patience may be a virtue, but it's not one of mine.

Erin stops at the door. "I hope it works out, Drew."

"Thanks, Erin."

And then she leaves. And I wait. And think. I think about the look on Kate's face when she was crying at her desk. I think about the panic she was in when she saw Warren at the bar.

Was that all I was to Kate? A distraction? A means to my own end?

I start pacing again. And praying. To a God I haven't spoken to since I was ten years old. But I talk to him now. I promise and I swear. I barter and beg—fervently.

For Kate to choose me.

The longest ninety minutes of my life later, Erin's voice hisses out of the intercom on my desk.

"Incoming! Incoming! Kate, nine o'clock."

I dive across my desk, knocking pens and paper clips to the floor. I push my chair up, smooth my hair down, and shuffle some papers around so it looks like I've been working. Then I take a deep breath. *Pull it together*.

It's game time.

Kate opens the door and walks in.

She looks . . . normal. Completely herself. No guilt. No anxiety. Not a care in the world.

She stands in front of my desk. "Hi."

"Hey." I force myself to smile casually. Even though my heart's pounding in my chest. Kind of like a dog's would—just before he's put down.

I should make small talk so I don't look too eager—too interested. But I just can't manage it. "So . . . how'd things go with Billy?"

She smiles softly. "We talked. We said some things that I think we both needed to hear. And now we're good. Really good, actually."

God. Can you see the knife sticking out of my chest? Yeah—the one she just twisted. They talked—they're good—*really* good. She took him back.

Fuck.

"That's great, Kate. Mission accomplished, then, huh?" I should have been an actor. I deserve a goddamn Academy Award after this.

Her brow wrinkles. "Mission?"

My cell phone rings. Saving me from this nightmare of a conversation.

"Hello?" It's Steven. But Kate doesn't know that. I force my voice to sound strong. Energized. "Hey, Stacey. Yeah, baby, I'm glad you called."

Always score first. Remember?

"Sorry I missed you on Saturday. What was I doing? Nothing important—a little project of mine. Something I've been trying to get done for a while. Yeah, I'm finished with it now. Turned out it wasn't as good as I thought it'd be."

Yes, my words are calculated. Yes, I hope they hurt her. What did you expect me to say? This is *me* you're talking to here. Did you really think I'd sit back like a chump while Kate gave me the brush-off?

No fucking way.

I ignore Steven's confusion on the other line and compel my lungs to laugh. "Tonight? Sure, I'd love to see you. Right, I'll bring the taxi."

Why are you looking at me like *I'm* the bastard? I gave Kate everything I have, everything I'm capable of. And she kicked me in the fucking teeth with it. I opened up my soul to her—and I know how pussified that sounds. But it's true. So don't look at me like I'm the bad guy, because—for once—I'm not.

I loved her. God, I fucking *love* her. And right now, it's killing me. I feel like one of those patients on ER who get their chests cracked open with a freaking rib spreader.

With the phone still on my ear, I finally look up at Kate. And for a second, I can't draw a breath. I thought she'd be pissed, maybe disappointed that I tossed her to the curb first. But that's not how she looks.

Have you ever seen someone get hit?

I have. Matthew, in our younger years. And Jack, on occasion, hasn't moved fast enough after coming on too strong to the wrong woman. When they got smacked—there was this expression. It only lasted a few seconds. Their whole face just went white . . . and blank.

I guess it's shock, like they can't believe what just happened actually happened to them.

That's what Kate looks like.

Like I slapped her across the face.

You think I should feel guilty about that? You want me to be sorry? Well too fucking bad. I can't. I won't. She made her decision. She made her choice.

Now she can choke on it.

I cover the mouthpiece of the phone. "Sorry, Kate, I have to take this. I'll see you at lunch, okay?"

She blinks twice. Then turns and walks out of my office without a word.

Chapter 18

After Kate leaves, things are . . . hazy. Isn't that how they always describe it? Victims of some catastrophic train wreck? That, in the moments after, it's all unclear. Unreal.

I tell Erin I'm sick. Her smile is sad and pitying. Before I get in the elevator, I look back at Kate's office, hoping to see her again. Just to torment myself.

But her door is closed.

It's raining outside. A winter downpour. The kind that soaks your clothes and chills you from the inside out. It doesn't bother me.

I walk back to my apartment, numb and dazed. Like a zombie from some low-budget horror film who doesn't react, even when he cuts his own foot off with a chain saw.

But when I make it through the door—that's when my senses kick back in. When I start to feel again. And I feel Kate.

Everywhere.

I can still see her eyes, heavy lidded with heat. I hear her whisper in my ear as I fall on the bed. Her scent covers my pillow. And I just can't get past the fact that she was right here a few hours ago. And I could touch her and look at her and kiss her.

And now I . . . can't.

It's like when someone dies. And you can't believe they're really gone because you just ran into them yesterday. They were right there with you, alive and real. And that's the memory you hold on to—the moment you mourn the most.

Because it was the last.

When did it happen?

That's what I can't figure out. When did Kate become so important to me that I can't function without her? Was it when I saw her crying in her office? Or the first time I kissed her in my office? Maybe it happened when Anderson insulted her, and I wanted to kick his ass for it. Was it that first night at the bar? The first time I looked into those endless brown eyes and knew I had to have her?

Or was it here? In my apartment? In any one of the hundred times I touched her . . .

God, why didn't I see it sooner?

All those weeks—all those months—wasted. All those women I fucked, whose faces I can't even remember. All the times I pissed her off when I could have been making her smile. All those days I could have been loving her. And getting her to love me.

Gone.

Women fall in love quicker than men. Easier and more often. But when guys fall? We go down harder. And when things go bad? When it's not us who ends it? We don't get to walk away.

We crawl.

I shouldn't have said those things. In my office. Kate didn't deserve that. It's not her fault she doesn't want what I want. That she doesn't feel what I feel.

Christ, this is awful. Just fucking kill me.

Where's a stray bullet from a random drive-by shooting when you need one?

Have you ever felt like this? Have you ever held something that meant . . . everything to you? Maybe you caught a home-run ball as it flew over the fence? Or looked at a picture of yourself from some sweet, unforgettable time? Maybe your mother gave you a ring that belonged to your grandma's grandmother? Whatever it is—you look at it and swear you'll keep it forever. Because it's that special. Precious.

Irreplaceable.

And then one day—you don't know how or when it happened—you realize it's gone.

Lost.

And you ache for it. You'd give anything to find it again. To have it back with you, where it was always supposed to be.

I curl myself around the pillow. I don't know how long I stay there like that, but the next time I open my eyes and look out the window, it's dark. What do you think they're doing right now? Celebrating probably. Going out. Or maybe staying in.

I stare at the ceiling. Yes, those are tears. Liquid regret.

Go ahead—call me a pussy. Call me a bitch. I deserve it. And I don't care.

Not anymore.

Do you think he has any idea how lucky he is? How blessed?

Of course he doesn't. He was the idiot who let her go. And I was the idiot who couldn't keep her.

Maybe they won't last. Maybe they'll break up again. When Kate realizes she deserves better. But I guess that won't make a difference for me, huh? Not after what I said. Not after I put that look on her face.

Jesus.

I roll off the bed and fall toward the trash can. I barely make it before I retch and heave. And anything that was in my stomach isn't.

And that's the moment—there on my knees. That's when I tell myself I have the flu. Because this . . . this broken wreck can't really be me.

Not forever.

If I'm just sick, then I can take some aspirin, get some sleep, and I'll feel better. I'll be me again. Eventually. But if I admit I'm crushed, if I acknowledge that my heart has been shattered into a thousand fucking shards . . . then I don't know when I'll ever be all right again. Maybe never.

So I get back into bed. To wait it out.

Till I'm over the flu.

Chapter 19

So that's it. That's my story. The rise. The fall. The end. And now—here I am—in this lousy restaurant Alexandra and Matthew dragged me to, where I just finished telling them pretty much the same story I told you.

When I was six, I learned how to ride a bike. Like all kids when they first take the training wheels off, I fell. A lot. Any time it happened, Alexandra was the one who was there. She dusted me off, kissed the scrapes away, and convinced me to climb back on. So it's only natural that I expect my sister to be compassionate about my heartache. Gentle. Sympathetic.

What I get is, "You're a goddamn idiot, you know that, Drew?"

I bet you were starting to wonder why we call her The Bitch. Well, here you go.

"I'm sorry?"

"Yes, sorry is exactly what you are. Do you have any idea what a mess you've made? I always knew you were spoiled and self-centered. Hell, I was one of the people who made you that way. But I never thought you were stupid."

Huh?

"And I could have sworn you were born with testicles."

I choke on my drink. And Matthew laughs.

"I'm serious. I distinctly remember changing your diaper and seeing those cute little guys hanging there. What happened to them? Did they shrink? Disappear? Because that's the only reason I can think of to explain why you would behave like such a pathetic no-balls coward."

"Jesus Christ, Alexandra!"

"No, I don't think even He can fix this."

Defensive anger seeps into my chest. "I really don't need this right now. Not from you. I'm already down—why the fuck are you kicking me?"

She scoffs. "Because a swift kick in the ass is exactly what you need. Did you ever even consider that when Kate said they were 'really good,' perhaps she meant they were civil? That they had decided to be friends? Part amicably? If you knew half as much about women as you think you do, you'd understand that no woman would want to end a ten-year relationship on bad terms."

That doesn't even make any sense. Why would anyone want to be friends with someone they used to be able to fuck and can't anymore? What would be the frigging point? "No. You're totally off base."

She shakes her head. "Regardless, if you had acted like a man instead of a wounded little boy, you would have told her how you felt."

Now she's just pissing me off. "Do I look like a fucking asshole to you? 'Cause I'm not. And there's no way I'm going to put myself out there and chase after someone who wants to be with somebody else."

A look washes over Alexandra's face that I've never seen before. At least not directed at me.

It's disappointment.

"Of course not, Drew. Why should you chase anyone, when you're so content to let everyone chase you?"

"What the hell is that supposed to mean?"

"It means everything has always been easy for you. You're handsome, intelligent, you have a family who loves you and women who lie down for you like sacrificial lambs. And the one time you have to struggle for something you want—the one time you have to risk your heart for someone who's finally worth it—what do you do? You give up. You shoot first and ask questions later. You curl up in a ball and wallow in self-pity."

She shakes her head slightly, and her voice softens. "You didn't even try, Drew. After all that. You just . . . threw her away."

I look down at my drink. My voice is quiet. With remorse.

"I know."

Don't think I haven't thought about it. Don't think I haven't regretted my words or lack thereof. Because I have. Bitterly. "I wish . . . But it's too late now."

Matthew finally speaks up. "It's never too late, man. The game's not over; it's just rain delayed."

I look at him. "Has Delores said anything to you? About Kate and Billy?"

He shakes his head. "Not about them . . . but she's had a whole lot to say about you."

"What do you mean?"

"I mean Dee hates your guts. She thinks you're a scumbag. Seriously, dude, if you were on fire in the street? I don't think she'd spit on you."

I roll that information around for a minute. "Maybe she hates me because I fucked her cousin's fiancé?"

"Maybe she hates you because you broke her best friend's heart?"

Yeah. It's a toss-up. No help there.

"Are you in love with Kate, Drew?"

My eyes meet Alexandra's. "Yes."

"Is there a chance that she feels the same way?"

"I think so." The more I thought about Kate's words and actions that weekend, the more certain I became that Kate felt something for me. Something real and deep.

At least she did before I shot it all to hell.

"Do you want to be with her?"

"God, yes."

"Then whether she's back with her ex or not is irrelevant. The question you need to ask yourself is what are you willing to do—willing to risk—to make this right? To get her back."

And my answer to that is simple: Anything. Everything. My throat is tight as I confess, "I'd give anything to have Kate back."

"Then, for God's sake, fight for her! Tell her."

As her words sink in, Matthew grips my shoulder. "In times like this, I always ask myself, 'What would William Wallace do?'" His eyes are serious. Stirring. Then his voice takes on a Scottish accent he doesn't have. "Aye . . . run, and you won't get rejected . . . but years from now, would you be willin' to trade all the days from now to then for a chance—just one chance—to go back and tell Kate she can take your balls and hang them from the rearview mirror of her car, but she can never take . . . your freedom!"

Alexandra rolls her eyes at the *Braveheart* speech, and I actually laugh. The black cloud that's been sitting on my shoulders all week long finally starts to lift. In its place is . . . hope. Confidence. Determination. All the things that make me . . . me. All the things I've been missing since the morning I watched Billy Warren sing.

Matthew smacks me on the back. "Go get her, man. I mean, look at you—what have you got to lose?"

He's right. Who needs dignity? Pride? They're overrated. When you've got nothing, you've got nothing left to lose.

"I have to go see Kate. Right now."

And if I strike out? At least I'll go down swinging. If I crash and burn and she grinds my ashes into the dirt with her heel? So be it. But I have to try. Because . . .

Well, because she's worth it.

When Alexandra turned sixteen, my parents rented out Six Flags Great Adventure for the day. Excessive? Yes. But that's one of the perks of a privileged upbringing. It was awesome. No lines, no crowds. Just our family, some business associates, and a hundred and fifty of our closest friends. Anyway, there was this one roller coaster—the Scream Machine.

Remember how I said I never ride the same coaster twice? This was the exception.

Matthew, Steven, and I rode it until we puked. Then we climbed back on and rode it again. The first hill was nasty. A long, torturous incline that ended in a twisting, gut-dropping, one-hundred-and-fifty-five-foot vertical plunge. No matter how many times we rode that bad boy—every time we climbed that first hill—it felt the same. My palms got sweaty, my stomach turned over. It was the perfect combination of excitement and dread.

And that's exactly how I feel right now.

See me there? The guy jogging through Times Square.

Just the thought of seeing Kate again . . . I'm pumped about it, I won't lie. But I'm nervous too. Because I have no idea what's on the other side of this hill, how far the drop might be for me.

No sympathy, huh? Tough crowd. You think I got what I deserved? Maybe I still deserve worse?

It's a compelling argument. I fucked up. No question about it. It was a slump—all the greats have them. But those days are over now. I'm off the bench and back in the game.

I just hope Kate will give me another chance at bat.

Panting from the seven-block sprint, I nod my head in greeting to the security guard and make my way through the empty lobby. I use the brief elevator ride up to catch my breath and practice what I'm going to say. Then I step out onto the fortieth floor.

There's only one place Kate Brooks would be at ten thirty on a Monday night. And that's right here, where it all started. The offices are dark. It's quiet, except for the music coming from her office. I walk down the hall and stop outside her closed door.

Then I see her. Through the glass.

Christ Almighty.

She's sitting at her desk, staring at the computer screen. She's biting her lip in that way that brings me to my fucking knees. Her hair is pulled back, exposing every flawless feature on her face. I've missed looking at her. You have no idea. It feels like . . . like I've been underwater, holding my breath. And now I can finally breathe again.

She looks up. And her eyes meet mine.

See how she stares for a few seconds longer than necessary? How her head tilts to the side, and her eyes squint? Like she doesn't quite believe what she's seeing.

She's surprised. Then the surprise morphs into distaste. Like she just ate something rotten. And that's when I know. When I'm certain of what you've probably already figured out. That I am a complete fucking idiot.

She didn't take Warren back. There's no way.

If she had? If our weekend had meant nothing to her? If *I* meant nothing? She wouldn't be looking at me like I'm the goddamn devil. She wouldn't be affected at all. It's simple guy logic: If a woman is angry? It means she cares. If you're in a relationship and a chick can't even be bothered to yell at you? You're screwed. Indifference is a woman's kiss of death. It's the equivalent of a man not interested in sex. In either case—it's over. You're done.

So, if Kate is upset, it's because I hurt her. And the only reason I was able to do that is because she wanted to be with me.

That may seem like a twisted way to think—but it's the way it is. Trust me, I know. I've spent my life screwing women I felt nothing for. If they fucked another guy right after me? Good for them. If they told me they never wanted to see me again? Even better. You can't get blood from a stone. You can't get a reaction from someone who doesn't give a shit.

Kate, on the other hand, is overflowing with emotion. Anger, distrust, betrayal—it simmers in her eyes and shines on her face. The fact that she still feels something for me—even if it's hatred—gives me hope. Because that I can work with.

I open the door to her office and walk in. Kate looks back to her laptop and hits a few keys.

"What do you want, Drew?"

"I need to talk to you."

She doesn't look up. "I'm working. I don't have time for you."

I step forward and close her laptop. "Make time."

She turns her eyes on me. They're hard. Glacial, like black ice.

"Go to hell."

I smirk, even though there's nothing remotely funny about any of this. "Been there. All week."

She leans back in her chair, looking me up and down. "That's right. Erin told us about your mysterious illness."

"I stayed home because—"

"Cab ride take too much out of you? Needed a few days to recover?"

I shake my head. "What I said that day was a mistake."

She stands up. "No. The only mistake here was mine. That I ever thought there was anything more to you. That I actually let myself believe there was something . . . beautiful underneath all your cocky charm and big-dick attitude. I was wrong. You're hollow inside. Empty."

Remember when I said Kate and I are a lot alike? We are. And I don't mean just in bed or at the office. We both have the uncanny ability to say just the right things—to wound. To find that weak spot inside every one of us and nail it with a verbal frigging grenade.

"Kate, I—"

She cuts me off. And her voice is tight. Clogged.

"You know, Drew, I'm not stupid. I wasn't expecting a marriage proposal. I knew what you were like. But, you seemed so . . . And that night at the bar? The way you looked at me. I thought . . ."

Her voice breaks, and I want to fucking kill myself.

". . . I thought I meant something to you."

I step closer, wanting to touch her. To comfort her. To take it all back.

Make it all better.

"You did. You do."

She nods stiffly. "Right. That's why you—"

"I didn't do anything! There was no hookup. No goddamn taxi ride. It was all bullshit. It was Steven on the phone that day, not Stacey. I just said those things so you would think it was her."

She goes pale, and I know she believes me. "Why . . . why would you do that?"

I blow out a breath. My voice is soft and strained. Begging her to understand.

"Because . . . I'm in love with you. I've been in love with you for a long time. I didn't know it until that Sunday night. And then when Billy showed up here . . . I thought you took him back. And it fucking crushed me. It hurt so much that I wanted to make you . . . feel as bad as I did."

Not my best moment, huh? Yeah, I know—I'm an asshole. Believe me, I know.

"So I said those things on purpose, so you would think you were nothing to me. That you were just another girl. But you're not, Kate. You're not like anyone I've ever known. I want to be with you . . . really be with you. Only you. I've never felt this way about anyone. And I know I sound like a freaking Hallmark card, but it's true. I've never wanted all the things I want to have when I'm with you."

She doesn't say anything. She just stares at me. And I can't take it anymore. I put my hands on her shoulders, on her arms. Just to feel her.

She stiffens but doesn't pull away. I bring my hands to her face. My thumb smooths over her cheeks and her lips.

Jesus.

Her eyes close at the contact, and the lump in my throat feels like it's strangling me.

"Please, Kate, can we just . . . go back? Everything was so good before. It was perfect. I want us to be like that again. I want that so much."

I've never believed in regret. In guilt. I used to think they were just in a person's head. Like a fear of heights. Nothing you can't get past if you have the determination. The strength. But I've never had someone—hurt someone—who meant more to me than . . . me. And to know that I messed this up because of my fear, my fucking stupidity, it's just . . . unbearable.

She knocks my hands away. And steps back.

"No."

Kate picks her bag up off the floor.

"Why?" I clear my throat. "Why not?"

"Do you remember when I first started working here? And you told me your father wanted me to put together a 'practice' presentation?"

I nod.

"You said that because you didn't want me to get the client. Right?"

"That's right."

"And then the night we met with Anderson, you told me that I was shoving my tits in his face because . . . How did you put it? You wanted to 'get a rise out of me.' Yes or no?"

Where's she going with this?

"Yes."

"And then last week—after everything—you made me believe that you were talking to that woman because you wanted to hurt me?"

"I did, but—"

"And now, now you're telling me you're in love with me?"

"I am."

She shakes her head softly. "And why on earth should I believe you, Drew?"

I stand there. Silent. Because I've got nothing. No defense. No reasons that would make any real difference. Not to her.

She turns to leave. And I panic. "Kate, please wait. . . ."

I step in front of her. She stops but looks past me—through me. Like I'm not even here.

"I know I fucked up. Badly. The taxi-girl thing was stupid and cruel. And I'm sorry. More sorry than you'll ever understand. But . . . you can't let that ruin what we could have."

She laughs in my face. "What we could have? What do we have, Drew? All we've ever had are arguments and competition and lust. . . ."

"No. It's more than that. I felt it that weekend, and I know you felt it too. What we have could be . . . spectacular. If you just give it a chance. Give us—me—one more chance. Please."

You know that song the Rolling Stones play, "Ain't Too Proud to Beg"? It's my new theme song.

Her lips fold against one another. Then she moves around me.

But I grab her arm.

"Let me go, Drew."

"I can't." And I don't just mean her arm.

She jerks away. "Try harder. You did it once. I'm sure you can manage it again."

Then she walks out the door.

And I don't follow her.

Chapter 20

Okay. So that didn't go very well.

You're right—it was a goddamn disaster. You think I should have gone after her? Well, you're wrong. Have you ever read *The Art of War* by Sun Tzu? I have. It's a book about military strategy. A good general knows when to attack. A great general knows when to pull back. To regroup.

I've told Kate what I needed to. Now I have to show her.

Actions win wars. Actions heal wounds. Not words. Words are cheap. Mine, in particular, have the combined value of pocket lint at the moment.

So . . . I have a plan. And failure's not an option. Because this isn't just about me, about what I want. Not anymore. It's about what Kate wants too. And she wants me. Sure, she's fighting it—but it's there. Like it's always been.

No one will ever be to Kate what I can be. And—before you take my head off—I'm not saying that because of my overdeveloped sense of confidence. I'm saying it because behind the anger, under the hurt . . . Kate is just as in love with me as I am with her.

Looking at her was like looking in a goddamn mirror.

So I won't quit. I won't throw in the towel. Not until we both have what we want.

Each other.

Hey—you know what else a great general knows how to do? Call in the reserves.

Here's a fact for you: Most men can't multitask.

It's true.

That's why you won't catch many guys trying to make a full-course Thanksgiving dinner. That's the reason mothers all over the world come home to a disaster area when they leave their kids with the hubby for a few hours. Most of us can only really focus on one thing at a time.

Most of us—but not me.

Before I'm out the door of the office, I've got Erin on the cell. No, I'm not a slave driver. If you're an assistant to one of the most successful I-bankers in New York City, late-night calls are part of the job description. Now that my head has been removed from its weeklong vacation up my ass, I need to find out if I have any clients left to work with.

Lucky for me, I do.

"I hope you can grow a third kidney, Drew," Erin says. "Because if Matthew, Jack, and Steven ever need one at the same time, you're going to have to hand them over."

Apparently, they're the ones who've been covering for me while I was making that permanent dent in my couch.

"Book Jack a table at Scores this weekend. On me."

Nothing says thank you like a prepaid stripper.

As for Matthew and Steven—I'm going to need to think about that one. I have a feeling titty bars are outlawed on the Dark Side.

After Erin updates me about work, I tell her to clear my schedule and give her a list of the things I'll need for tomorrow. I've got a hell of a day planned—but it's got nothing to do with investment banking.

By the time we hang up, I'm walking through the door of my apartment. *Jesus Christ.* I cover my nose with my hand. How the hell did I live with that smell for seven days?

Oh, that's right—I was a vegetable.

I take a good look around. Garbage bags line one wall. Empty bottles are stacked on the table. Dirty dishes fill the sink, and the air reeks like that stale scent that seeps through your car vents when you're stuck in traffic behind a garbage truck. Alexandra did her best to clean up, but it's still a disaster.

Kind of like my life at the moment, huh? How's that for symbolism.

I walk to the bedroom, where I can actually breathe through my nose. I sit on the edge of the bed and stare at the phone. Remember those reserves I mentioned? Time to call them up.

I pick up the phone and dial. A soothing voice greets me after the second ring. The perfect combination of strength and comfort, and I answer back.

"Hi, Mom."

You thought I was calling someone else, didn't you?

Deep down—I'm a momma's boy. I'm man enough to admit it. And trust me, I'm not the only one. Explains a lot, doesn't it? That's the reason your boyfriend can't manage to get his socks or underwear actually in the hamper—because he grew up with Mommy doing it for him. That's why your pasta sauce is good, but not great—because his taste buds have been finely tuned to Mom's Sunday gravy.

Plus, you know that saying "Mother knows best"? Yes, it's annoying. But is it accurate? Abso-fucking-lutely. I've never known my mother to be wrong. About anything. So at this moment, her opinion is my most valuable resource. *I* know what I *think* I should do to fix things with Kate, but I want confirmation that it's actually the *right* thing to do. This is new territory for me. And I can't afford to screw it up.

Again.

My mother starts talking about chicken soup and cold compresses. But I cut her off.

"Mom—I haven't been sick. Not like you think, anyway."

With a sigh, I dive into the whole sordid tale. The abridged, G-rated version.

Sort of feels like confession.

After I describe the morning in my office where I screwed the pooch with Kate—okay, you're right, where I pretty much fucked the whole kennel—my mother lets loose a sorrowful "Oh, Drew."

My stomach flips with regret and disappointment. What I wouldn't give for a time machine.

I finish the story of my downfall and go on to explain my plans to unfuck myself tomorrow. After I'm done, she's quiet for a few seconds. And then she does the last thing I'd expect my polite, reserved mother to do.

She laughs. "You're so much like your father. Sometimes I wonder if you got any of my DNA at all."

I've never really seen any similarities between my dad and me. Except our love of business—our drive to succeed. We've always been evenly matched in that respect. Otherwise, my father's as straitlaced as they come. A dedicated, loyal family man through and through. Pretty much the opposite of me in every way.

"I am?"

She's still chuckling. "One day I'll tell you how your dad and I really ended up together at Columbia. And I'll include all the dirty little details he never wanted you to know."

If that story involves sex in any way, I don't want to hear it.

Ever.

As far as I'm concerned, my parents have had sex two times in their entire lives. Once for Alexandra, and once for me. That's it. On some level I realize I'm deluding myself, but this is one topic where I prefer to live in denial.

"As for you and Kate, I imagine she'll be quite . . . impressed with what you have planned. Eventually. At first, I'm guessing she'll be livid. You should be prepared for that, Drew."

I'm kind of counting on it. Remember that fine line Matthew talked about?

"I have to ask you though, dear—are you sure? Are you absolutely positive that Kate Brooks is the young lady for you? Not just as a lover but as a friend, a companion, a partner? You need to be certain, Drew. It's wrong to toy with someone's feelings; you don't need me to tell you that."

There's reproach in her voice now—the same tone she used when I was eight and got caught reading Alexandra's diary.

"I'm a hundred percent sure. It's Kate or . . . nothing."

I'm still shocked by how true this is. And, frankly, scared shitless.

I mean, even before I nailed Kate, my interest in fucking any other woman had started to fade. Drastically. And it wasn't really because they were bad lays. It was because they weren't Kate. If, by some catastrophe, Kate won't take me back, I might as well shave my head and move to frigging Tibet.

I hear the monks are hiring.

"Well then, here's my advice: Be relentless. Unyielding. Absolutely persistent in your pursuit. If your confidence wavers at all, Kate will take that as a sign that your affection may waver as well. You've already given her several reasons not to believe in you; don't let your insecurities give her more. Be sweet, Drew. Be honest. Act like the man I raised you to be. The man I know you are."

I smile. And just like that, I know—without question—that somehow, some way, I'll make this right.

"Thanks, Mom."

As I'm about to say good-bye, she adds, "And for goodness' sake, as soon as you clear up this situation, I want both of you over at the house for dinner. I want to meet the woman who's got my son wrapped around her finger. She must be extraordinary."

A hundred snapshots of Kate jump into my head at once. . . .

Kate at her desk, glasses on. All brilliance and determination. A force to be reckoned with.

Kate laughing at one of my inappropriate comments. Introducing Matthew to Dee-Dee. Helping Steven out of a jam.

Kate in my arms—so fucking passionate and giving. Trusting and open. Her below me, above me, around me, matching me move for move, moan for moan.

I smile wider.

"She is, Mom. She really is."

Time for a history lesson, kids.

Back in the olden days, when two clans were at war, they would send their noblemen onto the field before a battle to try and negotiate a nonviolent resolution. If the lords could figure out a compromise, then there wouldn't be a fight. But if they couldn't reach an agreement—it was on.

And I'm talking old-school battle-axes, flaming arrows, cannonballs-that-will-take-your-legs-off-at-the-knee kind of on.

Yes, this was a scene in *Braveheart.* But it's still historically accurate.

My point is, for every goal, there are two ways of reaching it: the hard way and the easy way. The men back then understood that. And so do I. Which is why I'm standing outside my office building waiting to catch Kate before she walks through the door. To extend the olive branch. To work out a peaceful solution.

We'll call this my "easy way."

And here she comes. See her down the block? Apparently, I'm not the only one who came to work today ready for war. Kate definitely has her armor on.

She's wearing a black pantsuit and heels so high she'll be eye level with me. Her hair is twisted into a tight bun with just a few wisps caressing her face. Her chin's raised, her eyes are hard, and she's walking with fierce, purposeful strides.

Fucking magnificent.

My heartbeat speeds up, and my cock rises to half-mast, but I ignore it. True, it's been a freaking millennium since I've gotten any, but I'll get into that later. Right now, my focus is completely on Kate and my next move.

I push off from the building and meet her halfway.

"Hi, Kate. You're looking especially edible this morning."

I smile and hold out a purple lavender flower. She doesn't take it. Instead, she brushes past me without a word.

I backtrack so I'm still in front of her. "Morning, Kate."

She tries to go around me, but I block her in. And I smirk.

Can't help it.

"What? You're not speaking to me? You really think that's feasible considering we work together?"

Her voice is flat and rehearsed, like a robot's. "Of course not, Mr. Evans. If you have business to discuss with me, I'd be happy to converse with you. But if it's not regarding work, then I'd really prefer—"

"Mr. Evans?" *I don't think so.* "Is this like a kinky role-play thing? I'm the bad boss and you're the sexy secretary?"

Her jaw clenches, and her hand tightens on her briefcase.

"Or you can be the boss, if you like. And I could be the submissive assistant who needs punishing. I could definitely get into the dominatrix thing."

She makes a disgusted sound.

And walks away.

I easily catch up to her. "No, wait—I'm kidding. It was a joke. Please wait. I really do need to talk to you."

Her voice is sharp—annoyed. "What do you want?"

I smile and hold out the flower again. "Have dinner with me on Saturday."

Her brow wrinkles. "Are you taking some kind of medication that I'm not aware of?"

"Why do you ask?"

"Did I not make myself clear last night? Why would you think I would ever consider going out with you again?"

I shrug. "I was hoping you'd be in a better mood this morning. That maybe after a good night's sleep you'd realize that you still . . . like me."

She snorts. "Don't hold your breath."

She takes a step. Then stops and turns back to me.

"No, on second thought—do."

I keep pace beside her as she continues toward the building. I've got two minutes here, maybe less. I talk fast.

"Seriously, Kate, I've been thinking—"

"Will wonders never cease."

Was she always this much of a smart-ass?

"I want to start over. Do things right this time. I want to take you out. Tell you all the things I should have said before. About how amazing I think you are. How important you are to me. Oh, and I'm never going to lie to you again."

Ever.

I mean it.

Ten years from now, if Kate asks me if a certain pair of jeans makes her ass look fat—and they do? I'm going to take my life in my hands and say yes.

I swear.

She looks straight ahead as she answers, "Thanks for the offer, but no thanks. Being made to feel stupid and used really isn't high on my to-do list this week. Been there, done that. Not looking for a repeat."

I grasp her elbow gently and turn her toward me. I try to catch her eyes, but she refuses to meet mine. My voice is low. And sincere.

"Kate . . . I panicked. I got scared, and I screwed up. It'll never happen again. I learn from my mistakes."

"What a coincidence." She looks me up and down meaningfully. "So do I."

Then she walks away. And I blow out a big breath.

Okay.

Hard way it is.

Why am I not surprised?

Chapter 21

When Kate opens the door to the building, I'm right behind her. As soon as she crosses the threshold, the music starts.

And she stops dead in her tracks.

They're called the Three Man Band. They're traveling musicians. Literally. The lead singer's got a guitar hanging from a strap across his shoulders and a microphone attached to his chest. The drummer has a six-piece set harnessed in front—like a kid in a marching band, but much cooler. The last guy has a combination bass guitar and keyboard sitting on a platform at his waist.

It's really not as corny as it sounds. They're good. Like one of those cover bands that play down the Jersey shore in the summer. And they're playing "Caught Up in You" by .38 Special.

Kate hisses at me through her teeth, "What the hell is this?"

I shrug. "Well, I don't know how to play the guitar. And I can't sing. So . . ."

I know what you're thinking. *Music, Drew? That's the big plan? Didn't Billy already try that?* Yes, Warren tried this strategy and failed. But this will be different.

Better.

Longer.

The Three Man Band is mobile. Which means they can—and will—follow Kate all day. Serenading her with not just one but dozens of carefully chosen songs. And no—this isn't the whole plan. This is just the first step. There's more.

"I hate you."

No, she doesn't.

I slide my unclaimed flower behind her ear. "Listen to the words, Kate."

The singer croons about a man on his knees, who's so in love he wants to change, to be better—more. For her.

Kate rips the flower out of her hair and drops it on the floor. Then she shoves past me toward the elevator and gets in.

And the Three Man Band crowds in around her. Still playing.

She looks horrified, doesn't she? As the doors close, I almost feel bad.

Almost.

I take the next elevator up to the fortieth. By then, the sounds of "Angel" by Aerosmith fill the air. Apparently, Kate has barred the Three Man Band from her office. So they're stationed outside her closed door.

I stop at Erin's desk. She hands me my coffee.

"Good song."

"Thanks. Everything set?"

"Locked and loaded, boss." Then she snaps her fingers. "Oh, and I brought this for you." She hands me a medium-size box filled with DVDs. Lying on top are *Gone with the Wind, Say Anything, Beauty and the Beast, Casablanca, Titanic,* and . . . *The Notebook*.

"What's this?"

"Research. For you. I figured you might need it."

I smile. "What would I do without you, Erin?"

"Spend the rest of your life miserable and alone?"

She's not far off the mark.

"Give yourself another week's vacation, okay?"

I take my box of goodies into my office and prepare for phase two.

Flowers. Lots of women say they don't want them. But every woman is happy when she gets them.

Which is why I've arranged to have them delivered to Kate's office, every hour on the hour. Seven dozen at a time. That's one dozen for every day we were apart.

Romantic, right? I thought so too.

And although I know Kate's favorite are white daisies, I specifically told the florist to avoid them. Instead, I've chosen exotics—bouquets with brightly colored petals and strange shapes. The kinds of flowers Kate has probably never seen in her life, from places she's never been.

Places I want to take her to.

At first I kept the notes simple and generic. Take a look:

Kate,

I'm sorry.

Drew

Kate,

Let me make it up to you.

Drew

Kate,

I miss you. Please forgive me.

Drew.

But after a few hours I figured I needed to step it up a notch. Get more creative. What do you think?

Kate,

You're turning me into a stalker.

Drew

Kate,

Go out with me on Saturday and I'll give you all of my clients.

Every. Single. One.

Drew

Kate,

If I throw myself in front of a bus, will you come visit me at the hospital?

Drew

P.S.–Try not to feel too guilty if I don't survive. Really.

That last batch was delivered forty-five minutes ago. Now I'm just sitting at my desk, waiting. Waiting for what, you ask? You'll see. Kate may be stubborn, but she's not made of stone.

My office door slams open, leaving a dent in the drywall.

Here we go.

"*You* are driving me crazy!"

Her cheeks are flushed, her breathing's fast, and she's got murder in her eyes.

Beautiful.

I raise my brows hopefully. "Crazy? Like you want to rip my shirt open again?"

"No. Crazy like the itch of a yeast infection that just won't go away."

I flinch. Can't help it.

I mean—*Christ.*

Kate steps toward my desk. "I am trying to work. I need to focus. And you've got Huey, Dewey, and Louie outside my office door playing every cheesy eighties song ever written!"

"Cheesy? Really? Huh. I so had you pegged for an eighties kind of girl."

Well, you live and learn.

"I'm serious, Drew. This is a place of business; I can't be the only one this noise is bothering."

Good. We're back to Drew. Progress.

And as far as disturbing the rest of the staff? I thought of that. I spoke with most of the people on this floor and gave them a heads-up about the entertainment for the day. They didn't seem to mind.

"I'm serious too, Kate. You shouldn't be working. You should be listening. I chose this playlist myself. It's my grand gesture. To show you how I feel."

"I don't give a shit about how you feel!"

"Well, that's harsh."

She crosses her arms, and her foot taps on the floor.

"You know, I didn't want to do this, but you've left me no choice. You're obviously too immature to handle this like an adult. So . . . I'm going to tell your father."

Right.

She's the one who's going to tell Daddy on me, but *I'm* being immature.

Of course.

And I thought of that already too. "My father's in California for the next two weeks. I'm not overly concerned about what he might do to me via telephone." She opens her mouth to try again, but I continue. "You could try talking to Frank. But he's in the Hamptons, at that year-round golf course Trump just opened. George is in his office." She turns, but my next words make her pause. "I should warn you, though . . . he's got a real soft spot for romantics. I wouldn't get my hopes up if I were you. And he's my godfather."

She stares at me a minute. She's trying to think of a comeback. I'm just glad I cleared all the heavy objects off my desk.

You know, the ones she probably wants to chuck at my head right about now.

"You can't do this. This is sexual harassment."

I stand up and lean across my desk. "Sue me."

Her mouth opens to spew what I'm sure will be a tirade of volcanic proportions. But I cut her off. And my voice is calm. Rational.

"Or, you can save yourself the trouble and just go out with me on Saturday. One date. One night, and all this goes away. After that, if you still don't want to have anything to do with me, I'll leave you alone. Scout's honor."

Technically, this isn't a lie. We've already established Boy Scouting was not my thing. Loopholes, remember?

Her face contorts into a mask of disgust. "Absolutely not. I won't be blackmailed into going out with you."

I sit back down. "That is the strong choice. The feminist, I-am-woman-hear-me-roar decision. I'm proud of you, Kate."

Her eyes narrow suspiciously.

Smart girl.

"Plus, I can't wait for you to see what I have planned for tomorrow. I wouldn't schedule any meetings, though. Might be too loud."

Her voice rises with every word. Like thunder from a storm that's moving closer. "You are a manipulative, childish, vindictive bastard!"

"I'm not trying to be."

She makes her way around my desk, and I stand up to meet her.

"A selfish, self-centered, egotistical son of a bitch!"

"I know."

She hits me on the chest with both fists.

Whack.

"I wish I'd never seen you at that stupid club!"

Whack.

"I wish I never got this job!"

Whack.

"I wish I never met you!"

I grip her wrists and pull her close.

Now here's when we usually start kissing.

Were you looking forward to that part? Sorry. Not gonna happen. Because this isn't just about me and my raging hard-on. Not anymore. And I have to prove that to Kate.

So I hold back. But don't think it's easy, 'cause it's not. There's nothing I want more than to mold my mouth to hers and remind her of how good it was between us. How good it can still be.

I lean in and rest my forehead against hers. She closes her eyes. I brush my nose against hers and inhale, needing a fix. She smells even better than I remember. Like warm cookies in the Garden of fucking Eden.

And then I whisper, "I'm sorry I hurt you. I didn't mean any of it. Not a single goddamn word. Please believe that."

Kate opens her eyes. There's surprise in those brown beauties. And fear, like a deer that just caught a hunter's scent. Because she *wants* to believe me. And she knows I know that.

Then she blinks. And her eyes go hard. It's difficult to tell if she's more pissed at me or herself.

Probably me.

She shoves my chest, and I fall back into my chair.

"Fuck you!"

She stalks back around my desk toward the door.

"Here? Now?" I look up at the ceiling, like I'm debating the prospect. "Well . . . okay. But be gentle. My couch is a virgin."

I loosen my tie and start to unbutton my shirt.

She stutters. Then she points her finger at me and practically growls.

Yeah—it's fucking hot.

"Ugh!" Then she walks out of my office. She stops in front of the Three Man Band, who've been waiting outside. "And don't follow me!"

As she disappears down the hall, the lead singer looks at me.

I nod.

And they follow in Kate's footsteps, belting out "Heat of the Moment" by Asia.

Hey—what's wrong? You look worried. Don't be. I know what I'm doing. It's all part of the plan.

Chapter 22

I bet you didn't know this, but lots of guys have a thing for Ariel. You know, from *The Little Mermaid*? I've never been into her myself, but I can understand the attraction: She fills out her shells nicely, she's a redhead, and she spends most of the movie unable to speak.

In light of this, I'm not too disturbed about the semi I'm sporting while watching *Beauty and the Beast*—part of the homework Erin gave me. I like Belle. She's hot. Well . . . for a cartoon, anyway. She reminds me of Kate. She's resourceful. Smart. And she doesn't take any shit from the Beast or that douche bag with the freakishly large arms.

I stare at the television as Belle bends over to feed a bird. Then I lean forward, hoping for a nice cleavage shot. . . .

I'm going to hell, aren't I?

I can't help it. I'm desperate. Frustrated.

Horny.

I said I'd get to this later, remember? Well, it's later. I feel like a shaken can of soda that's about to explode. I know my previous record is twelve days—but this is different.

Worse.

I've gone cold turkey. Completely. I haven't even jerked off. Not once. In *nine frigging days*. I think the buildup of semen is starting to affect my brain. Like sugar to a diabetic.

Why haven't I used the hand God gave me, you ask?

It's a new rule. My own self-imposed penance for my stupidity. I refuse to come until Kate comes with me. Seemed like a good idea yesterday. But after seeing her today, I'm pretty sure the wait is going to kill me.

Don't roll your eyes.

You don't understand. Unless you're a guy, you can't. You have no idea how important regular sexual gratification is for us. It's crucial. Vital.

I'll explain.

In 2004, UCLA conducted a survey to determine how highly women valued getting off in relation to other daily activities. You know what they found? Eight in ten—that's eighty percent—said if given the choice between sex or sleep, they would choose sleep.

In that same year, NYU conducted its own study. With rats. They implanted electrodes in the brains of male rats and put two buttons in their cages. When the lucky little bastards pushed the blue button, the electrodes triggered an orgasm. When they pushed a red button, they were given food.

Care to guess what happened to all the rats?

They died.

They fucking starved to death.

They *never* pushed the red button.

Need I say more?

Anyway, here I am. Stuck in my own little cage with no goddamn blue button. But . . .

Maybe I can have the next best thing. I pause the movie. Then I pick up the phone and dial.

"Hello?" Her voice is sleepy. Husky.

"Hi, Kate."

"Drew? How . . . how did you get my home number?"

"I looked in your personnel file."

Yes, those things are supposed to be confidential, but I called in a favor. I play to win. Never said I play fair.

I lie back on the couch while images of Kate in bed dance in my head.

"So . . . what are you wearing?"

Click.

That went well.

I dial again.

"Hello."

"You were thinking about me before I called, weren't you?"

Click.

I smile. And dial again.

"*What?*"

"Just in case you're wondering, I still have them."

"You still have what?"

"Your underwear. The black lace ones. They're in my drawer. Sometimes I sleep with them under my pillow."

Sick? Possibly.

"You keep trophies from all your victims? How very serial killer-ish of you."

"No, not from all of them. Just you."

"Am I supposed to be flattered? Nauseated is more like it."

"I was hoping we could add another one to the collection."

Click.

Now this is just getting ridiculous.

I dial again.

"What. Do. You. Want?"

You.

And me.

Stranded on a luxurious deserted island for about a week.

"Don't hang up. I'll just keep calling back."

"Then I'll take the phone off the hook."

The challenge in her voice brings my semi full throttle. Did I say a week? I meant a month.

At least.

"Then I'll come over. I'll plant myself outside your door and talk through it. It won't make you very popular with the neighbors."

For a few seconds, she doesn't speak. It's after midnight. She's probably wondering if I'm serious.

I am.

Then she huffs, "Fine. I'll stay on the phone. Do you actually have a reason for calling, or do you just want to annoy me—more?"

I tell her the bare, honest truth. "I just wanted to hear your voice."

Not too long ago, I could stop by Kate's office whenever I wanted. I could talk to her. Look at her. Listen to her.

I miss that. A lot.

"What are you doing?" I ask.

"Working."

"Me too. Kind of. What are you working on?"

"A proposal for a new client. Jeffrey Davies."

"The millionaire? Isn't he . . . like, crazy?"

"He's very eccentric, yes."

I heard he's a fucking nutcase. Like one of those Trekkie fanatics who know the Klingon language or surgically alter their ears to look like Mr. Spock.

"What's he interested in?"

"Technology. Life-prolonging scientific research, to be exact."

Her voice is comfortable now. Normal. Almost friendly.

"I have some contacts in cryogenics. I could hook you up. We should discuss it over dinner on Saturday."

"Are you trying to bribe me?"

"Would you prefer breakfast? Lunch works for me too."

At this point, I'd settle for a light midday snack.

She snorts. It's not a laugh, but it's close. "Let it go, Drew."

I smirk even though she can't see it. "Not going to happen. I can keep this up forever. I have amazing stamina—but then you already know that."

"Do I have to hang up again?"

I whine, "No. I'll be good."

I turn on my side. My apartment is dim and still. It feels . . . intimate. Like one of those late-night conversations you had in high school under the covers because you weren't supposed to still be on the phone.

"So what are you doing for Christmas?"

There's a smile in her voice when she answers. "My mom's coming to visit. Dee-Dee's is too, so we're all going out together for Christmas dinner. And then my lease is up next month, so I plan on doing some apartment hunting while Mom's here. I'm hoping New York will impress her. Maybe I'll find a place that will entice her to stay."

"What about Warren? Is he still staying with Delores?"

Don't want any sneak attacks, now, do we?

The edge is back in her tone as she tells me, "Not that it's any of your business, but Billy moved to L.A. three days ago."

Well, doesn't that just make me want to stand up and do the happy dance on my dining room table?

"Do you guys still . . . talk?"

"He's going to email me once he's settled. Let me know how things are going."

"Kate . . . what happened between you two, that day in your office?"

I should have had the balls to listen to her that day. I should have asked her this question then. At the time I thought it'd be easier to pretend I didn't care than to hear her say *she* didn't.

I was wrong.

She sounds sad when she answers. And weary. "We talked, Drew. I told him that I loved him, that a part of me always would. I said that I knew he loved me too. But that we weren't . . . *in* love anymore. Not the way we were supposed to be . . . not for a long time. It took awhile, but eventually Billy agreed with me. And"—she blows out an annoyed breath—"I don't even know why I'm telling you any of this."

We're both quiet for a moment. And then I just can't help myself.

"I'm *in* love with you, Kate."

She's silent. She doesn't respond at all.

And my chest tightens because I know why.

"You don't believe me, do you?"

"I think you're an excellent liar when you want to be, Drew."

Ouch. So this is what it feels like to sleep in the bed you made, huh? It sucks.

But my voice is firm. Determined and un-fucking-wavering. "I'm not lying to you now, Kate. But it's okay. Do what you need to do. Curse me out, slap me around—get it all out of your system. I can take it. Because the more you push me away, the harder I'm going to fight to prove to you that this is real. That I'm not going anywhere and that what I feel for you isn't going to change. And then someday—maybe not anytime soon, but one day—I'm going to tell you that you, Kate Brooks, are the love of my life, and you won't have any doubt that it's true."

After a minute, Kate clears her throat. "I should go. It's late. And I have a lot of work to finish."

"Yeah. Okay. Me too."

"Good night, Drew."

I grin. "It could have been. But you're across town."

She laughs then. It's quick and muffled, but it's genuine. And I'm pretty sure it's the best sound I've ever heard.

"Sweet dreams, Kate. You know, the ones with you and me in them. Naked."

Click.

Chapter 23

The most important game in a rookie pitcher's career isn't his debut. It's his follow-up. The second showing. He has to prove that he's consistent. Reliable.

Today is my follow-up game. The day I show Kate she's not getting rid of me and that I'm one hell of a clutch player. I've started with something simple. Elegant. Something less in-your-face than the Three Man Band. After all, you don't always need to drop a nuke to win the war.

I had Kate's office filled with balloons.

A thousand of them.

Each printed with I'M SORRY.

Too much? I don't think so either.

Then I had a little something delivered to her office. From Tiffany. A small blue box with a note:

You already own mine.
Drew

Inside the box, on a platinum chain, is a flawless two-carat diamond heart.

Sappy? Sure it is. But women love sappy shit like that. At least according to the films I stayed up until three o'clock in the goddamn morning watching, they do.

I'm hoping it'll knock Kate off her feet. Right onto her back—and I'm sure I don't have to tell you how much I like her in that position.

Just kidding.

Kind of.

Besides, I get the feeling Kate isn't used to getting presents, at least not of that caliber. And she should be. She deserves to be spoiled. To have nice things. Beautiful things. Things her dipshit ex-boyfriend couldn't afford and probably wouldn't have thought to give her.

Things I can. And will.

I wanted to be there when she opened it. To see the look on her face. But I have a meeting.

"Andrew Evans. Still as handsome as the devil himself. How are you, m'boy?"

See that woman hugging me in my office? Yes, the auburn-haired, blue-eyed lady who's still a knockout, even in her fifties? She used to be my sixth-grade teacher. Back then, her skin was as smooth and creamy as her Irish brogue. And she had a body that begged for sin. Lots and lots of sin.

She was my first crush. The first woman I ever masturbated about. My first Mrs. Robinson-like, older-woman fantasy.

Sister Mary Beatrice Dugan.

Yep, you heard me right—she's a nun. But not just any nun, kiddies. Sister Beatrice was a NILF. I don't need to spell that one out for you, do I?

In those days, she was the youngest nun any of us had ever laid eyes on—unlike the bitter, black-robed hags who looked like they were old enough to have actually been around when Jesus was alive. The fact that she was a woman of the cloth—forbidden—and in a position of power over us naughty Catholic boys just made it all that much more erotic.

She could've spanked me with a ruler anytime.

And I wasn't the only one who thought so. Just ask Matthew.

When we were thirteen, Estelle noticed Matthew was wincing when he walked. She dragged him bitching and moaning to the doctor's, where he was promptly diagnosed with CPS.

Chafed Penis Syndrome.

The doc told Estelle the condition had been caused by leaving wet swim trunks on too long. And she believed him. Even though it was November. Matthew's dick was raw all right, but it wasn't because of a fucking bathing suit.

It was because of Sister Beatrice.

"You're as stunning as ever, Sister B. You decide to leave the order yet?"

I don't go to church. Not anymore. I'm a lot of things, but a hypocrite really isn't one of them. If you're not going to play by the rules, you don't show up for team meetings. Over the years, however, I've kept in touch with Sister Beatrice. She's the principal at St. Mary's now, and my family has always donated generously.

She taps my face. "Cheeky boy."

I wink. "Come on, Sister, be fair. God's had you for, what? Thirty years? Don't you think it's time you gave the rest of us a shot?"

She shakes her head and grins. "Ah, Andrew, yer charms would tempt the virtue of a saint."

I hand her a cup of tea, and we sit down on my unadulterated couch.

"I was surprised by yer phone call. And more than a bit curious. What hole 'ave you dug yerself into, m'boy?"

I called her yesterday. And told her I needed her help.

"I have a friend I'd like you to speak with."

Her eyes twinkle. "Would this be a lady friend, now?"

I smile. "Yes. Katherine Brooks."

"You always were the one kissin' the lasses and makin' 'em cry. And about what would you like me to speak with Miss Katherine about? You haven't gotten her in the family way, have you?"

"Christ, no."

She raises a stern brow at me.

"Sorry."

She nods, and I go on. "I was hoping you could talk to her about . . . forgiveness. Second chances. Redemption."

She takes a sip of tea and looks thoughtful. "'To err is human; to forgive, divine.'"

Exactly. I thought about sending Matthew or Steven to plead my case. But they're too biased. Kate would never buy it. And before you ask—no—I would never send The Bitch. Too risky. When it comes to persuasion, my sister's kind of like a pet lion. Sweet and playful one minute, but if you make the wrong move? She'll rip your frigging face off.

Sister Beatrice is a religious woman. Kind. Honest. If anyone can convince Kate that men are—that I am—capable of changing, it's her. The fact that she adores me almost as much as the woman who gave birth to me doesn't hurt either.

"And who does the young lady need to forgive?"

I raise my hand. "That would be me."

"Played the cad, did you?"

I shrug in the affirmative. "And I've been trying everything I can think of since to make up for it—short of tattooing her name on my ass and streaking across Yankee Stadium."

I was saving that for next week.

"Men often want what they can no longer have, Andrew. I like to think that you are not that type of man. So if I speak to the young lady and convince her to trust you with her heart again, what are you intendin' to do with it?"

I look into her cerulean eyes. And speak without a trace of doubt.

"I'll cherish it. I'll do anything I have to to make her happy. For as long as she'll let me."

A slow smile spreads across Sister Beatrice's face. "And they say miracles don't happen anymore." She sets her cup aside and stands up. "It appears I have the Lord's work to do. Where are you hidin' the dear girl? Is she expectin' me?"

"I took the liberty of speaking with Kate's secretary. She's expecting someone. She just doesn't know it's you."

She chuckles. "Don't you think that'll ruffle her feathers a bit?"

"Probably. But she won't take it out on you. She'll save all her feathers for me."

We make our way to the door.

"Have you tried praying, Andrew? Prayer is a powerful thing."

"I think your prayers are a little more powerful than mine these days."

She smiles and touches my cheek like a mother would.

"We're all sinners, m'boy. Some of us just enjoy it more than others."

I laugh as I open the door.

And then the smile slides off my face as I stare at Erin's back. She's standing in front of my office with her arms out. Blocking it. From the woman in front of her.

Who just happens to be Delores Warren.

After Erin escorts Sister B to Kate's office, I turn toward Delores. She's wearing a black bustier, tight leather pants, and red stiletto heels. If this is what she wears to work, I can't fucking imagine what she wears in the bedroom. Must be interesting.

Steven walks up to us, his eyes on the retreating forms down the hallway.

"Was that Sister Beatrice?"

"Yep."

He nods appreciatively. "Nice."

See? NILF. Told you.

He smiles evilly at Delores. "Hey, Dee, did Matthew tell you about Sister B?"

"Kind of. He introduced us at church last week."

Unlike me, Matthew still attends church regularly. He likes to keep his bases covered, just in case.

Steven smiles wider. Like a toddler who's about to tattle on a sibling.

"Did he tell you about CPS?"

Her brow wrinkles. "What's CPS?"

"Ask Matthew. He'll tell you. He's kind of an expert on it." He nudges me with an elbow. "Alexandra and Mackenzie are coming by later. You want to join us for lunch?"

I scratch behind my ear. "Can't. I've got a meeting . . . with a guy . . . about a thing."

He's a skywriter. He's supposed to fly over the building at four. I just need to work out what he's going to write. But I don't want Delores to know. Can't have her warning Kate ahead of time.

Steven nods. "All right. Later."

I look Delores in the eyes. And flash her one of my classic smiles.

She just glares back.

I must be losing my touch.

"We need to talk."

There are only a few reasons why Delores Warren would want to talk to me at this point in my life. None of them are pleasant.

I motion toward my office. "Come on in."

This is how it must feel to invite a vampire into your house.

I sit down behind my desk. She stands.

"What can I do for you, Delores?"

"Self-castration would be great. But I'll settle for a flying leap off a bridge. I hear the Brooklyn is nice this time of year."

Oh yeah—this is going to be fun.

"Besides that."

She braces her hands on my desk and leans over, like a snake getting ready to strike. "You can stop fucking with my best friend's head."

Not a problem. Kate's head isn't the body part I'm looking to fuck at the moment. Think I should tell her that? Probably not.

"I don't know what you're talking about."

"I'm talking about last week, when you treated her like a used condom. And now, all of a sudden, you're all flowers and music and love notes."

Heard about those, did she? That's a good sign.

"So I'm thinking you're either a split personality—caused by the raging syphilis coursing through your bloodstream—or you've got an itch for a good challenge. In either case, move along, jerk-off. Kate isn't interested."

I'm not into challenges. When Kate blew me off that first night at REM, did I chase her? No, I went with the sure thing. The easy out.

Or in that particular case—the double play.

"Let's not bullshit each other here. We both know Kate is very interested. You wouldn't be so eager to rip into me if she wasn't. As for the rest of your concerns, I don't do head games. And there's a line of women around the block willing to scratch any itch I can think of. This isn't about getting laid."

I lean forward on my desk. And my tone is straightforward and persuasive, like she's a client on the fence. One I need to sway to my side. "I'll admit, my feelings for Kate caught me off guard, and at first, I handled things badly. That's why I'm doing all this—to show her that I care about her."

"You care about your dick."

Can't really argue with that.

She sits down across from me. "Kate and I are like sisters. Closer even. She's not a one-night-stand kind of girl—she never was. She's a relationship kind. It's very important to me that she's with someone who treats her right. A man."

Couldn't agree more. Most guys would sacrifice a limb for some juicy girl-on-girl action. It's a turn-on—big-time. But when it comes to Kate? I don't plan on sharing. With either sex.

"Last time I checked, that's what I was."

"No. You're a dog. She needs a good man. A nice man."

Good guys are boring. You need a little bad to keep things fun. And nice guys? Nice guys have something to hide.

Jeffrey Dahmer's neighbors thought he was a nice guy. Until they found those heads in his freezer.

She crosses her arms, and her voice turns triumphant. Gloating. "And I know someone who's perfect for her. He works in my lab. He's smart. He's funny. His name is Bert."

Bert?

Is she fucking kidding me? What kind of sick son of a bitch names his kid Bert in this day and age? That's just cruel.

"He'll show Kate a good time. I plan on setting them up this weekend."

And I plan on handcuffing myself to Kate's ankle and eating the key. Let's see what kind of good time Bert can show Kate when she's dragging me around behind her like a Siamese twin.

"I have a better idea. How about we double. You and Matthew, me and Kate. We'll hang out. It'll give me the chance to show you how perfect Kate and I are for each other."

"Okay, now you sound like a stalker. You had your chance, you fucked up, get over it. Pick some other number out of your little black book and leave Kate alone."

I stand up. "Contrary to what you think you know, I'm not some serial scumbag. I don't lead women on—I don't need to. You want me to tell Kate I'm sorry? I have. You want a guarantee that I'll never hurt her again? I can write you one, and I'll sign it in blood if it makes you happy. But don't ask me to leave her alone, because I won't. I can't."

She doesn't move. Her face is as still and hard as a pissed-off statue. And my argument is making about as much of a dent as a goddamn toothpick.

"Did Matthew tell you what I was like? Do I look like the type of guy who goes catatonic over just any woman? God, Delores, I fucking worship her."

She snorts. "Today. You worship her today. But what happens if she gives in? When the novelty wears off and the sex gets old? And some new bitch in heat crosses your path and wants you to sniff her ass?"

Sex doesn't get old. Not if you're doing it right.

"I don't want anyone else. And I don't see that changing any-time . . . ever."

"I think you're full of shit."

"I'm sure you do. If you dicked Matthew around the way I did Kate, I'd pretty much write you off too. But what you think doesn't change what Kate wants. And deep down, even if she won't admit it yet, that's me."

"Could you be any more full of yourself? You may have money, but it can't buy you class. Or integrity. You're not even close to good enough for Kate."

"But you think your cousin is?"

"No, I don't. Billy's an immature jackass, and that relationship was going nowhere fast for a long time. Over the years I tried to tell her. To make her see that she and their relationship had become more about friendship than real love. But by then our lives, our families, were so intertwined, I think they were both afraid of rocking the boat and losing more than just each other. But he did—*does* love her. I'm sure of that. He's just always loved his guitar more."

She starts to pace in front of my desk. Like a professor in a lecture hall.

"See, Drew, there are three kinds of males in this world: boys, guys, and men. Boys—like Billy—never grow up, never get serious. They only care about themselves, their music, their cars. Guys—like you—are all about numbers and variety. Like an assembly line, it's just one one-night stand after another. Then there are men—like Matthew. They're not perfect, but they appreciate women for more than their flexibility and mouth suction."

She's not wrong. You should listen to her.

The only part she doesn't get, though, is that sometimes a guy can't become a man until he's met the right woman.

"You can't make that call. You barely know me."

"Oh, I know you. Believe me. I was conceived by a guy just like you."

Crap. Daddy issues. They're the worst.

"Kate and I look out for each other," she goes on. "We always have. And I'm not going to let her be another notch on your STD-coated bedpost."

You ever bang your head against a wall?

No?

Watch closely. This is what it looks like.

"She's not. That's what I've been trying to tell you! What fucking language would you like to hear it in?"

"I don't know. Do you speak anything besides Asshole?"

I pinch the bridge of my nose. I feel an aneurysm coming on.

"Okay, look—you don't trust me? Fine. Talk to Matthew. You trust him, right? He wouldn't want me screwing around with his girlfriend's best friend if I wasn't playing for keeps."

She waves her hand in the air. "That doesn't prove anything. Penises stick together."

Jesus, Mary, and Joseph.

I scrub my hand down my face. Then I take a deep, calming breath. Time to lay it on the line. Put my cards on the table. Throw the Hail Mary pass.

I walk to the window, gathering my thoughts as I watch the traffic far below. I'm still looking at it as I tell her, "You know what I saw yesterday when I was coming to work? I saw a pregnant woman, getting a cab."

I used to think pregnant women were kind of grotesque. Deformed. You should have seen Alexandra. When she was knocked up with Mackenzie, she looked like she'd eaten Humpty Dumpty for breakfast. And the way she was chowing down at the time, she totally could have.

"And all I could think about was how adorable Kate would look pregnant. And about how I wanted to do things for her. Like . . . if she gets sick, I want to be the guy making her tea and bringing her tissues. I want to know how she got that small scar on her chin and if she's afraid of spiders . . . and what she dreams about at night. Everything. It's fucking insane—don't think I don't know that. It's never happened to me before. And I don't want it to ever happen again—with anybody else. Just Kate."

I turn my head from the window and look her in the eyes.

If you're ever in the woods and come face-to-face with a pissed-off momma bear, it's always better to look her in the eyes. Run away? She'll feed you to the cubs. One arm at a time. But if you stand your ground, you just might make it out alive.

"You want to hear that Kate has me whipped? 'Cause she does. She's got me on my knees and under her thumb, and I don't want to get out."

We're both quiet after that. Delores just stares at me. For a while. Searching my face for . . . something. I'm not exactly sure what it is, but I know the moment she finds it. Because something shifts in her eyes. They become softer. Just a little. And her shoulders relax. And then she nods.

"Okay, then."

Some battles don't have a winner. Sometimes the best a good general can hope for is a cease-fire.

"Kate makes her own choices," she says. "And if those choices turn out to be rotten, then I'll help her clean up the mess. Because that's what best friends do—help bury the body."

She stands up. Walks a few steps to the door. Then she stops and spins around with her finger pointing in my direction.

"You just remember one thing, buddy. I don't care if it's ten days down the road or ten years, I'll be watching you. And if I ever find out that you've fucked her over? I'll make you sorry. And I work in a lab, Drew. With chemicals. Odorless, tasteless chemicals that can permanently shrink your nuts so small, you'll have to start calling yourself Drewsilla. Are we clear?"

Matthew is out of his fucking mind. Delores Warren is scary. Definite psycho-bitch potential. She and Alexandra should totally hang out.

And she's put way too much thought into that little plan for my liking.

I swallow hard. "Crystal."

She nods again. "Glad we understand each other."

And with that, she breezes out of my office. And I collapse back into my chair and stare at the ceiling.

Christ.

This relationship shit is exhausting. I feel like I just ran a marathon. With hurdles.

But you know what? I'm pretty sure the finish line's in sight.

Chapter 24

After Delores leaves, I pick up my briefcase and head out the door. To my meeting with the skywriter. I still have to figure out how to get Kate on the roof. Speaking of Kate . . .

Want to swing by her office on the way out? See how her and the good sister are getting along?

Her door's open. I brace my hands on the frame and lean in. Can you see her through the balloons? Sitting at her desk, with her hands folded on top—a smile stuck on her face as she nods obediently to whatever Sister Beatrice is saying.

"Ladies. How are we doing this afternoon?"

Kate turns to me. And her voice is strained. "Drew. There you are. I was just thinking about you"—from the way she's gripping her hands together, it looks like she was thinking about strangling me—"while Sister Beatrice here was telling me the fascinating tale of glass houses. And how those of us who live in them shouldn't throw stones."

She's still smiling. But her eyes say something else entirely.

It's a little creepy.

You know in *Texas Chainsaw Massacre* when the old man smiles just before he slits the girl's throat? Yeah—it's kind of like that.

Sister Beatrice looks at the ceiling. "We are all imperfect in the eyes of the Lord. Katherine, may I use yer facilities, dear? Nature is calling."

"Of course, Sister." They stand, and Kate opens the door to her adjoining washroom.

And as soon as that door closes, Smiley Kate goes bye-bye. Mad Kate takes her place. She marches toward me.

And the balloons run for their lives.

"I'm going to ask you this one time, and if you lie to me, I swear I'll let Delores poison you."

"Okay."

"Is she a real nun? Or some actress you hired?"

I laugh. I didn't even think of that. "No, she's real."

Kate is not pleased. "God, Drew! A nun? A fucking nun? This is low. Even for you."

"I think she's technically a mother superior now."

I lean in closer to Kate because . . . well, just because I can . . . and the smell of her lotion hits me. Hard. I resist the urge to put my nose against her skin and sniff like a cocaine addict.

"Is there any level you won't sink to to get your way?"

Nope. Sorry. Not a one. I don't mind getting down and dirty.

Actually, I prefer it that way.

"Desperate times . . . I had to call out the big guns."

"You want to see guns? As soon as the Flying Nun leaves my office, I'll show you guns! I can't believe—"

God, she's beautiful. I mean, look at her. She's like a volcano going off—fierce and fiery and breathtaking. If she doesn't find a way to ugly herself down, I'm going to be spending an awful lot of time pissing her off.

Which might not be such a bad thing in the end. Angry sex is awesome.

I cut off Kate's rant. "As titillating as this conversation has been—and believe me, it's been very—I have a meeting to get to."

Before I go, I motion toward her bare neck. "Hey, why aren't you wearing your necklace?"

She folds her arms and smiles proudly. "I donated it to Sister Beatrice. For the less fortunate."

Played that one well, didn't she?

I can play too.

"That's very generous. Of course, I'll have to replace it for you.

With something . . . bigger. You should expect another delivery tomorrow."

Her smile turns upside down. And she smacks a rogue balloon out of the way.

Then she slams the door in my face.

I wait two seconds before calling through it, "Okay. I'll see you later, Kate. Good talk."

From inside, I hear Sister Beatrice's voice: "Did Andrew leave already? Such a sweet boy he is. And devoted too, when he sets his heart to a task. Let me tell you about the time he weeded the convent's garden. It's a long story, but we 'ave all afternoon. There was a scuffle in the lunchroom, you see. . . ."

Traffic was a bitch and a half. Both ways. But I worked out the particulars with the skywriter. He was suiting up when I left. I now have just enough time to get to Kate's office and get her to the roof. If she won't come willingly, I'm just going to pick her up and carry her. Although I'd feel a lot better about the idea if I had a cup on.

Kate is definitely a kicker.

I sprint through the lobby and push the button for the elevator. But what I see when the doors open stops me cold.

It's The Bitch, with Mackenzie at her side. And in my niece's perfect little hands are strings. A dozen of them. Strings that are tied to balloons. Kate's balloons.

"Fuck me."

"Well, that's a nice way to greet your doting sister and her daughter."

Had I said that out loud? Doesn't matter.

Fuck fuck fuckity fuck.

This is bad—very bad. Like F5-tornado kind of bad, except my sister is capable of leaving more damage behind.

"Hi, Uncle Drew!"

I smile. "Hi, sweetheart." Then I scowl. "What the hell did you do, Alexandra?"

Her eyes widen innocently. Like she's surprised. "Me? I came to meet my husband for lunch. Is that a crime?"

When I was in junior high, a kid named Chris Whittle sucker punched me when I was coming out of trigonometry. I had hooked up with his girlfriend. She had talented hands.

Anyway, the next day, Alexandra paid Chris a little visit—and made him piss his pants.

Literally.

See, according to The Bitch Code, she can fuck with me all she wants to, but no one else is allowed. Now do you see why I'm concerned?

"You went to see Kate, didn't you?"

Mackenzie answers for her. "We did, Uncle Drew! She's great. Kate gave me dees balloons and a calculator! See?" She holds it over her head like it's the Stanley Cup, and I can't help but smile.

"That's terrific, Mackenzie."

Then I glare at Alexandra again.

She's not concerned. "You said you wanted Mackenzie to meet Kate."

If you put two pregnant hamsters in the same cage, you know what they'll do? Eat each other. Female hormones are like undetonated warheads. There's just no way to tell when they're going to go the fuck off.

"Yes, I wanted *Mackenzie* to meet Kate. I didn't want *you* meeting Kate until I was done smoothing things the hell over."

Mackenzie takes my friend the Bad Word Jar out of her backpack and holds it up. I put two dollars in.

She sticks her face in the mouth of the jar and looks up at me with a frown. "Um . . . Uncle Drew? Bad words no cost one dollar no more. They cost ten."

"Ten? Since when?"

She's excited. "It was Kate's idea. She say the maconomy is bad."

What the hell is the *maconomy*?

"She calls it *in . . . in . . .*"

"Inflation," Alexandra finishes with a smile.

"Yeah, that."

Inflation.

Great.

Thanks, Kate.

I raise my brows at Mackenzie. "Do you take American Express?" She giggles. I pay my fine in cash. "How about you add up the rest on your calculator, honey?"

She's going to need it. I have a feeling this little discussion is going to put me in the triple digits.

"What did you say to Kate?" I ask Alexandra.

She shrugs. "We talked, one woman to another. I appealed to her business sense. It went well. You really don't need to know all the details."

"Why don't you let me decide what I need to know. Considering you shouldn't have fucking talked to her at all."

Tap-tap-tap goes the calculator.

"Ungrateful much? I was just trying to help."

Dr. Kevorkian was just trying to help his patients too. And we all know how they turned out.

"I don't need your help. I have a plan."

Alexandra's hands go to her hips. "Right. Your master plan that entails what, exactly? Annoying Kate until she agrees to go out with you? You gonna call her names on the playground too? Pull on her braids? I have to admit, Sister Beatrice was an interesting touch. I can't believe Kate isn't falling on her knees, begging you to take her back after that. Very romantic, Drew."

My jaw clenches. "It's. Working."

She raises a brow. "That's not what Kate said."

And there she is. Take a good look.

The Bitch in all her glory.

And you thought I was overreacting.

"Did she say something to you? About me? What did she say?"

She waves her hand in the air. "Oh, this and that."

You know how some kids like to tease their dogs by showing them a bone and then yanking it away before they can bite it? My sister was one of those kids.

"Goddamn it, Lex."

Tap-tap-tap.

"I like her, by the way," she says. "She really doesn't take any shit does she?"

Tap-tap-tap.

"How do you know she doesn't take any shit?"

Tap-tap-tap.

"Did you give her shit, Lex?"

Tap-tap-tap.

"What kind of shit did you give her, Alexandra?"

Tap-tap-tap.

She laughs. "My God, would you relax. I haven't seen you this wound up in . . . well, never. Now that you're not pathetic and sad, it's actually kind of fun."

My status with Kate at the moment is like a house of cards. I've managed to build myself up a few floors, but one small tremor and the whole damn thing could fall apart.

"If you fucked this up for me, I'll—"

Tap-tap-tap.

"You know stress causes premature gray hair. If you keep this up, you're going to look like Daddy before you turn thirty."

"I'm glad you find this so amusing. I don't. We're talking about my frigging life here."

That sobers her up. She tilts her head to the side. Appraising me. And then her voice isn't teasing anymore.

It's tender, sincere.

"I'm proud of you, you know. You're sticking this out. Seeing it through. You're . . . all grown up." She smiles softly. "Never thought I'd see the day." And then she hugs me. "It'll be okay, Drew. Promise."

When I was eight, my grandfather had a heart attack. After my parents left for the hospital, Alexandra promised me everything would be okay.

It wasn't.

"Did Kate tell you that?"

She shakes her head. "Not in so many words."

"Then how do you know?"

She shrugs again. "It's the estrogen. It gives us ESP. If you had a vagina, you'd know too."

Mackenzie raises her hand proudly. "I have a bagina."

I smirk. "Yes, you do, sweetheart. And someday, it's gonna help you rule the world."

"Johnny Fitzgerald has a penis. He say his penis is better than my bagina."

"Johnny Fitzgerald's an idiot. Vaginas beat penises every time. They're like kryptonite. Penises are defenseless against them."

My sister puts an end to our discussion. "O-kay. That's enough of that lovely conversation. Although I'm sure Mackenzie's preschool teacher will enjoy hearing all about it. Right before she calls Child Protective Services on me."

I put my hands up. "I'm just trying to tell her like it is. The sooner she realizes the power she has, the better off she'll be." I check my watch; I need to get upstairs. I look at Mackenzie. "What's the damage, sweetie?"

"Eighty dollars."

Ouch.

I need to start billing my clients more. Or work out some kind of payment plan.

As the bills fall into the jar, Alexandra takes her hand. "Come on, Mackenzie, let's go to the American Girl store and spend some of Uncle Drew's money."

"Okay!"

They walk across the lobby but stop at the double doors. Mackenzie whispers something to Alexandra and hands over her balloons.

Then she runs back to me.

I scoop her up and hold her tight as her little arms come around my shoulders and squeeze.

"I love you, Uncle Drew."

You ever drink brandy? Usually I'm more of a whiskey man myself. But a good glass of brandy warms you all over, from the inside. And that's me—right now.

"I love you too, Mackenzie."

She pulls back. "Guess what?"

"What?"

"Kate ask me what I wanna be when I grown up."

I nod. "And did you tell her you want to be a princess?"

Her forehead creases adorably, and she shakes her head. "I no wanna be a princess no more."

"Well, that's a relief. What do you want to be?"

She grins. "A banker."

"Fantastic choice. What made you change your mind?"

Her fingers play with the collar of my shirt as she tells me, "Well, Kate is a immessment banker, and you say you be proud of me to be jus' like her. So tha's what I wanna be."

After her words sink in, I ask her seriously, "Mackenzie? Did you tell Kate that I said I wanted you to grow up to be just like her?"

You see that smile? That's not the smile of a four-year-old child. That, ladies and gentlemen, is the smile of a genius.

"Yep."

I close my eyes. And chuckle. I can't believe I didn't think of this myself. Mackenzie is the perfect weapon. My very own baby Borg. *Resistance is futile.*

"Sweetheart," I say, "you did Uncle Drew a huge favor. Anything you want for Christmas—name it and it's yours. And I mean anything."

Her eyes widen at the possibilities. She glances at my sister and then whispers conspiratorially, "Can I have a pony?"

Oh, boy.

I think about it for exactly one second.

"Absolutely."

She squeezes me tighter and squeals.

"Only . . . don't tell Mommy until after it's delivered, okay?"

I may have to enter the witness protection program after this one.

Mackenzie kisses my cheek, and I set her on her feet. She skips back to Alexandra, and I wave as they walk out the door.

Chapter 25

I walk into Kate's office like a soldier storming the beach at Normandy. She's at her desk writing rapidly on a yellow legal pad.

"I'm back. Miss me?"

She doesn't look up. "Desperately."

Sarcasm is the oldest defense in the book. I play along. "I knew I was wearing you down. What put me over the top? Sister B?"

Kate pushes back from her desk and crosses her legs. She's wearing new shoes. I didn't notice before. Black Mary Janes with a wicked high heel and a strap around the ankle. *Good God.* They're the perfect blend of naughty and nice. Sweetness and sex. And my poor, neglected cock convulses as I picture all the fantastic—and semi-illegal—things I could do to her in those shoes.

I've never had a fetish, but I'm thinking about starting one.

Kate's voice drags me away from my impure thoughts. "No. It was the visit from your sister, actually. Subtlety doesn't run in your family, does it?"

Uh-oh. I was afraid of this.

"Alexandra has deep-seated psychological issues. She's unstable. You shouldn't listen to anything she says. No one in my family does."

"She seemed completely lucid when she was here."

I shrug. "Mental illness is a tricky thing."

Her eyes squint doubtfully. "You're not serious, are you?"

Crap. No lying.

"Technically, she's never been diagnosed. But her ideas about justice and revenge are certifiable. Imagine Delores . . . with a decade more experience to perfect her technique."

Kate's face goes slack with understanding. "Oh."

Yep—welcome to my world, sweetheart.

"She brought me coffee," Kate says. "Should I drink it?"

We both eye the Starbucks cup on her desk suspiciously.

When I was thirteen, I auctioned off a pair of Alexandra's underwear in the boys' locker room. Dirty ones. When she found out through the grapevine of older sisters, she played it cool—never let on that she knew. And then she spiked my Cocoa Pebbles with chocolate-flavored laxatives. I didn't leave the bathroom for three days.

Now, I realize she's not carrying that kind of grudge against Kate, but still . . .

"I wouldn't."

She nods stiffly and slides the cup back away from her.

"What'd you think of Mackenzie? I really wanted to be here when you met her."

Her smile is warm and genuine. "I think she's amazing."

"I'm sure you'll be thrilled to hear she used your calculator on me when I ran into them downstairs."

Her smile widens. "That's nice."

I shake my head, and Kate says, "I see now why Alexandra started the Bad Word Jar, since you seem to spend so much time with Mackenzie."

"What do you mean?"

She shrugs. "She talks like you. It's not every day you hear a four-year-old say Prince Charming is a douche bag who's only holding Cinderella back."

That's my girl.

"Swearing is good for the soul."

Kate stifles a laugh. And she looks so tempting I can't help but lean over her chair, trapping her with my arms. Small talk is over. Time to get back to business.

"Come for a walk with me."

My voice is low. Persuasive.

"No way."

And utterly ineffective.

"Come on, Kate, it'll just take a minute. I want to show you something."

She snorts. "What'd you do? Hire Ringling Brothers to do a show in the lobby? Organize a ticker-tape parade in my honor?"

I laugh. "Don't be ridiculous. I wouldn't do that."

Kate raises one skeptical brow.

"Okay, you're right—I would *so* do that. But not today."

She pushes me back and stands up. I let her.

"You're not scared, are you?" I ask. "Afraid you won't be able to control yourself if you're alone with me?"

To people like Kate and me, a dare is kind of like a hooker at a sex addicts' convention. There's almost no chance they're going to get turned down.

"If you mean am I afraid I'll kill you if there aren't any witnesses to testify against me, then the answer's yes. Although I must admit, twenty-to-life is looking like a small price to pay at the moment."

Do you think she enjoys the verbal foreplay as much as I do? She's got to. She's so good at it.

She circles around, putting her desk between us.

"Look, Drew, I have a new client. I told you that. You know how it is. I can't afford these . . . distractions right now."

I take that as a compliment. "I distract you?"

She huffs. "That's not what I meant." Then her face changes. And she's imploring. "You have to stop this"—her hands wave in the air—"this mission you're on. Just let it go. Please."

When Steven was eleven, he ran into a tree during a game of touch football in his backyard—and busted his forehead open. For as long as I live, I'll never forget the sound of him begging, pleading with his mother not to take him to the hospital. Because he knew he needed stitches. And stitches just—suck. At any age.

But Janey Reinhart didn't give in. She brought him anyway. Because even though Steven was terrified—even though it wasn't what he wanted—she knew it was what he needed.

You see where I'm going with this?

"The ball's in your court, Kate. I told you that from the beginning. You want me gone, all you have to do is go out with me on Saturday."

She bites her lip. And looks down at her desk.

"Okay."

Come again?

Sure, I'd love to. With Kate.

Okay—not the time to joke.

"I'm sorry? Could you repeat that, please?"

Her eyes meet mine. They look hesitant but resigned. Like someone waiting in line for a roller coaster. Determined to get on but not exactly sure what the hell they've gotten themselves into. "I said yes. I'll have dinner with you on Saturday."

It's official. Brace yourselves. Hell has actually frozen the fuck over.

"After talking with your sister, I realized a few things. . . ."

You love me? You need me? You can't live without me?

"I think you need closure, Drew."

Oh no. Not closure. Anything but fucking closure.

Closure is a made-up word that women invented so they can overanalyze something and talk about it—to death. And then, after it's been blessed and buried, closure gives them the excuse to dig the poor fucker up and talk about it—some more.

Guys don't do that. Ever.

It's over. Fade to black. The end.

That's all the goddamn closure we need.

"Closure?"

She walks toward me. "I think things with us started and stopped so fast, you didn't have time to acclimate yourself. Maybe if we spend some time . . . if we talk away from the office . . . you'll understand that after everything that's happened, the best we can hope to be is friends."

I'm pretty sure she means without benefits. And that just doesn't work for me.

A guy can't be friends with a woman he's actively attracted to. Not really. Because at some point his dick will take over. It'll walk like him and talk like him, but—like one of the poor schmucks infected by those freaky face-sucking things in *Alien*—it won't be him. And from that point on, every move, every gesture will be geared toward accomplishing the dick's goal. Which sure as shit won't have anything to do with friendship.

Besides, I have friends—Matthew, Steven, Jack. I don't want to fuck any of them.

"Friends?"

She doesn't notice my disgust with the idea. Or she just doesn't give a damn.

"Yes. We should get reacquainted as coworkers. Equals. Not a date. Kind of more like a business meeting between colleagues."

Denial is a powerful thing. But at this point I'll take what I can get. "So, what you're telling me is you'll go out with me on Saturday? That's the bottom line, right?"

She hesitates. And then nods. "Yes."

"Perfect. Don't say anything else. I'll pick you up at seven."

"No."

"No?"

"No. I'll meet you."

Interesting.

I speak slowly. "Now, Kate, I know you haven't been on many dates, considering the moron you called a boyfriend had you engaged before you were out of a training bra. But in cases like this, the guy—that's me—is supposed to pick you—the girl—up. It's an unwritten law."

See how her lips press together? How her shoulders square off? Oh yeah, she's ready to rumble.

"I just told you this isn't a date."

I shrug. "Semantics."

"Let's say hypothetically it is a date. It would be a *first* date. And I would never have a man that I didn't know come to my apartment to pick me up for a first date."

I push a hand through my hair. "That doesn't make any sense. You know me. We did sixty-nine. I'd say you know me pretty damn well."

"Look, these are my terms. If you can't live with them, we can just forget the whole—"

"Wait, wait. Let's not be hasty. I give. You can meet me at my apartment. At seven. Sharp."

"Okay."

"But I have some terms of my own."

She jumps down my throat. "I'm not having sex with you!"

I force myself to look surprised. "I'm wounded. Really. Who said anything about sex? I would never require sex as part of our agreement."

And then I smile.

"It's optional. Clothing too."

She rolls her eyes. "Is that it?"

"Nope."

"What else do you want?"

Oh, baby. If she only knew. Though it's probably better that she doesn't. Don't want to scare her away.

"I want four hours. At least. Uninterrupted. I want conversation, dinner—appetizers, entrée, dessert—wine, dancing . . ."

She holds up her hand. "No dancing."

"One dance. That's nonnegotiable."

She looks at the ceiling, weighing her options. "Fine. One dance." She points her finger at me. "But if your hands go anywhere near my ass, I'm out of there."

Now it's my turn to think it over. "Well . . . okay. But if you renege on any of my stipulations, I reserve the right to call do-over."

She waits a moment. Her eyes narrow distrustfully. "And you'll leave me alone—completely—until Saturday? No priests popping in to say hello? No ice sculptures melting outside my door?"

I smirk. "It'll be like we never met. Like I don't even work here."

Chances are I won't *be* here. I'm going to be a very busy boy.

Kate nods. "Okay."

I hold out my hand. She shakes it and says, "It's a deal."

I turn her hand over gently and kiss the back—like I did the first night we met. "It's a date."

Have you ever walked into a room to get something, but once you're there, you have no idea what you came for? Good. Then you'll understand why I turn and start to walk out of the room.

Until Kate's voice stops me. "Drew?"

I look back at her. "Yeah?"

Her face is downcast. "I don't . . . I don't enjoy hurting people. So . . . don't get your hopes up about Saturday."

Before I can open my mouth, movement out the window catches my eye. And I can't believe I almost forgot. Wordlessly, I walk forward and take Kate's hand. I bring her to the window and stand behind her, resting my hands on her shoulders.

I bring my mouth to her ear. My breath gives her goose bumps. The good kind.

"Too late."

I wanted it to be simple. Something I would have carved on a tree or spray-painted on a wall if we were kids. But I needed it to be clear. A proclamation. Telling Kate and every other woman out there that I, Drew Evans, am off the field.

Kate gasps when she sees it.

Up there in the sky, in huge white letters, for the whole city to see:

Always go out on top. Have I told you this yet?

No? Well I'm telling you now.

I don't care if you're a businessman, a singer, or a top-rated television show—leave them wanting more. Never overplay your hand. You can always go back later for an encore, but once they're sick of you, there's no taking it back.

I kiss the top of her head. "I'll see you Saturday, Kate."

And she's still staring out the window as I walk out.

Don't worry—the show's not over yet. I still have a few tricks up my sleeve, and I always save the best for last. You're really not going to want to miss this.

I head straight for Erin's desk. "I need you to get the florist on the phone. And the caterer. And set up an appointment for me—tonight—with that interior designer we talked about yesterday."

She picks up her phone and dials. "I'm on it."

Yes, I said interior designer. You don't know what that's for, do you?

It's the grand finale. My winning move.

You'll see.

On Saturday night.

Chapter 26

See that rakishly handsome guy in the charcoal slacks and black shirt with the sleeves half rolled up? The one arranging the china plates on that table?

That's me. Drew Evans.

Well, not really. Not the old me. I'm new and improved. This is DAK. Can you guess what that stands for? Half the women in this city would give their left tit to have me where I am right now. Pussy whipped. Obsessed.

In love.

But there's only one woman who was able to put me here. Now I just need to show her I'm here to stay. I haven't seen her for two days. Two long, excruciating days. It wasn't as bad as the seven, but it was close.

Anyway, take a look around. What do you think? Am I missing anything?

Fresh flowers cover every available surface. White daisies. Before, I thought seeing them would remind her of Warren, but I'm not worried about that now. They're Kate's favorite, so they're the only kind here. Bocelli plays softly on the sound system. Candles light the room. Hundreds of them—glass-enclosed.

You can't go wrong with candles. They make everyone look better. They make everything smell better.

Knock-knock.

That would be Kate. Right on time. I scan the room once more. This is it. My Super Bowl. Game Seven. And everything's ready. I'm ready. As I'll ever be. I blow out a deep breath. And open the door.

And then I can't move. I can't think. Breathing? That's not a frigging option either.

Kate's dark hair is piled high on her head. Elegant tendrils kiss her neck, caressing the very spot that I spent hours nibbling on not so long ago. Her dress is dark red—shiny—maybe satin. It hangs from delicate straps that bridge her shoulders and fall low in back. The bottom rests above her knee, exposing her smooth legs inch by delectable inch.

And her shoes . . . *Mother of Christ* . . . Her shoes are all heel, held on by an intricate black bow tied at the back of her ankle.

When I'm actually able to form words, my voice is rough. "Is there any way we could renegotiate the no-ass-grabbing clause? 'Cause I have to tell you, in that dress? It's going to be hard."

And it's not the only thing, if you catch my drift.

She smiles and shakes her head. "All previous stipulations stand."

I stand back as she walks in, looking me over out of the corner of her eye. Watch her face closely. See how her eyes darken? How she licks her lips without realizing it? Like a lioness that just spotted a gazelle in the high grass.

She likes what she sees. She wants to compliment me. She wants to, but she won't. This is Kate we're talking about here. Post-my-colossal-foot-in-mouth-fuckup Kate. And despite my recent progress, she's still defensive. Untrusting. On guard.

And that's okay. I'm not offended. Her eyes tell me everything she won't let herself say.

I lead her toward the living room, and she bites her lip as she asks, "So, where are we going?"

And then she stops short when she spots the candles. And the flowers. And the perfectly set table for two.

I tell her softly, "We're already here."

She gazes around the room. "Wow. It's . . . it's beautiful, Drew."

I shrug. "The room's nice. *You're* beautiful."

She blushes. And it's amazing.

I want to kiss her. Badly.

You ever been thirsty? Really thirsty? Like on a ninety-eight-degree summer day when you don't have enough spit in your mouth to even swallow? Now imagine somebody puts an ice-cold glass of water in front of you. And you can look at it, and you can picture how perfect it would taste—but you can't touch it. And you definitely can't drink it.

That's pretty much the hell I'm in at the moment.

I tear my eyes away from Kate's face and hand her a glass of red wine. Then I take a long drink of my own.

"What happened to your fingers?" She's referring to the Band-Aids that cover four of my ten digits.

"Mushrooms. Spongy little bastards don't appreciate being sliced."

She looks surprised. "You cooked?"

I was going to take Kate to a restaurant. The best in the city. But she's about quality, remember? And I figure she'll appreciate my effort a hell of a lot more than anything a gourmet chef could come up with.

I smile. "I have many talents. You've only seen a few."

And this might remain true. I've never cooked before.

Which reminds me—Martha Stewart? She's my new idol. Seriously. I used to think her whole deal was a joke. Who becomes a billionaire by showing people how to fold goddamn dinner napkins correctly? But that was before. Before I actually tried to use my oven or set a table.

Now Martha's a fucking god. Like Buddha. And if her recipe helps me pull this off? I'll worship at her pudgy, sandaled feet every day for the rest of my life.

Kate and I sit on the couch.

"So . . . how are things at the office?" I ask.

She sips her wine and brushes nonexistent wrinkles off her dress. "Good. Things have been good. You know . . . quiet."

"In other words, you've been bored out of your mind without me."

"No. It's been . . . productive. I've gotten a lot done."

I smirk. "You've missed me."

She snorts. "I didn't say that."

She didn't have to.

"Come on, Kate, I've taken a vow of honesty here. It's only fair that you do the same." I lean forward. "Look me in the eyes and tell me you haven't thought about me—at all—in the last few days."

"I—"

Buzzzzz . . . buzzzzz . . . buzzzzz.

Dinner's ready. Kate takes another drink from her glass.

"You should get that, Drew. Don't want it to burn."

And she's saved by the buzzer.

For now.

The chicken marsala I made looks . . . *unique* now that it's actually out of the oven and on our plates.

Okay, it's fucking frightening. I admit it.

Kate's brow is furrowed as she pushes at the brown lumps like she's dissecting a frog in biology. "Did you mix the flour with water before you added it?"

Water? Martha didn't say anything about water. *That bitch.*

"You know, Drew, some of the best culinary dishes in history looked disgusting. Presentation doesn't count for much. It's all about the taste."

"Really?"

She picks up her fork and takes a deep breath. "No. I was just trying to make you feel better."

I stare at my plate. "Thanks for trying."

Before she takes a bite, I reach across the table and put my hand on hers. "Wait. I'll go first."

That way, if the food makes me keel over like bad blowfish, at least one of us will be conscious to call 911. Plus, if I'm hospitalized, I think there's an excellent chance Kate would throw a pity fuck my way.

And don't think for a second that I wouldn't take it. In a freaking heartbeat.

I try not to breathe through my nose as I take a bite. Kate stares at me. I chew.

And then I smile slowly. "It's not bad."

She seems relieved. Maybe even a little proud. She slides her fork through her lips. Then she nods. "It's really good. I'm impressed."

"Yeah—I get that a lot."

Through the entire meal, our conversation flows easily. Comfortably. I keep the topics safe. We talk about her new client, Matthew and Delores's burgeoning relationship, and the never-ending political antics going on in D.C.

For dessert, I serve strawberries and whipped cream. Strawberries are Kate's favorite. I knew that from our Lost Weekend. Originally, I was going for strawberry shortcake. But you don't want to know how the pudding turned out. I don't think even Matthew would've eaten it. When Martha said stir constantly, she wasn't screwing around.

While we enjoy our last course, I mention Mackenzie's impending Christmas present.

Kate laughs. Unbelieving. "You're not really going to buy her a pony, are you?"

"Of course I am. She's a little girl. Every girl should have a pony."

She sips her wine. We're halfway through our second bottle.

"And I'm going to get one of those carts like the horses in Central Park. That way they can train it to take her to school."

"This is New York City, Drew. Where are they going to keep it?"

"They have a five-bedroom condo. Two of the rooms are filled with Alexandra's useless shit. I figure they can clean one out and make it the pony's room."

She looks at me straight-faced. "The pony's room?"

"Yeah. Why not?"

"How are they going to get it to their floor?"

"Freight elevator. All the older buildings have one."

She sits back in her chair. "Well, you've thought of everything, haven't you?"

I take a drink. "I always do."

"Have you thought about what method your sister will use to kill you?"

"I'm sure she'll surprise me. Will you defend me when she tries?"

She fingers her wineglass and glances up at me through those insanely long lashes. "No way, Pony Boy. She's bigger than I am. You're on your own."

I put my hand over my heart. "I'm crushed."

She's not buying it. "You'll get over it."

Our laughter fades into relaxed smiles. And I'm content to just watch her for a moment. She's staring at me too.

Then she clears her throat and looks away. "This is a good CD."

She's talking about the music that's been playing in the background for the last few hours.

"I can't take all the credit. The guys helped me burn it."

On cue, "I Touch Myself" by the Divinyls pours out from the speakers.

"Jack picked that one."

Kate laughs, and I stand up and press the button on the CD player, changing the song.

"And since I most likely only have a few weeks to live"—I hold my hand out to Kate—"may I have this dance?"

A new song fills the room: "Then" by Brad Paisley. I'm not really into country music, but Brad's pretty cool. He's a guy's guy, even for a singer.

She takes my hand and stands up. Her arms go around my neck. And my hands rest at her waist—trying not to squeeze. Gently, we start to sway.

I swallow hard as her round, dark eyes look up at me without frustration or anger or hurt. They're all warmth, like liquid chocolate. And my fucking knees go weak. I trail my hand up her spine to the back of her head. She turns her cheek and lays her head on my chest. And I pull her against me even closer—tighter.

I'd like to tell you what it feels like. To hold her again. To have my arms wrapped around her, at last, and her body pressed against mine.

I'd like to, but I can't.

Because there aren't words—in English or any other language—that could even come close to describing it.

I inhale the sweet flowery scent of her hair. If the poison in the gas chamber smelled like Kate? Every death row inmate would die with a smile on his face.

She doesn't lift her head as she whispers, "Drew?"

"Mmmm?"

"I want you to know . . . I forgive you . . . for what you said that day in your office. I believe you, that you didn't mean it."

"Thank you."

"And, in hindsight, I realize that I didn't help the situation. I could've said something, given you . . . reassurance about how I felt . . . before I went to talk to Billy. I'm sorry that I didn't."

"I appreciate that."

And then her voice changes—becomes lower.

Mournful.

"But it doesn't change anything."

My thumb sweeps back and forth across the bare skin of her neck. "Of course it does. It changes everything."

She raises her head. "I can't do this with you, Drew."

"Yes, you can."

She stares at my chest as she tries to explain. "I have goals. Aspirations. That I've worked hard for—sacrificed for."

"And I want to watch you meet those goals, Kate. I want to help make your dreams come true. Every goddamn one."

She looks up. And her eyes are begging now—for understanding. For mercy.

"When Billy broke up with me, I was sad. It hurt. But I was able to keep going. I didn't miss a beat. This thing with you . . . it's different. It's . . . more. And I'm not too proud to admit that if it doesn't work out, I'm not going to be able to just pick myself up and move on. You can . . . you could break me, Drew."

"But I won't."

My hand moves to her cheek. And she leans into it.

"I know what it feels like to think I've lost you, Kate. And I don't ever want to feel that way again. I'm a man who knows what he wants, remember? And I want you."

She shakes her head slowly. "You want me tonight. But what about—"

"I want you tonight, and I'll want you tomorrow and the next day. And ten thousand days after that. Didn't you get the memo in the sky?"

"You might change your mind."

"I might get struck by lightning. Or eaten by a shark. And both of those things are a hell of a lot more likely than a day ever coming when I won't want you. Trust me."

And I guess that's the problem, isn't it?

She stares at me for several moments, then her gaze falls to the floor. The song ends. And she starts to pull away. "I'm sorry. I just . . . can't."

I try to hold on. Like a drowning man gripping a life preserver.

"Kate . . ."

"I should go."

No no no no no. I'm losing her.

"Don't do this."

Her eyes harden like molten lava when it cools to black rock. "Your time's almost up. This was lovely. But . . ."

This is not fucking happening. It's like watching your receiver fumble the ball when you're up by three with twenty seconds left on the clock. She turns toward the door. But I grab her arm and force her to look at me. My voice sounds desperate. Because I am.

"Just hold on. You can't go yet. There's one more thing I have to show you. Give me ten more minutes—please."

Look at her face. Right now.

She wants to stay. No—she wants me to *convince* her to stay. To give her a reason to believe in me again. And if this doesn't do it, nothing on God's green earth ever will.

"Okay, Drew. Ten more minutes."

The breath rushes out of me. "Thank you."

I let go of her arm, grab a black silk scarf off the chair, and hold it up. "You can't take this off until I tell you, okay?"

Suspicion washes over her face. "Is this some kind of weird sex thing?"

I chuckle. "No. But I like the way you think."

She rolls her eyes to the ceiling right before I cover them with the scarf, and the world as she knows it fades to black.

Chapter 27

Every new associate at Evans, Reinhart and Fisher gets to redecorate his or her office. We're not the only firm with this kind of policy. It's good business. Makes employees feel comfortable, like a piece of the company belongs to them. The choices of paint colors and furniture patterns aren't unlimited—but at a firm like ours, the palette is pretty vast. That's how I got my inspiration. How I was able to figure out what Kate prefers.

She's not into florals, and I thank Christ for that. She likes stripes, paisleys, and earth tones. Why am I telling you this, you ask? What does it have to do with anything?

You remember the Bat Cave, don't you? My home office. My firstborn. My strictly dickly, men-only region? Well, it's gotten a sex change. No, that's not really accurate. It's more of a hermaphrodite now.

Watch.

I turn the light on and bring Kate to the middle of the room. Then I untie the scarf.

Her eyes widen. "Oh, my . . ."

The once burgundy walls are now a majestic blue. The English leather couches are history. In their place are two sofas, striped in warm tan and the same deep blue as the walls. My desk is shifted to the left—to make room for the lighter cherry one that sits next to it, side by side, like a bride next to her groom on their wedding day. The picture window behind them is framed with drapes in the same material as the sofas. And the poker table's still in the corner. But now it's got a stiff brown cover over it—to support the large, leafy plant that sits on top. I don't usually do live plants. My thumb's about as green as Morticia Adams's. But the interior decorator said women are into them. Some shit about the nurturing instinct.

Pretty amazing what you can accomplish in a short time when you've got an interior decorator with a team of workers at your disposal and money isn't an issue, right? But curtains are a real bitch to hang. I did those myself—wanted to personally add a few touches. And I almost put the rod through the frigging window a dozen times before I got them straight.

I watch Kate's face closely. But I can't tell what she's thinking. She's blank. Stunned. Like an eyewitness to a double homicide.

I swallow hard. And start the most important pitch of my life:

"I watched *The Notebook* again."

It's still *so* fucking gay.

However . . .

"I get it now. Why Noah put that art room together for Allie. It wasn't because he was a vagina; it was because he didn't have a choice. She was it for him. No matter what he did, there was never gonna be anyone but her. So all he could do was set up the room and hope to God that one day she'd show up to use it. And that pretty much sums up exactly how I feel about you. So I did this"—I gesture around the room—"because I want you in my life, Kate. Permanently."

Her eyes settle on me. And they're shining with tears.

"I want you to move in here with me. I want to fall asleep with your hair in my face every night. And I want to wake up wrapped around you every morning. I want us to spend whole weekends without any clothes on at all. I want to have clean fights and dirty makeup sex."

She laughs at that one. And a single tear slips silently down her cheek.

"I want to talk to you until the sun comes up, and I want to bring you cereal in bed every Sunday. I want to work long, endless hours in this office, but only if you're here next to me."

Her voice is barely a whisper. "Like a partnership? Fifty-fifty split?"

I shake my head. "No. Not fifty-fifty. You don't get just half of me. You get all of me. A hundred percent."

She breathes deep. And bites her lip. And glances down at her desk. Then her face goes slack.

"Where did you get that?"

It's her parents' wedding picture.

"I stole it from your office and had it copied while you were at lunch."

She shakes her head slowly. And looks back up at me. In awe. "I can't believe you did all this."

I take a step forward. "I know you just got out of a relationship, and I've never been in one. And I know I'm supposed to tell you that if you're not ready, that it's okay. That I'll be patient and wait. But . . . if I say those things . . . I'll be lying. Because . . . I'm just not a waiting kind of guy. I'm more of a take-the-bull-by-the-horns, keep-at-you-until-you-break-or-go-insane kind of guy."

She chuckles again.

"So if this isn't enough, if you need something more—tell me. No matter what it is, I'll do it. For you."

When I'm done, she just stands there. Staring at me.

She licks her lips and wipes her eyes. "I have some conditions."

I nod cautiously.

"No lying. I mean it, Drew. When you tell me something, I have to know that it's the truth. That you don't have some ulterior motive."

"Okay."

"And no other women. I think I'm pretty adventurous in bed when it comes to you, but I'm monogamous. I don't swing. I don't do threesomes."

Not a problem. My dick only has eyes for Kate.

"Me neither. Well, you know, not anymore. I mean . . . agreed."

And then she smiles. And it's blinding. Luminous.

Fucking incandescent.

And she steps toward me. "Well, Mr. Evans . . . it looks like you've got yourself a merger."

And that's all I need to hear.

I move like a spring that's been cocked too tight for too long. And before Kate can take a breath, I've got her crushed against me—I'm holding her, lifting her right off her feet.

Our mouths snap together like two magnets. She grips my shirt. And my tongue slides into her welcoming mouth.

Jesus. The taste of her—my memory was unforgivably inadequate. I feel like a recovering crack addict who just fell off the wagon and never wants to climb back on.

Our hands grope at each other. It's explosive. Combustible.

Burn, baby, burn.

I drag my lips across her jaw. She tilts her head to give me more room, and I attack her neck. She's panting. We both are. My hands are in her hair, loosening all the pins that kept it styled, holding her hostage. And her hands are on my chest skimming my ribs and waist. I have no fucking clue how she got my shirt open. I'm just glad she did. My fingers whisper down her back to the hem of her dress. Then I slide them under it, cupping her smooth, firm ass.

She must be wearing a thong.

I massage and squeeze, pressing our hips together. Kate's mouth replaces her hands, moving across my chest and lower. And I start to really fucking lose it. I grab the back of her dress in both hands and pull—ripping it almost in two. Kind of like the Incredible Hulk.

"I'll buy you a new one, I swear."

It falls to her waist. And our bare chests crash together.

Fuck me. I missed this. How in Christ did I ever go an hour—let alone days—without feeling her against me like this? Too fucking long.

"God, Drew."

Her hands are across my back now. Scratching and kneading. My mouth is at her ear, demanding, "Whatever underwear you've got on? I'm keeping them." I drop to my knees, scorching a path between her breasts and down her stomach.

Kate gasps. "That could be a problem."

"Why?"

I drag her dress down to the floor. And then I stare—mesmerized—at Kate's bare snatch.

"Because I'm not wearing any."

My cock moans in agony. And then I look up at her. "You always go commando to business meetings with friends?"

She smiles shyly. "I guess I was hoping you'd change my mind about that."

For a second, I'm stunned. She wanted this. Just as badly as I did. And I wasted all that time eating chicken marsala—when I could have been eating her.

God.

Damn.

Without another word, I dive in. Like a toddler getting his first luscious taste of birthday cake. I sink my face—my tongue—into her pussy. She tastes warm and silky, like the liquid sugar on top of a cinnamon bun, but sweeter.

Kate's knees buckle, but I brace my hands at the small of her back and slide her legs over my shoulder. And then I lie back on the floor so she's straddling my face.

Like I've dreamed of every damn night.

She writhes and gasps above me. Unabashedly. And I devour her in a starving frenzy. Her whimpers get higher. Louder. Her hand reaches back. And she strokes my cock over my pants.

You ever heard of a two-pump chump? Well, if she doesn't stop touching me real frigging quickly, you're going to get a bird's-eye view of one.

I grab her hand and lock our fingers together. Kate uses them for leverage as she rotates her hips, rubbing her gorgeous cunt against my mouth. She moves once, twice . . . and then she's coming. Screaming my name brokenly.

She breathes deep as she comes back down. Then she slides sinuously over my body till our mouths line up. And we're kissing. It's savage and rough—all tongue and teeth. My hands push through her hair, pulling it loose. Her hips grind against my dick, and her wetness soaks through my pants.

"Fuck, Kate. I'm going to come so fucking hard."

I just hope I'm actually inside her when I do.

She swirls her tongue around my nipple before she tells me, "Pants, Drew. Off."

My hips bow off the floor as I tear at the button on my pants. I manage to push them and my boxers down to my knees, but I'm too out of my mind to get them off completely.

I grab her hips and bring them lower. And my cock slides effortlessly inside her.

Christ Almighty.

We freeze—our faces just millimeters apart—our breaths harsh and entwined. My eyes hold hers. And then she moves. Slowly. Drawing me almost completely out—before surging back down. My head falls back, and my lids close.

It's perfect. Divine.

My hands are splayed across her hips. Helping her. Gripping hard enough to bruise. And then she sits up, arching her back till her hair brushes my knees. I force my eyes open, needing to see her. Her head's back, her breasts are high, and her lips are open as euphoric moans and nonsensical words slip out.

You know how sometimes you read about naked pictures of some moron's wife getting leaked on to the Internet? I never got that.

But now I do. Because if I had a camera? I'd be snapping that shutter like the freaking paparazzi. To capture this moment. To remember how Kate looks right now. Because she's just that magnificent. More stunning than any masterpiece in the Louvre—more breathtaking than all the Seven Wonders combined.

She moves faster, harder. And I feel the pressure building low in my gut.

"Yeah, Kate. Ride me . . . just like that."

Her tits bounce with each thrust. Hypnotically. And I just can't resist a taste. I sit up and cover one tip with my mouth, laving and flicking her pointy little peak with my tongue. She screams as her legs wrap around my back—pulling me tighter—rubbing her clit along my happy trail.

She's close. *We're* fucking close. But I don't want it to end. Not yet.

So I roll her under me, cradling the back of her head in my hands, protecting it from the wood floor, as I lie on top of her. Kate's welcoming thighs open wide, and I push even deeper inside her.

"Oh God . . . oh God . . ."

The sounds of our bodies slapping together and her breathy

voice fill the room like an erotic symphony. The New York Philharmonic's got nothing on us.

"God! Oh God!"

I smile as I pick up the pace, "God's not the one fucking you, baby."

Sure, I'm in love, but this is still *me* here.

"Drew . . . Drew . . . yes . . . Drew!"

Much better.

You didn't think I was going to start spewing sickeningly sweet, asswipe-like phrases, now, did you? Sorry to disappoint.

Besides, I like the word *fuck*. It implies a certain level of heat. Passion. And it's specific. If Congress had asked Bill Clinton if he fucked Monica Lewinski, there wouldn't have been any question about just what the hell they were talking about, now, would there?

It doesn't much matter what you say when you're screwing anyway. Or how you do it. Slow and gentle or fast and violent—it's the feelings behind it that make it mean something. That make it mean everything.

Christ, am I enlightened or what? Aren't you proud of me? You should be.

I bend my arms and cover her mouth in a devouring, harsh kiss. Then I lick my way to her shoulder and, caught up in the moment, bite down. Not hard enough to break the skin but with just enough pressure to send Kate flying over the fucking edge again.

I straighten my arms so I can watch her. She bucks up one more time before she goes stiff and tight beneath me. Her perfectly painted toes curl in the air as she comes. Her muscles squeeze me hard from base to tip, like desperate hands milking a tube of toothpaste from the bottom up, wringing out every last drop.

My head rolls back and my eyes close as I grunt and curse. And I'm helpless—like a grain of sand in the grip of a tsunami. Pleasure pounds out of every pore in my body as I come with the force of a frigging geyser.

Incredible.

We ride out the wave of ecstasy together until we're both gulping for air. And then I collapse on top of her. My cheek lies in the valley between her breasts, my stomach between her thighs. And a few seconds later, Kate's hands come up my back before sliding down my spine in the most soothing fucking way.

I cup her face with my hands and kiss her. Slowly this time. Languidly. Her doe eyes stare into mine. But neither of us speaks. We don't need to.

And then I feel it.

Have you ever seen a racehorse after it's been sidelined for a while? I have. When they get back on the track, it's like fire's been shot into their veins. They can just run and run—countless laps—miles at a time.

You see where I'm going with this?

I flip us over so Kate's once again on top, her knees straddling my hips, her head against my chest. We really should move this to the bed—the floor's damn hard. But, then again, so am I. And that takes precedence.

Kate lifts her head and her eyes widen. "Already?"

I raise my brows. "We've missed a lot of quality time lately. Apparently my dick would like to make up for every second of it. You game?"

I rotate my hips, and she moans just a little.

I'll take that as a yes.

Chapter 28

We made it to the bed. Eventually.

A few hours and three orgasms later, we're lying side by side, facing each other. Sharing a pillow. *The* pillow.

"Say it again."

It's the tenth time she's asked me. But I don't mind. I'll say it till I'm blue in the face if she wants me to.

"I love you, Kate."

She sighs. It sounds contented. "I'm going to be really clingy and needy for the next few weeks. You should be prepared."

"I'll be insecure and jealous. It'll work out great."

There's a smile in her voice. "You told me you don't get jealous."

I shrug. "I also told you I wasn't going to lie to you ever again."

Her hands comb through the back of my hair gently. "When did you know?"

I smile. "The first time you let me come inside you without a rubber."

She yanks my hair. Hard.

"Ow! Jesus!"

Her voice is exasperated, like a mother who just caught her kid snagging an off-limits cookie for the tenth time.

"Drew. That doesn't sound very romantic."

"You don't think so?"

I find the strength to lift my head, and then I lower it down over her already hardened nipple. I suck at it, tease it with my teeth, before slowly letting it go with a pop.

"Because I happen to think coming inside you is very, very romantic."

As I start to give the other beauty the same treatment, she gasps. "That's a good point."

I chuckle. "They all are, sweetheart."

Laying my head back down, I drag my fingertip up her arm, fascinated by the goose bumps that rise up as I go.

"Aren't you going to ask me when I knew?" she asks.

"When you knew what?"

Kate rolls onto her stomach. And her hair swings over her shoulder, reaching the skin on my ribs. Tickling it like a feather. It's arousing. Sensual. And just like that, I'm ready to go again.

Edward Cullen can take his stupid heroin and OD on it. Kate is my own personal brand of Viagra.

"When I knew I was in love with you."

Have you noticed that Kate hasn't returned any of my "I love yous"? I certainly have. But like I said—I try not to put much faith in words. Actions tell you more. And every move Kate makes tells me that we're on the same page.

Still, I'm kind of curious.

"When?"

She leans forward and kisses my eyes . . . my cheeks . . . and then the tip of my nose before planting a sweet one on my lips. Then she leans back. "Do you remember that day in my office? After Billy and I broke up, and I was crying?"

I nod.

"I should have been devastated—I was—for a little while. But then you came in, and you put your arms around me. And I never wanted you to let go. It was like everything I'd always needed, anything I'd ever wanted, was right there in front of me. And that's when I knew. That, somehow, you'd sucked me in, and I was totally in love with you." She laughs softly. "I was so scared . . ."

I bet.

". . . because I never in a million years thought you'd feel the same way."

I brush my thumb across her beautiful bottom lip. "I already did, Kate. I just didn't know it."

She smiles and lays her head back down on the pillow. Her voice is soft and sincere.

"Yeah. You can be a real dumbass sometimes."

Was that what you thought she was going to say? Me neither.

"Excuse me?"

She cocks a brow smugly. "I'm just saying, if you look at our history—"

Before she can finish, I've got her pinned under me, her back to my chest. "Those are fighting words, Kate." My fingers travel down her ribs slowly. Torturously. She starts to squirm, and her ass rubs against my cock.

It's nice.

"Take it back."

"No."

My fingers move light and fast over her. Tickling her without mercy.

"Say, 'Drew Evans is a god. A brilliant, genius god.'"

She bucks and shrieks, "Drew! Stop! Stop!"

I don't let up. "Ask me nicely and maybe I will. Beg me for it."

She laughs even while she's screaming. "Never!"

You know what they say about *never,* don't you?

Oh yeah—this is going to be fun.

She begged.

Did you have any doubt? Then she got on top of me, and I was the one begging.

Now I'm lying with my head at Kate's feet, massaging them. Her head's on my thigh. Want to know how we ended up in this position? Nah—I'll let you use your imagination.

"So, what did Alexandra say to you?" I ask her.

"Mmm?"

I bend my elbow and rest my head on my hand so I can see

Kate's face. She looks completely exhausted. Worn out. Un-gently used. It's a really good look for her.

"The other day, in your office, before you agreed to go out with me. You seemed different. More . . . receptive. Did she threaten you?"

She chuckles drowsily and cracks her eyes open. "No, no threats. She told me to think like the professional woman I am. To look at you like a business venture. That every investment has risks, but I have to weigh them against the payoff. She said based on your most recent performance, you're a risk worth taking."

Good strategy. I should have thought of that.

"I should send her flowers."

Her hand rubs my thigh. "But that's not what convinced me to give you another chance."

My brow wrinkles. "No?"

"Nope."

"Then what did?"

She swings around till her head's on my chest, and there's not a breath of space between us.

"Mackenzie."

"How'd she pull it off?"

"She told me a story about how you took her to Central Park last summer. And a boy threw sand at her."

I remember that day. I was just about to offer a six-year-old fifty bucks to drop kick the little fucker.

"And then he came up to her and said he was sorry. But she wasn't sure if she wanted to play with him again. And she said that you told her that sometimes boys are stupid. And a lot of times they do stupid things. So, once in a while, she should take pity on them. And if they say they're sorry, she should give them a second chance. Not a third or a fourth . . . but you told her that everyone deserves a second chance." She pauses. And laughs. "And then you told her if he did it again she should kick him in the balls."

All girls should know how to defend themselves. A well-aimed kick will do it every time.

It's kind of amazing, don't you think? If it wasn't for my perfect niece, we might not be here right now.

"Maybe I should buy her two ponies."

Kate smiles. And her eyes gaze up at me in that way I now crave. Like I mean everything to her.

"You have no sense of self-preservation, do you?"

I shake my head. "No, not at the moment. I'm too focused on . . . fornication."

She brings her knee up around my hip. "I'm going to make you so happy, Drew Evans."

My arms tighten around her. "You already have. After this? Heaven's going to be a major disappointment."

I dip my head and kiss her. It's wet and slow and wonderful. And she's kissing me back. Like she never wants to stop. And you know something?

That works really well for me.

So there you go. Thanks for coming along for the ride. But you really should leave now. No more living vicariously through my sex life. Because, remember when I said all guys talk to their friends about sex?

Well, we do.

But no guy talks to his friends about sex with his girlfriend. Ever.

You really think I want somebody jerking off to what Kate lets me do to her? Or what she does to me? No fucking way.

So this is where you get off. Not in the fantastic way I'm about to, of course, but that's just too bad for you.

Still . . . after all the pointers I've given you, I feel like I owe you some final words of wisdom. A lesson. Something meaningful. So here we go:

Assume nothing. Even if you think you know everything. Even if you're sure that you're right. Get confirmation. That whole "ass" cliché about assuming? It's right on the money. And if you're not careful, it could end up costing you the best thing that's ever going to happen to you.

And another thing—don't get too comfortable. Take chances.

Don't be afraid to lay it on the line. Even if you're happy. Even if you think life is freaking perfect.

Because I had a life once. A life I loved. It was consistent. Fun.

It was reliable. Safe.

And then one night, a beautiful dark-haired girl came along and blew it all to kingdom come. Now my life is a mess. In a good way. A giant unpredictable web of screwups and makeups. Frustration and tenderness. Annoyance and affection. Lust and love.

But that's okay. Because as long as Kate Brooks is tangled up in that web with me?

Well, I can't imagine anything fucking better than that.

Turn the page for a sneak peek

at the continuation of Kate and Drew's story

in Emma Chase's next book

Twisted

COMING SOON FROM GALLERY BOOKS

5 weeks earlier

"Well, hot damn, looks like we got ourselves a deal!"

The guy in the cowboy hat? Signing that stack of papers, across from me at the conference table? That's Jackson Howard Sr. The younger version in the black hat, sitting next to him? That's his son, Jack Jr.

They're cattle ranchers. Owners of the largest cattle ranch in North America, and they've just acquired the most innovative developer of GPS tracking software in the country. Now, you may ask yourself, why would two already wealthy businessmen travel across the country to expand their empire?

Because they want the best. And I'm the best.

Or should I say *we* are.

Drew takes the final document from him. "Sure do, Jack. I'd start looking into yachts for business travel, if I were you. When the profit reports roll in, your tax adviser's going to want something big to write off."

Kate and Drew.

The dream team of Evans, Reinhart and Fisher.

John Evans, Drew's father, definitely knew what he was doing when he put us together. A fact he proudly loves to remind us of.

To hear him tell it, he knew all along that Drew and I would be an unbeatable team—unless we killed each other. Apparently that was a chance John was willing to take. Of course, he didn't know we'd end up together like we are now, but . . . he takes credit for that part too. Starting to see where Drew gets it from, aren't you?

Erin walks in now with our clients' coats. She makes eye contact with Drew and taps her watch. He nods discreetly.

"I say we go out and celebrate—paint this town red! See if you city folk can keep up with the likes of me," Jackson Howard says.

Even though he's pushing seventy, he's got the energy of a twenty-year-old. And I suspect he's got more than a few bull-riding stories up his sleeve.

I open my mouth to accept the invite, but Drew cuts me off.

"We'd love to, Jack, but unfortunately Kate and I have a previously scheduled appointment. There's a car waiting for you downstairs to take you to the finest establishments in the city. Enjoy yourselves. And of course the tab's on us."

They stand and Jack tips his hat to Drew. "That's damn fine of you, son."

"It's our pleasure."

As we walk to the door, Jack Jr. turns to me and holds out his card. "It was a real pleasure working with you, Miss Brooks. The next time you're in my neck of the woods, I'd be honored to show around. I have a feelin' Texas would agree with you. Maybe you'll even decide to stay and put down some roots."

Yep, he's coming on to me. Maybe you think that's sleazy. I would have, two years ago. But like Drew told me then, it happens all the time. Businessmen are slick, cocky. They kind of have to be.

It's one of the reasons this field has the third-highest rate of infidelity—right after truck drivers and police officers. The long hours, the frequent traveling, hooking up almost becomes inevitable. A foregone conclusion.

It's how Drew and I started, remember?

But Jack Jr.'s not like the other jerks who've propositioned me. He seems sincere. Sweet. So I smile and reach out to take his card, just to be polite.

But Drew's hand is faster than mine. "We'd love to. We don't get a lot of work down South, but the next time we do, we'll cash in that rain check."

He's trying to be professional, unemotional. But his jaw is clenched. Sure, he's smiling, but have you ever seen *Lord of the Rings*? Gollum smiled too.

Just before he bit that guy's hand off who was holding his "precious."

Drew is territorial and possessive. That's just who he is.

Matthew once told me a story: For Drew's first day of kindergarten, his mother bought him a lunch box. A Yoda one. On the playground, Drew wouldn't put it down because it was his and he was afraid someone would break it. Or steal it. It took Matthew a week to convince him that nobody would—or that together, they could beat the everlasting hell out of anyone who did.

At times like this, I know just how that lunch box felt.

I smile kindly at Jack Jr. and he tips his hat. And then they're out the door.

As soon as it's closed behind them, Drew tears John Jr.'s card in half. "Dickhead."

I push his shoulder. "Stop it. He was nice."

Drew's eyes snap to mine. "You thought Luke and Daisy Duke's inbred love child was nice? Really?" He takes a step forward.

"As a matter of fact, yes."

His voice morphs into an over-the-top southern drawl. "Maybe I should buy myself some chaps. And a cowboy hat." Then he drops the accent. "Oohh—or better yet, we'll get *you* one. I can be your wild stallion and you can be the brazen cowgirl who rides me."

And the funniest thing of all? He's really not kidding.

I shake my head with a smile. "So what's this mysterious meeting we have? There's nothing on my schedule."

He smiles widely. "We have an appointment at the airport." He slides two airline tickets out of his suit pocket.

First class—to Cabo San Lucas.

I inhale quickly. "Cabo?"

His eyes sparkle. "Surprise."

I've traveled more in the last two years than I had in my entire life before—the cherry blossoms blooming in Japan, the crystal waters of Portugal. . . . All things Drew had already seen, places he'd already been to.

Places he wanted to share—with me.

I look closer at the tickets and frown. "Drew, this flight leaves in three hours. I'll never have time to pack."

He takes two bags out of the closet. "So it's a good thing that I already have."

I wrap my arms around his neck and squeeze. "You are the best boyfriend ever."

He smirks in that way that makes me want to kiss him and slap him at the same time.

"Yeah, I know."

The hotel is stunning. With views I've only seen on a postcard. We're on the top floor—penthouse. Like Richard Gere in *Pretty Woman,* Drew is a big believer in "only the best."

It's late when we get in, but after a nap on the plane, we're both wired. Energized.

And hungry.

All the airlines are cutting back these days, even in first class. The sandwiches may be complimentary, but that doesn't mean they're edible.

While Drew is in the shower, I start to unpack. Why aren't we showering together? I really don't need to answer that, do I?

I put the bags on the bed and open them. Most men look at an empty suitcase like it's some kind of physics equation—they can stare at it for hours, but still have no frigging clue what they're supposed to do with it.

But not Drew.

He's Mr. I-Think-of-Everything.

He packed all the incidentals that most men wouldn't think of. Everything I'll need to make my vacation comfortable and fun.

Except for underwear. There isn't a single pair of underwear in this entire suitcase.

And it's not an oversight.

My boyfriend happens to hold a serious grudge against undergarments. If he had his way, we'd both be walking around like Adam and Eve—minus the fig leaves, of course.

But he did bring the rest of the essentials. Deodorant, shaving cream, a razor, makeup, birth control pills, moisturizer, the rest of my antibiotic for the ear infection I had last week, eye cream—and so on.

And we should pause here, for a brief public service announcement.

I have a few clients who are in the pharmaceutical field. And those companies have whole departments whose sole job is writing.

Writing what, you ask? You know those little inserts that come with your prescription? The ones that list every possible side effect and what you should do, should any of them occur? May cause drowsiness, don't operate large machinery, contact doctor immediately, blah blah blah.

Most of us just open the little paper bag, take out our pills, and throw the insert away. Most of us do . . . but we shouldn't. I'm not going to bore you with a lecture. All I'll say at the moment is: Read the insert. You'll be glad you did.